In the DARKEST of Shadows

Richard Allen

RICHARD ALLEN

Richard Allen is a retired police Superintendent who, in addition to uniformed duties, saw service with the CID, the Vice Squad, the Drug Squad and Special Branch. Richard is the author of two best-selling works dealing with police management and leadership, which were listed as recommended reading by both the US Department of Justice and the Police Staff College.

'In the DARKEST of Shadows' is the fourth in the ***Mark Faraday Collection***.

By the same author:

Non-Fiction:

Effective Supervision in the Police Service

Leading from the Middle

Fiction:

DIRTY Business

DIE Back

DARKER than Death

First published 2016
Second Edition 2018

Published by MARS Associates

www.richard-allen-author.com

Member: Crime Writers Association (UK)
Member: International Thriller Writers (USA)

to:
my ever wonderful wife
Ann
our caring and beautiful daughter
Suzi
and our exceptional son-in-law
Phiroze

'Police duties require men of sound judgement, of sturdy character, clear of conscience and desirous of justice; their higher authorities should spare them anything likely to diminish or dull in them these rare and precious qualities'

Célestin Hennion CVO
1862-1915
Prefect of Police (Paris)

Prologue

St John the Baptist Day

48˚ 42’ N 53˚ 05’ W

THEY KNEW NOT THE EXACT TIME. But it was past dawn on the 24th June. Nor did these eighteen men know the exact place. But they had triumphed. They had crossed The Sea of Darkness. They had suffered too, grievously weakened and desperately weary. But they had arrived by the Grace of God.

Now they knelt in supplication and thanked Him for their deliverance. They raised their banners in recognition of their dread sovereign Lord their King and the blessed Holy Father. The standards of St George and of St Peter were humbly thrust into the ground and these banners trembled and beat in the breeze. And, from amongst the trees, wide eyes looked and they marvelled at what they saw.

Chapter 1

Tuesday, 19th April – more than 500 years later.

Washington, United States of America.

THE WALLS WERE GREY. So too were the furnishings. And the carpeting. With the ceiling lights dimmed, Samantha Hayden looked ghost-like as she stood behind the lectern, her face illuminated by the pale green lectern light, and addressed the members of the Strategic Intelligence Group 7B. It had been a long, tedious morning – they always were with Colonel Hayden. They had overrun again and they were going to overrun some.

'The final item for this morning is simply a reminder to us all of the continuing interest of Putin's Russia in the Bering Straits, and the Bering and Beaufort Seas.' As she spoke, a large map of America's 49th state, Alaska, and the Canadian North West Territories appeared on the screen behind her. 'The Russians view this whole area,' she continued, her right hand sweeping a large arc over the screen, 'as part of their territorial waters, arguing that the continental shelf here is a continuation of the Khrebet Kolymskiy mountain range. Their submersibles continue to scoot about and our Coast Guard are continuing to monitor their activities. The position of the United States remains as ever that these seas constitute international waters.'

'The bottom line is that it's all about resources, ma'am,' offered Lieutenant-Colonel Trumbell, who, hitherto had appeared content to doze in the gloom.

‘Resources are always a component to be considered, Hank,’ said Commander Walt Bergman.

‘Thank you, Walt,’ interjected Colonel Samantha Hayden. ‘Eighty per cent of Alaska’s state revenue is derived from oil and gas. There is believed to be 4.3TM3 of gas below the Artic Islands and 178 billion barrels of oil. So, yes, the United States is naturally alert to and wary of any Russian activity hereabout.’

‘And our Canadian cousins?’ questioned Trumbell mischievously.

‘Our relations with our northern ally remain vital to the interests of the United States, although they consider what is known as the Canadian Arctic Archipelago and, particularly, the Parry Channel as an integral part of Canada.’ She raised her hand so as to halt the anticipated interruption by Colonel Trumbell. ‘The North West Passage was first free of ice in 2007. With global warming, these waterways will shortly be no different than those of the English Channel. In any event, there is another legal avenue I intend to pursue in this regard. For now we will break for lunch and resume at two. Thank you all for your attention.’

The ceiling lights brightened as the delegates shuffled their papers and made their eager way to the restaurant. ‘Walt,’ summoned Samantha Hayden.

‘Yes, colonel,’ he said as he approached the lectern.

'You are shipping out at the end of the month I hear.' It was a statement, not a question, as Hayden attempted to give the impression of being caring and thoughtful. She was neither.

'Yes, ma'am. I'm looking forward to my time in London, but maybe not so much the weather.'

Walt's attempt at conversation was wasted. 'And Lucy and Debbie-Anne will remain in Marriotville.' Again, not a question but a remark intended to demonstrate that Colonel Hayden was aware of all things connected with her command. Walt answered anyway.

'Well that's right, ma'am. Lucy will remain in the family home,' adding proudly, 'Debbie-Anne has gained her bachelor's and will continue with a Master's in Applied Economics at Washington State for the next two years and so a very suitable arrangement.'

A father's pride and a daughter's achievements and aspirations were of no interest to a rather sour-faced Colonel Hayden whose life was the United States Army and nothing else. 'I mentioned a legal argument. I know you are shipping out but you are still a lawyer. Spend a few days researching Section 35 of the Constitution Act for me.' Then added, together with a contrived smile reminiscent of a ventriloquist's dummy, 'I would be most grateful.'

'Of course, ma'am,' he replied as the colonel walked from the briefing room leaving Commander Walt Bergman with his grey thoughts, as grey as the grey walls and grey carpet.

He returned to his grey chair and slumped down. He thought of his beautiful wife, Lucy, or more correctly ex-wife, who was never satisfied with her comfortable life with a dependable husband and lovely daughter. Lucy idled her time away with one admirer after another, or simply bought more and more handbags, dresses and particularly shoes. She would always find fault with loving Walt who had worshipped her. She had become indignant blaming Walt for what she termed 'distractions' – the golf club pro, the personal trainer and so many others. And if it wasn't Walt's fault it had been the navy's fault for the disruptive inconvenience of their postings. Walt had thought that Lucy, the daughter of a rear-admiral, would have accepted and understood navy life. But no. And Walt had been real stupid. He had had one affair, just one short-lived affair with Sarah. Sarah, the pretty temptress from the HR Department. And Walt had been tempted. And Walt had been indiscreet. And Lucy had been alert. And Lucy had seized upon Walt's indiscretion and taken the opportunity to assume the role of the betrayed and wronged woman, suing for divorce, and Walt, out of embarrassment or pride, had not fought it; in fact, Walt had hidden his embarrassment behind the rumour that he was some sort of secret gigolo. Now Lucy had what had been their family home. But Walt consoled himself. At least he still had Debbie-Anne, his career and a posting to the UK.

Chapter 2

Tuesday, 19th April – and one year on.

Rome, Italy.

UNDER THE MID-MORNING SUN and cloudless blue sky, the two men concealed themselves in plain sight. At the Caffe San Sebastiano they sat in the shade, with many others, in the wooden and canvas seats at the pleasant tables with pure white linen. Both were dressed in clothing common to their surroundings. They made no exaggerated gestures. They were casual in manner and appeared comfortable. They simply observed the tourists teaming along the Via di San Gregorio towards the Colosseum following their guides, guides who held aloft their symbol of office – the umbrella. Of course, there were, probably, three hundred bobbing and waving umbrellas. The two men smiled. The guides did not exhibit the organisational skills and discipline that their own lives demanded. Far from reducing the chaos, the umbrellas simply contributed to it, as did their charges, most of whom seemed determined to photograph everything, even the irrelevant. The two men ordered coffees and alfresco salads. They were at ease, although always alert, searching the passers-by for any anomalies. They detected none, even in those who appeared content to be idle.

Both men were not ostentatious in their appearance, although the American wore a Breitling Navitimer watch, reflecting his affiliation to all things nautical, but this did not look that out of place at all. They spoke of family and fine wines, the Italian of his home city of Naples on the Tyrrhenian coast and the American of San Diego in California. The coffees were brought to their tables as they spoke, then the salads and a dish of green and black olives. Their speech was muted but full of smiles. They spoke for a little over forty minutes. Their conversation was pleasant and relaxed but punctuated by, what would appear to most observers, innocuous questions and equally mundane answers. There was one question that was certainly not mundane but central to their meeting, a question the significance of which could, and probably would, create a regional conflict, certainly regional instability, many, many miles away.

'You ask the information regarding business papers, the most significant,' said the Italian, referring to a document written by the banker, Giovanni Antonio de Carbonariis. 'The paper, it can no longer be found again.'

'You say "again"?' asked the American incredulously, the manner of his question failing to mask his frustration.

'The restorations at the office are, how you say, much extensive.' He gestured almost gracefully to emphasise the magnitude of the work. 'The papers, much papers, remove to allow work the smooth progress. Some, they were lost, now they found,' he remarked with a shrug as if such occurrences were to be accepted as the understandable norm and quite reasonable. 'This one you seek,' he continued, 'is certainly the missing. There is no doubting.'

For the American this situation was not at all understandable and quite unreasonable. This was not how it worked in his world. To the American the papers were vital. To the Italian simply another theft amongst many. The American tried to remain calm as he asked: 'Any idea when you might recover the papers so that our business can move forward?'

'There is the office worker,' he replied, a description that did not describe the thief accurately at all, but this was understood by the American, 'who has been the much help. The papers, they go, but … ,' he paused, '… I know when and how they go.' The Italian lent back in his creaking canvas chair, pleased that he was about to reveal the efficiency of the Corpo della Gendarmeria.

Chapter 3

Friday 29th April.

Bristol, England.

HER MOBILE PHONE RANG. Not her bed-side phone. She woke and automatically checked the bed-side clock. 01:47. A strange hour for such a call, she thought. As the District's senior detective and Duty Officer, she would have anticipated calls, but on her house phone not her mobile. She picked up her mobile and read the name and number of the caller. Her lover, at her side, stirred under the warm duvet.

Detective Chief Inspector Kay Yin switched on her bed-side lamp and pressed the green button on her phone, the lamp's light enhancing and silhouetting her beautiful Oriental features. 'Yes, David?' she asked as she opened her little note pad.

'Do you need a moment to gather your thoughts, ma'am?' asked Inspector David Grant, the night tour uniformed inspector, as Mark Faraday got out of their bed and walked towards the hallway and into the kitchen – their routine. She put her phone on speaker.

'No, I'm fine thank you, David. Go ahead.'

'There's been a fatal RTA,' then added quickly, 'not one of ours, ma'am.' Relieved that none of her officers had been killed in a road accident, she focused, her pencil still hovering over her entry: *'01:47. Insp DG'*. Grant continued at a steady, pedantic pace. 'I'm at the Portway, about three hundred yards west of its junction with Bridge Valley Road,' explained Grant who was standing on the pavement of the main arterial road leading from Avonmouth Docks and the M5 motorway, running parallel with the River Avon, and into the heart of the city of Bristol. 'Reported to us by a passing lorry driver. The deceased, forty-three years of age, appears to have had a heart attack or stroke at the wheel of his private car as he was driving out of the city. No apparent signs of foul play or another party. His vehicle, a Volvo saloon, has a manual box and was in second gear, consistent with him having pulled away from the traffic lights at the junction and then crashing, or more accurately, drifting sideways to his left, coming to rest up against the railings alongside the river.' She listened patiently as she jotted succinct notes onto her little pad. 'The reason for the call is that PNC lists the vehicle's keeper as Adrian Harvey of Hotwells, Bristol. The driver's licence found on the deceased confirms this but I have also found a French passport in an overnight bag in the boot of the car.' She remained silent as he continued. 'The photograph on the driver's licence and the French passport are of the same person, as are the dates and places of birth: 9th January 1971 at Alsace, France, but the names are different. The passport identifies the deceased as Edouard Melies.'

The inspector paused so as to allow Kay to absorb the information. Then she spoke. 'Why the mobile, David?' she probed, sensing that there was more.

‘Well, ma’am. We know that the press monitor our calls and I thought I should use my mobile as I also found a MoD Procurement HQ security pass for Harvey in the deceased’s wallet,’ he said, referring to the ultra-sensitive Ministry of Defence centre at Abbeywood on the outskirts of Bristol.

‘Excellent. Who knows?’

‘Just one of my sergeants. Wallace, ma’am.’

‘Keep it that way,’ she ordered, then asked: ‘Where’s the deceased now?’

‘Pronounced at the scene and photographed in situ,’ he replied as he looked behind him towards the deceased’s car and the mortuary van. ‘Just about to be taken to the mortuary.’

‘Okay,’ she said, ‘let Sergeant Wallace deal with the accident report in the usual way. Inform Comms Centre of the details and that the death is apparently the result of a coronary. As we are not *absolutely* certain as to his identity, detail the driver at this stage as “unknown male – enquiries continuing” with Wallace as the officer dealing. That should keep it low key. Are we clear?’

‘Yes, ma’am.’

‘Just the overnight bag in the boot you say, nothing else?’

‘A standard tool kit, spare wheel, some jump leads, hiking boots with heavy-duty socks neatly tucked into each boot and an empty Mach 8 fishing rod case. Nothing else, ma'am.'

'Good. Have the vehicle removed to the secure compound at forensics HQ, but I want the overnight bag and all the keys, except the ignition key. I will be at the mortuary in twenty. Is that time good for you, David?'

'Yes, ma'am,' he answered, then asked: 'Are there any other instructions?'

Her response was immediate. 'I think that Special Branch should be in the mix, but not at the scene. That may attract too much interest. I will speak with Detective Superintendent Faraday and see if he wishes to attend.'

Grant had heard rumours that the chief inspector and the Head of Special Branch were lovers, but he said nothing other than: 'Thank you, ma'am.'

'No, thank you, David. Good job.' Then she rang off.

Mark, who was now dressed in a pair of fine cord, navy-blue trousers and a dark grey-coloured Crew jumper, stood silently at the bedroom door holding two mugs of Carte Noir coffee in his hands.

'Did I miss anything?' she asked.

'No, not at all,' he reassured with a huge smile. 'Interesting though. It could simply be a heart attack, but we will have to await the PM and a full tox screen. He could be MI5 or

MI6 working out of Abbeywood I suppose. We know they do. If he is a legitimate MoD employee, what was his role? Why the passport in another name? Where had he been and where was he going, particularly at this time? Lots and lots of interesting little questions to pose.'

As she dressed, she asked: 'Will you inform the ACC?'

He looked at her as if in deep thought, but he wasn't. He had already decided. 'No, not yet. Let's see what the deceased looks like on the slab and what's in his bag. No sense in disturbing Robert's beauty sleep with what we have so far.'

'And the French embassy?' she posed, aware of the protocol that requires foreign embassies to be informed in the event of the death of one of their nationals.

'Certainly not,' he said firmly, then added in a lighter tone: 'Nor the MoD.'

***

They went by separate cars, approaching the mortuary from different routes, he from the direction he would take from his apartment in Sneyd Park if he had been sleeping there, she from the direction of her apartment in Redland. Maybe an unnecessary subterfuge but one born out of habit and an understandable, if unnecessary, desire to protect her. Kay arrived first, followed by Mark. Grant was already there in a black police anorak and peaked cap. The black mortuary van was not. They stood together for a moment in the chill of the early Spring morning, Mark Faraday six foot four inches tall, dark brown hair and piercing coal-black eyes; Kay Yin five foot three inches and petite, with exquisite teeth, Oriental features and beautiful large eyes; and David Grant, a little shorter than Faraday but heavier built. Pleasantries were exchanged as they entered the cold building.

There is always an unpleasant and distinct odour in any mortuary. Maybe it's the cleansing fluids and disinfectants. Maybe just the odour of death. Whatever, a distasteful odour that assails the nose and lingers for many, many hours.

They walked along a central corridor of white walls, bright ceiling lights and pale-blue floor tiles, their footsteps a hollow echo as they approached the double, pale-blue doors at the end of the corridor.

Inspector Grant had already had the body placed on its back, lying to attention, on the cold, stainless steel gurney.

Before he had become a policeman, Faraday had always assumed that a deceased's facial expression would have shown signs of pain or fear. But no, the deceased had an expression of composure and tranquillity. There was no evidence of impact injuries, but if his vehicle had indeed drifted into the barrier as they surmised there probably would be none at all. Faraday gloved-up then leaned in close to the deceased's head and noted that he was clean shaven – extremely clean shaven – as if he had shaved only a few hours before his death. The scent of after-shave was strong. Faraday examined the deceased's hands. The hands appeared smooth and fingernails neatly manicured. The deceased's green v-neck jumper, navy and green check long-sleeved shirt and blue jeans were mid-range quality and the light-brown loafers well-worn.

'Have you searched the body?' asked Faraday.

'No, sir. I thought I should wait.'

'That's fine,' replied Faraday without censure, conscious that his manner was often perceived as aloof and his stare intimidating. 'What I propose, if you agree chief inspector, is that we simply search the clothing and his overnight bag. As there appears to be no suspicious causes of death, I think it best to leave his clothes in situ until the PM. I don't want in any way to compromise the integrity of the PM. Once we have done that, then we can consider what we have found, if anything.'

'And his home address, sir?' offered Kay.

'Absolutely, you and me as soon as we are finished here, then return for the PM.'

'And the car, sir?' asked Grant.

'Yes, the car. You can leave that with me. I want the full skinny on the vehicle which will eat into your district budget and so, leave it with me and I will clear the expenditure with Force HQ.'

‘You have some worries, sir?’ persisted Grant.

‘No particular worries other than anything to do with the security services will, inevitably, be like one of two things. Either trying to pick up mercury in your fingers or handling horse manure.’ Grant smiled and was about to laugh, but thought better of it as Faraday continued in a serious tone. ‘In any case, I am never happy until I know how and why a person has died. We owe his family that,’ he replied. Then he turned to Kay and continued rhetorically, ‘Can I suggest we start with his clothing?’

Chief Inspector Yin gloved-up in pale-blue forensic gloves and began to methodically examine the deceased’s clothing with her petite, beautiful hands. She searched carefully through the outside pockets of a Peter Storm anorak that had been recovered from the front passenger seat. There was nothing other than a comb in the right-hand outer pocket, a black Thinsulate knitted hat in the left and in the only outer breast pocket a pair a Jaeger dark glasses in a case. The inside zipped pocket revealed a leather wallet. One trouser pocket contained some cash, the other some paper tissues. The leather belt carried what appeared to be an empty mobile phone pouch. On the deceased’s left wrist was a Tissot watch. He wore no socks but the brown loafers. Kay noted what she had found and then returned all the items to the appropriate pockets.

‘Observations, Kay? David?’ asked Faraday, following his well-established policy of asking subordinates their opinions, and not firstly presenting his with the possibility that subordinates would simply agree.

Grant remained silent, either out of deference or because he was a little out of his depth. Kay broke the silence.

'It's what isn't here that's interesting,' she said. Faraday smiled and waited for her to continue. 'There's £3.27p in loose change in his trouser pocket. There's a road-side parking meter ticket for last evening; a wallet containing a driver's licence, an RAC membership card and his MoD ID in the name of Harvey, and exactly £400 in £20 notes but no bank or credit cards. There is a mobile phone pouch on his belt but no mobile phone.' She stepped back from the gurney, paused for a moment assessing what lay before her, then gestured towards the clothing and observed objectively: 'His clothing and his watch are not excessively expensive, although his clothing suggests a hiker, a walker, someone like that.'

Faraday saw that Grant was about to speak, but remained silent. 'Go on, Inspector,' he said, 'you were about to say something.'

'Only that there were a pair of hiking boots in the boot of his car, all neatly stowed away Bristol fashion with some heavy duty socks.'

'Good. Okay, let's have a look at his overnight bag,' suggested Faraday.

They turned towards the adjacent stainless steel table, empty except for the large black, leather bag. Kay Yin unzipped the bag and gently removed each item, placing them neatly into little groups. After a few moments she stepped back and scrutinised the collection of personal items in front of her.

'Well, we have a WHSmith's A5, one-page-for-each-day diary,' she said examining the pages of this dark blue-coloured book quickly. Every few moments she paused to examine one page, then another more closely. She stopped and thumbed back through the pages for a short moment, then closed the diary and placed it back on the table. 'The entries are precise and neat. All in black biro, although what appears to be "to-do" items have been ticked off in red ink. There appears to be a pattern of entries,' she observed, then added: 'but these may be of no significance,' but she was already sure that they would prove to be very significant. 'There is also a list of contacts typed on white pieces of paper and these are glued very precisely and neatly into the last few pages of the diary at the rear.'

Kay Yin then concentrated methodically upon the other items. 'There are … yes, eight pairs of underpants, all John Lewis brand; three short-sleeved and seven long-sleeved casual shirts, various brands ranging from Primark to M&S; same size. Three pairs of socks, all brown and a flattened Australian bush hat, Barmah make. Then there's a toilet bag containing a Remington electric shaver and Body Shop aftershave.' She paused as she picked up two Sure roll-on deodorants. She unscrewed the black top and examined both. 'Two deodorants, both un-used; nail clippers and a nail file and a large pink-coloured comb.' She then pointed at the soaps. 'Four bars of Marseille Soap, a well-thumbed four hundred and forty-eight page copy of Collins' Bird

Guide and … ' she turned the final items in her hand reading the inscription on the shafts before she continued, 'a couple of Bic biros and no mobile phone.'

'The keys, David. Do you have them please?' asked Faraday.

Grant pulled a bunch of keys from his pocket and handed them to Faraday who examined each key in turn: a Chubb five-lever key and a Yale cylinder key on one ring; what appeared to be a desk or locker key on a separate ring; and a Union three-lever key together with an Ingersol cylinder key on a separate ring, all of which were attached to a larger ring. He placed the keys on the table.

'Not sure if any of this helps us understand what he's been up to, sir,' offered Inspector Grant.

'No, you are right, David,' he responded without deflating the inspector, 'but it does tell us a lot about *him*.'

'Sir?' queried a slightly bemused Grant.

Faraday remained still for a silent moment, then Kay asked: 'Where is the tooth brush and tooth paste?'

'The tooth brush and paste?' queried Grant. He looked at Chief Inspector Yin, confusion on his face. Then looked at the items on the table before answering. 'There isn't any, ma'am.'

'Precisely,' replied Faraday. 'I think that we can assume that he was packed for a weekend or more likely a week away. If I go away for a weekend or a few days, I would take my tooth brush and paste with me unless, of course, I was staying in a nice hotel that would provide that sort of thing. If that were the case, why would I take with me four bars of soap? One bar maybe, if I had some sort of skin allergy. Harvey doesn't appear to have an allergy, and so, why four?'

Faraday paused as if contemplating his own answer. 'No, he wasn't going to a hotel. He could have been heading for a girlfriend's home but, my guess is that he was going to his own place where he would have had a tooth brush. And he was taking with him a supply of his favourite French soap, which indicates, maybe, a close attachment to France.' Then added: 'And the keys?' He moved forward and picked them up from the shiny steel and fingered them before returning them to the cold surface. 'I think, at this stage, that we can assume that these are two sets of house keys, maybe a second home, where we will find his bird-spotting binoculars.'

'And there are no credit cards, sir,' observed Kay.

Faraday turned to Inspector Grant as if ignoring Kay's comments and asked: 'Was the deceased's car fitted with a satnav?'

'No, sir.'

'And no mobile phone?' asked Faraday, seeking confirmation.

'No, sir.'

'It was stolen do you think?'

'I don't think so, sir,' replied the inspector, an anxious edge to his voice, concerned that Faraday may suspect that he, or his sergeant, had stolen the mobile. 'The way the body was slumped, an opportunist thief would not have seen the pouch, more likely he would have rummaged through his anorak.'

'And no sign of a mobile phone charger?'

'No, sir.'

Faraday remained silent as so often was his way, then a slight smile creased his face as he considered the facts as he knew them so far. A pattern was emerging. 'Well, I think that we can reasonably assume that our Mister Harvey, or is it Monsieur Melies, is being a naughty boy. It's early days but, maybe, he's using cash and not credit cards because he does not want his movements to be traced.' He turned to the inspector. 'His car didn't have a built-in satnav, did it?'

'No, sir.'

'And there wasn't any satnav in the glove compartment or anywhere else?'

'No, sir.'

Faraday looked at the items on the table again, then nodded towards Kay Yin and said, as if to no one in particular: 'Without satnav or a mobile, tracking his movements becomes even more difficult ... although not impossible.'

Kay began to repack the items into the overnight bag but retained the French passport and MoD ID, the drivers licence and wallet, diary and keys. She recorded these items in her pocket book and asked Grant to counter-sign the entry.

'I think we are done here Mr Grant. Thank you,' suggested Faraday. 'The chief inspector and I can handle the PM, unless you want to attend, although there is no reason for you to do so, particularly as you will be on nights again tonight. And we will also take a quick look at his apartment.'

'That's fine with me, sir,' replied a relieved Inspector Grant – he didn't like post mortems.

'Meanwhile, you will say nothing to anyone about what you have seen or our conversation here tonight. I will speak with your superintendent later this morning after I have spoken with the ACC. Do we understand each other?'

'Of course, sir,' he said in compliance with this instruction, reinforced by that Faraday glare.

Superintendent Faraday and Chief Inspector Yin returned to their cars, then drove off towards Hotwells and the dock-side home of Adrian Harvey.

***

They had contacted the Force Communication Centre which had the details of The Great Engineer's House, the apartment block named after Isambard Kingdom Brunel, the famous Victorian engineer. Only three of the thirty-two apartments were alarmed. Number sixteen wasn't alarmed. The apartment block consisted of four floors. The approach to the main entrance was crisp, clean and sterile, perfectly laid concrete paving bordered by grey slate stones and spiky Yucca shrubs, shrubs which will survive in the sun and well-drained soil, ideal for an environment where the residents are unlikely to water and tend the plants. The main entrance door was pine, glass and stainless steel. Faraday put his leather pilot's case on the floor and selected the Ingersol from his pocket and inserted this key into the lock and turned it to the right. The door opened, but she looked at him and said with mocking praise: 'You are so clever.' They giggled as they entered the lobby. The lobby. Sterile again.

Kay double-checked her note book for the number that Grant had given her during his first call, then scrutinised the apartment numbers and floor allocation on the display board. 'Number sixteen, second floor,' she said as the lift doors immediately opened to her delicate touch on the button.

The second floor was identical to the ground floor – plush but sterile. They walked past identical doors and came to number sixteen on their right. The river side. The expensive side thought Faraday. The Union key opened the door. They stepped inside and closed the door quietly. They stood there in the darkness of the hallway allowing their senses to absorb their surroundings. Silent surroundings. Silent. Not suspect. Satisfied, Faraday gloved-up again and walked purposefully down the hallway into the lounge, found the light switch and pressed it downwards. Energy bulbs flickered and then brightened. Faraday checked the pleasant book-lined lounge with a large window overlooking the docks. It was open-plan, very modern as if all the furniture had been chosen from the same catalogue; neat and tidy, with a breakfast-cum-kitchen area to the left.

'Bathroom and the bedroom clear,' said Kay as she joined him in the lounge. Faraday was standing in the middle of the lounge – just looking.

'Okay,' he said. 'Will you do the bathroom and bedroom and I'll do here.'

Kay left Faraday as he silently circumnavigated the lounge in silence. One wall, the one to the right, was filled with books, floor to ceiling. He checked these, pulling some volumes from their shelves, thumbing through the pages or checking the index for content, then recording details in his pocket book as he did so. There were a large number of books, hundreds in fact, all arranged as if a library without the Dewey coding. His examination took some while, but satisfied – at least for the moment – Faraday then sat at a modern, pine bureaux. The desk was free of clutter; no post at the door but neatly opened and in an in-tray. The bin of the cross-cut shredder was empty. Pens and pencils, highlighters of various colours and envelopes of various sizes were neatly placed in their apertures. Faraday opened a little wooden box containing postage stamps. He closed the lid then examined a note pad which he removed and placed in an evidence bag, as he did with the Olympus pocket recorder and two framed photographs.

He sat back in the chair imagining how Harvey would have felt seated there at his desk. He glanced up at the framed certificates, examining each closely, then, as if awakened from his thoughts, he pulled open the filing drawer to his right and methodically looked through each maroon, blue and grey-coloured drop file. All twelve of the maroon files were empty; some of the blue and grey ones were empty too, whilst others were full of documents. He fingered the plastic identification tags of the drop files and examined the card inserts. He removed a bundle of bank statements and cash receipts; a mobile phone invoice; vehicle insurance, MOT and repair invoices, all in the name of Harvey. Whilst Faraday was preoccupied with the files, Kay checked the kitchen, the contents of the food cupboards, the fridge and freezer, rubbish bins and the washing machine.

After some thirty-five minutes, Faraday returned to the main part of the lounge and walked towards the large plate glass window which gave an impressive view out onto the river, the *Matthew* at her berth and the *SS Great Britain* in her dry dock, the illuminated spire of St Mary Redcliffe beyond, once referred to by Queen Elizabeth the First as 'the fairest parish church in the kingdom'. He lowered himself into the green leather arm chair and checked the answerphone on the machine to his right. There were no saved or new messages. But it was not the view of the church that preoccupied Faraday.

Finished in the kitchen area, Kay returned to the lounge carrying four exhibit bags. She didn't interrupt him until he looked around towards her and smiled. 'You are fascinated by the painting?' she asked.

He nodded in agreement, then asked, 'What do you have there?'

'A black and white photograph in a frame of a very striking Chinese woman. It was on the bedside table, along with a Valentine's card. And, in the drawer was a collection of erotic photographs of the same female together with a mobile phone.'

Faraday refrained from examining the photographs, maybe out of deference to his lover or, maybe, because he wanted nothing to distract him. 'Interesting about the Chinese female and the mobile phone,' he said without a smile. 'Why have a mobile phone in a drawer and have an empty mobile phone pouch on your trouser belt? There's another phone somewhere and we've missed it or it was stolen. Anyway,' he asked, 'your sense of this apartment?'

'Clothing is reasonably priced. John Lewis and Marks & Spencer. All stowed away neatly; shirts, underpants, socks, trousers, jackets and shoes all where they should be as if the maid had just finished up. The bed has been neatly made. The bathroom has a couple of little model sail boats on top of a wall cabinet and a collection of sea shells in a glass bowl.' She held up a forensic bag containing the shells and continued: 'Towels neat and tidy; nothing in the linen basket and the toilet has been cleaned with a blue cleaner – just as if it has been prepared for his return.'

'And the kitchen?'

'Larder all branded items. Freezer full. Fridge empty,' she replied. 'With the exception of an un-opened litre of long-life milk. Dishwasher empty. A mug and spoon, plate and knife on the drainer. Sink clean. Rubbish bin and food waste bin all empty with clean liners in both. Washing machine set to come on the 16th May at 0200. No significant contents. All utensils, pans and hob are really clean. I don't think he was in to cooking,' she speculated then continued: 'Sixteen bottles of wine, all French, and seem to be expensive. As with the bathroom and bedroom, no medication to speak of other than some headache and cold tablets, a partially used bottle of indigestion medicine, Elastoplasts, a small bottle of TCP and another small, brown plastic medicine bottle containing twenty-two Piroxicam 10mg capsules. In Harvey's name and local pharmacy's label. I checked on my mobile. Piroxicam is an anti-inflammatory.'

'Well, he was clearly planning on being away.'

'And the picture?' she asked, referring to the 52" x 20" oil painting hanging in a modern, gold-coloured frame over a mock fireplace depicting a river scene against low hills in the background.

Faraday didn't answer directly, his thoughts already racing ahead. 'This is his favourite place. This chair. This window. Seated here,' he said as he pointed to a scale model of the twelve-metre racing yacht *True North IV* of Canada, 'he is alongside this fine model of the yacht, with a romantic view of the harbour, the white porcelain head of a unicorn in the hearth, that canvas above the fireplace and his music centre. Maybe he would dream here.'

'And what do you have in your lap?' she asked.

'Oh, a laptop,' he said referring to a Sony at the bottom of a pile of exhibit bags. 'It is probably his but we can have it examined and see what it gives us. There are also some files which don't seem to be anything to get too excited about, but we'll see. We have a UK passport in Harvey's name and also his divorce papers and employment contract, plus a single mobile phone contract, so, maybe there isn't a second phone, but ... ,' he paused, losing his train of thought thinking of mobile phones. Typically dyslexic, it took Faraday a moment or two to get back on track. 'Yes, sorry, what intrigues me is that other than the canvas, the only things on the walls are right there above his desk,' he said pointing to the wall, 'and they are all identically framed ... , 'he paused for a moment and flicked through his note book, ' ... here we are, a First from Cambridge, a Dipôme de l'Institut Européen de Commerce et de Gestion de la Rochelle, his Masters from Southampton and a Doctorate from Bristol. But no photographs of him in cap and gown or with fellow students. He was obviously proud of his achievements to the extent that whilst his awards span many years, the frames are identical indicating perfection, pride and maybe arrogance. Whatever, they are very fine achievements, but nothing about his school days, no souvenirs - other than the ceramic head of a white unicorn – and only two photographs . One, I think could be of his mother. The other is of a naval officer, but not wearing a Royal Navy cap badge. Maybe a grand-father or uncle,' he said as he held up a brown paper exhibit bag, then asked: 'You plucked some cards off the kitchen pin board?'

'Yes, the business cards of a plumber, an electrician, a TV repair guy, a dentist and a barber. If he has a habit of chatting to anyone, it will always be a barber or a chiropodist. Worth a visit to the barber.'

'Okay. Are we done here do you think?'

'Yep,' she replied as they put the exhibits in the pilot's case, 'but we could check the communal bin bay on the way out.'

'Wow. A perfect ending to a perfect evening with my perfect girlfriend.'

Chapter 4

Saturday, 30th April.

Bristol, England and Rome, Italy.

IT WAS EXACTLY 10.30am as arranged. Kay Yin rang the doorbell and waited. She was expecting a dour, plain woman, but when Mrs Harvey opened the door Kay was met by a not unattractive, well-dressed, slim, smiling lady. The apartment was larger than Kay had imagined with roof-top views over the city where the night had surrendered to a glorious Spring day. The lounge had a very feminine feel about it, although business-like, with a brief case neatly placed against an easy chair, together with a laptop and numerous NHS files arranged on a low table.

They sat at the breakfast bar in the light oak-coloured kitchen and drank coffee from mugs as they talked. Kay carefully. Annette Harvey uneasily. Kay showed Mrs Harvey the British passport of her ex-husband and she readily confirmed his identity but with some anxiety. She was shocked at the news of his death and took many moments to compose herself. Like many who have received such news, Annette Harvey took refuge in immersing herself in the mechanics of what officialdom would now demand of her. She asked for more details of her ex-husband's death, the inquest procedure and funeral arrangements. She explained that her husband's parents had died a long while ago and he had no near relatives. She spoke proudly of Adrian's hobbies, his cleverness and time at Cambridge; of the early years of their marriage, the good times and high hopes they had harboured for their future together. There was contemplative silence followed by sadness as she explained that all that had changed when he was repeatedly overlooked for promotion. Her husband, she explained, became increasingly frustrated then bitter, particularly about six years ago when a female was appointed as his new boss.

Other than a photograph of an elderly couple, Annette's parents Kay assumed, there were no photographs of children. Nevertheless, Kay asked the question.

'You have no children, Annette?'

For a moment she was thoughtful, reflecting sadly: 'No ... no, there were no children. Probably for the best really.'

Conveniently changing the subject to what appeared to be a lighter topic, Kay asked: 'And where did you and Adrian go for your holidays? Would it be here or abroad?'

'Here in the UK,' she said slowly thinking of happier days. 'Devon, Norfolk and Dorset mostly. Walking, bird watching, that sort of thing. It was an interest that we both shared ... something we did together.' Her sadness returned, but Kay had to persist.

'Ah, they are lovely counties. Which would have been the favourite?'

'I've never thought about it really. Why do you ask?' she said, more out of curiosity than anything else.

'We think that Adrian may have had another house, a cottage maybe or an apartment somewhere. Can you help me here?'

Annette was surprised. 'I thought he only had the Hotwells' property,' she replied, bemused, 'but he was always going off somewhere at weekends.'

'We are not certain but if he had another, where do you think it would most likely be?'

'Dorset,' she said without hesitation. 'Most likely Dorset.'

'And would that be inland or along the coast, do you think?'

'Inland if there was a river or on the coast. The coast probably, anywhere where birds would be found.'

'And fish?' asked Kay casually.

'Fish?' she questioned incredulously.

'Yes, fishing. I don't know, maybe rod fishing?' she asked, making a gesture as if casting a line.

'Oh, no,' replied Annette, virtually disgusted by the thought. 'Fishing annoyed Adrian. Birds were always being fouled by lines or being killed by eating the small lead weights. No, we would never fish.'

‘You said that you used to live in Stoke Bishop. Where exactly would that have been?’

‘Ormerod Road.’

‘Ah, yes. I know it,’ she said remembering the houses in this expensive suburb.

‘And the Stoke Bishop house was sold when you divorced?’

‘Yes, I bought this place and Adrian bought the apartment in Hotwells.’

‘May I ask? Does he pay you any annual sum?’

‘Yes, £3,000 a year.’

The two women continued to talk and by the time they had finished their second mug of coffee, Annette had become more open about their marriage and her ex-husband’s sexual predilections, his constant accusations that she had not understood his needs as well as her suspicions that he was seeing a prostitute.

‘Do you know that for certain? Kay asked.

‘Not for certain. I knew that quite large sums of money would be drawn out every other Thursday and he would be out on those Thursday nights – all night.’

‘Can you recall how much?’

‘It was in the hundreds … two or three hundred, I think,’ she replied, then added: ‘It may have been more,’ embarrassed to contemplate such a large sum.

‘That’s a lot of money,’ queried Kay, not considering it necessary to add ‘for a prostitute.’

‘I think she was quite sophisticated and very … ,’ Annette paused for a moment with a painful memory, then continued: ‘He said that she was very understanding.’

‘In what way?’ probed Kay gently.

Tears filled her eyes before she answered. ‘I suppose I didn’t do enough … he wanted me to do things … I couldn’t do them.’ Annette cleared her throat and wiped away the tears. ‘He always kept saying that the people at work didn’t understand him and that I didn’t understand him either.’

Kay put her hand on Annette’s and said, ‘I think with Adrian that nothing anyone would do for him at work or in the home would ever have been enough.’

‘Will this be reported at the inquest? asked Annette suddenly anxious.

‘No,’ reassured Kay, ‘an inquest is really only concerned with the cause of death. I need to check out a few things and satisfy myself that this was simply a car accident as a result of a heart attack,’ she said, then adding gently: ‘If it is of any comfort, we are pretty sure that it was instantaneous. He wouldn’t have known anything about it.’

‘But you aren’t satisfied about the cause of him dying?’ she asked, an edge of anxiety in her voice.

‘I can’t be certain, but I am pretty sure that there is nothing suspicious about Adrian’s death, but we will have to await the normal tests and we will know the results very soon.’ Annette seemed satisfied with Kay’s explanation and so Kay asked one final question. ‘Oh, one last thing. I found a little bottle of Piroxican tablets in Adrian’s kitchen. What were they prescribed for, do you know?’

‘Oh, yes, Adrian had some sort of spinal sclerosis when he was younger, in his early twenties.’

‘I see. And how many tablets would he take a day?’

‘They weren’t tablets exactly, little capsules, about two a day, in the mornings. Is this important?’

‘I don’t think so, I just wondered that was all.’ Kay sensed that Annette was now sufficiently reassured and confident in her relationship with the policewoman to appeal to her for her co-operation. ‘Meanwhile,’ she continued, ‘it would be helpful to me personally if you did not discuss Adrian’s death with anyone at the moment, other than with Superintendent Faraday at headquarters or me. I’m sure you know what it’s like, the press will get hold of this and suggest that Adrian was some sort of James Bond and you will be hounded from dawn to dusk.’

For a moment a smile returned to her face at the ridiculous thought of her ex-husband being some sort of secret agent or spy. 'Yes, yes. I understand.'

Kay left Annette her card and the interview, tense but revealing, finished a little before twelve-forty-five.

***

The ATAC bus number NI crossed the River Tiber and travelled onwards along the Via del Tritone. Alessio Bianchi continued his animated conversation with his fellow plasterer, Marco Rossi, as they passed the fountain at the Piazza Gigli. Dominating the piazza was the magnificence of the Repobblica Teatro dell Opera. As craftsmen of the highest order, they admired and appreciated its beauty.

Further on at the Piazza Vittoorio Emanuele 11, the municipal bus slowed to a gentle halt. The automatic doors hissed open allowing passengers to exit and warm air to enter. Both men stepped down onto the pavement, the day's sun radiating brightly from the pavement and the mellow brick walls. They walked just a little further amongst little knots of gossiping pedestrians and casual strollers, stopping near the university's Facolta di Studi Orientali. In the cool shade of the Pinus pinea, the 'umbrella pine' trees, and overlooking the park, these old friends shared cigarettes as they reflected upon their immense good fortune. It had been hard work and both had been working six-day weeks for many months, but both had had full employment for three years working within the Sistine Hall of the Vatican Library and the Archivum

Secretum Vaticanum, and benefitted from the reputation that such skilled work had attracted. As a result of their skills and consciousness, Marco had gained a further contract at the Borghese Gallery and Alessio a prestigious contract at the Basilica di San Giovanni Laterano.

For Alessio, the older and shorter of the two men, this work represented the pinnacle of his career. He had always thought that the prestige of working at Windsor Castle in England between 1994 and 1996, after the fire there in 1992, could not be exceeded, but the last three years had been a triumph and a crowning glory. His skill as a plasterer in both cast and free-hand techniques, together with his uncanny ability to work quickly and precisely with rapidly drying stucco, had resulted in his elevation to that of renowned restoration chief.

Cigarettes finished, these good friends parted company for their short weekend, but not before they admired, as men of a certain age do, a girl – a girl to these middle-aged men – who walked past with beautiful legs and an equally beautifully strutting walk in light-blue soft shoes, a student they thought, with care-free blond hair and dressed in casual, non-descript clothes, a small canvas bag slung over a bare tanned shoulder. They would have expected the scent of her perfume as she passed them by, but there was none, she simply turned her head and crossed the road. She smiled. Her smile was natural and captivating. Their eyes followed her. They smiled the silly smiles of dreamers. Then she was out of their sight and then out of their thoughts.

Alession walked on alone towards the Viale Carlo Felice against the on-coming traffic in the one-way street. He entered this street of parked cars, faint shadows and tall apartment blocks of ochre-coloured walls and stone embossments. He walked on for another three-hundred yards in the shade of the pine trees until he arrived at the wrought-iron gates hanging open on their supporting pillars. He entered the courtyard within and made his way up just two steps to the open archway and stepped through into the cool vestibule of marble floors and steep, dark winding stairs. On the left-hand side of the vestibule were the forty post boxes of this residential block. He stood in front of his own, number thirty-two, and fumbled in his pocket for the little key. He felt excitement tinged with caution as he imagined the envelope that lay within, the envelope that would contain the last of four payments, each of $7,000. He inserted the key into the lock to the right of the oblong box. He turned the key once to the left and the little grey-coloured door sprang open with a sharp metallic click. Inside was the envelope. For a moment Alessio hesitated as he glanced furtively towards the entrance door and then up the winding staircase. The doorway and stairs were completely empty. He waited a moment longer. All was still. He removed the thick, brown-coloured envelope and quickly stuffed it in to his baggy trouser pocket, shut the little post box door and pressed the button for the lift. He glanced up above the doors and saw the display board illuminate the little numbers slowly in turn: '4', then '3', '2' and '1'. As the lift was about to reach the ground floor, Alessio stepped back a few paces.

The lift doors rattled open. Alessio stared at the woman transfixed, then recovered himself. He and Signorina Alvarez from the fourth floor exchanged pleasantries. The elderly lady told him how her rheumatism seemed to be worsening by the day. He, in return, hoped that the glorious weather that had been forecast for the weeks ahead would help her. She feigned gloom-ridden mournfulness, predicting with certainty that her pain and suffering would continue. Pleasantries completed, if that was how this exchange could be described, Alessio was thankful when the lift doors slid closed, his only thought now was to put the money safely under the false floor of his heavy, dark wooden wardrobe as quickly as he could.

He entered his apartment on the third floor. Once inside, panic seized him as he closed the door and fumbled with the two locks. Relieved that he was now safe, he leant back against the door and took a number of deep breaths, then, agitatedly he pulled the brown envelope from his pocket. He picked at the flap and crudely opened the envelope. He brought the opened envelope up to his nose and smelt the crispness of the US dollar bills. He thumbed and counted them with relief then walked into the bedroom, knelt before the wardrobe and opened both doors. Alessio removed some shoes then lifted the floor panel of the wardrobe and placed, almost reverently, the $7,000 in his secret hiding place. He replaced the wooden panel, rearranged his shoes carefully and began to close the doors.

‘I have a gun pointed at your head,’ said the American quietly but firmly. ‘Stand up very slowly with your hands where I can see them.’

Alessio looked around, startled, losing his balance, steadying himself with his left hand as he stumbled and sat back on the floor, his back against the wardrobe doors. For a fleeting moment he was totally confused. His apartment door had been securely locked with two locks. He had heard nothing. There was no aroma of delicate perfume. Of course there was none. That would have been a mistake. Now total confusion gave way to total fear. This could not be the same girl, he thought. But it was. He first recognised her soft light-blue shoes and beautiful tanned legs, then the business end of a black 2213 automatic pistol, the smallest automatic in the Smith & Wesson catalogue, although he had no idea of the manufacture, just its menacing intent. He notice again her care-free blond hair and bare, tanned shoulders, but, her smile was no longer captivating; her mouth was unsmiling, firm and uncompromising. She spoke again.

‘We have much to talk about, Alessio, you and me.’

Chapter 5

Sunday, 1st May.

Central London and Police Headquarters, Bristol, England.

AT 10.30am COMMANDER WALT BERGMAN, the Assistant Naval Attaché, or so proclaimed his accreditation to the Court of St James, although in reality a member of the Office of Naval Intelligence, parked the United States' embassy pool car on the seventh floor of the multi-storey car park in Holborne, Central London. He reversed into Bay 392 and waited. He always liked to arrive early for appointments, even when these appointments were with friends and old colleagues. Old habits. He had driven around the floors but had noticed nothing that gave him a warning that his activities may have been the subject of surveillance. In any case, Walt needed time to consider carefully his approach and the words he would shortly use at the meeting. He knew that these men could be relied upon. He needed them to be on-side and for them not to think that they were simply being treated disrespectfully as errand boys.

At 10.55am a black Mitsubishi L200 Animal approached up the ramp and drove into Bay 391, driver's door to driver's door. The electric window of each vehicle wound down simultaneously letting in the dank smell of oil and ever-present exhaust fumes.

‘Hi, Jim. Curt,’ said Walt. The two Americans nodded in recognition.

‘Good to see you, Walt,’ said the other driver, Jim Hogan. His passenger, Curt Olsen, leant forward and gave a casual salute in acknowledgement.

‘Kinda good to see you too,’ he replied.

‘You had in mind that we could maybe help you out some again?’ asked Jim, a thick-set, clean-shaven, square-jawed former US Marine with Colgate TV advertisement teeth.

‘We have a time-sensitive operation going down,’ replied Walt, ‘and it would be real useful if you guys could help us out a little.’

‘Okay. Is this off-the-books, Walt?’

‘Yep. Under the table again,’ replied Commander Bergman. ‘We are talking plausible deniability here guys. No e-mails or any trail, you understand?’

‘We always understand. That’s what we do. Hey, at the end of the day we are all helping Uncle Sam,’ said Jim Hogan, then asked: ‘What would you have us do?’

Bergman had already thought of a response to this inevitable question. He needed to be diplomatic. He didn’t want to offend or belittle these two men with whom he had worked so closely before. ‘We need to have a parcel collected out of town.’

‘A parcel you say?’ queried Hogan curiously.

‘That’s it. Just a parcel, a cardboard tube about so long,’ replied Bergman, extending his hands apart and indicating a length of about two feet.

‘We don’t normally do parcels, Walt, you know that,’ he said slightly dismissively.

‘I wouldn’t ask you guys if it wasn’t a *very* important parcel.’

Both ex-US Marines looked at each other and exchanged sceptical, if not offended, faces. Bergman wasn’t sure which. He was about to justify their involvement in the operation when Jim Hogan asked: ‘We would need to know what the tube contained?’

‘I have no knowledge, guys. Always best not to know,’ adding quickly and so as to reassure and confirm the importance of the operation, ‘although the grey suits at State seem to be more eager than usual.’

The mention of the State Department seemed to placate Hogan. ‘Well, you know State. They get the jitters if the brand of toilet paper is changed,’ then queried more seriously: ‘Is it heavy or light?’

‘It’s light, real light. Papers I think.’

Satisfied that the contents were not ordnance or drugs, Hogan asked: ‘Okay, is this a pick-up from a person or place?’

‘From a French sailor or a Brit,’ replied the naval attaché.

‘Okay, and are these guys likely to present a problem for us?’

‘Not to you,’ Bergman replied. ‘The Frenchman is a small-time playboy-type with a sail boat. The Brit’s a desk jockey,’ replied Bergman conveniently omitting the fact that the Brit was a researcher at the British Ministry of Defence Procurement Headquarters.

‘Is there a time-frame here?’ probed Hogan.

‘Yes, ideally mid-May. We hope to know more by the 3rd . The dates could change of course, a little earlier, a little later.’

‘And where would the pick-up be?’

‘Our judgement at the moment is along the south coast.’

Jim Hogan looked towards Curt Oslen. Oslen nodded in agreement to the unasked question. ‘Okay, Walt, that’s doable. What do you want us to do with the parcel when we have it?’

‘I will collect from you,’ Walt replied. ‘I’ll be able to give you a time and place soon.’

‘You say the south coast. Can you be more specific?’

‘No. Not at the moment. We had some intel from the Italians and a NSA bird is tracking the French guy right now,’ he said, referring to one of the United States’ National Security Agency satellites. ‘We are certain that it will be along the south coast but where exactly we’ll have to wait on the NSA boys a little longer.’

The involvement of the NSA impressed Hogan and Oslen. ‘Okay,’ acknowledged Jim displaying his Colgate teeth again. ‘The south coast is good for us and we like to get out of town from time to time. We’ll wait to hear from you, Walt, in the normal way.’

Jim Hogan started the 2.5 diesel engine and backed the pick-up out of the parking bay. The engine sounded harsh as Jim Hogan waved and drove down towards the exit. Commander Walt Bergman remained seated in the embassy car. He removed his personal mobile phone and called Atlas International Associates and asked to speak with their Executive Vice-President.

‘Good to hear from you, Walt,’ said William J L Kemper after he had deliberately made the commander wait. ‘Do you have any news for me?’

‘Always good news, sir,’ replied Walt warily but enthusiastically. ‘All the players are seated at the table.’

‘That’s good to hear, Walt,’ said Kemper, then added: ‘Only call me again when you’ve swept the board.’ Then the line went dead.

Forty minutes later, and one hundred and thirty-two miles away to the west, four people were about to gather in the Severnside Police Headquarters' office suite of Robert Perrin QPM, Assistant Chief Constable (Crime).

Perrin, a thinner version of the disgraced former Italian prime minister, Silvio Berlusconi, wearing a beautifully tailored double-breasted suit and slicked-down jet-back hair, stood with his back to the window which gave panoramic views over the Gordano Valley. At his side, perfectly silhouetted against the light, was the beautiful Helen Cave dressed in a black business suit. Faraday tapped on the polished pine door, opened it and allowed Chief Inspector Kay Yin to walk through into the imposing office. He could not see Helen's face but he knew it was her, instantly recognising her silhouette.

'Ah, good morning Mark, you know Helen Cave, I believe?' said the ACC introducing the MI5 agent.

Helen stepped forward extending her arm to shake his hand, her stance rigid, her shoulders back, defensive maybe, thought Mark or simply to forestall an embrace.

'Yes, sir. We worked together four years ago,' he said shaking her hand, thinking for a short moment of what had been.

'And this is Detective Chief Inspector Kay Yin,' said Perrin. Helen shook Kay's hand as she assessed the petite and alluring Chinese detective, noting her expensive blue blazer and light-blue Armani jeans. She had seen the fleeting but intimate deference Mark had shown to Kay Yin, as she had also noticed their body language and the hardness behind Kay's beautiful fawn-like eyes as the two women met. Mark and Kay were lovers. Helen had no doubt – as they had once been.

Coffee arrived and the quartet sat around the centrally placed, oval coffee table, Cave assessing the three police officers; Faraday and Yin assessing Cave, and Perrin assessing them all.

'Thank you all for coming in on a Sunday,' said Perrin, replacing his cup and saucer on the table. 'This meeting is to ensure that we are all in the loop on this. Let me summarise and please interrupt if I have any of the facts wrong.' He brushed imaginary crumbs from his trouser legs before speaking again. 'A forty-three year old male was found dead in the early hours of Friday morning on the Portway, one of the main western arterial roads serving the city. Preliminary examination indicates that he suffered a heart attack whilst driving his Volvo saloon. The car is registered in the name of Adrian Harvey of Hotwells,' then turned towards Helen Cave and said in his most affable and helpful manner: 'His address is in a pleasant, water-side apartment in the old Bristol docks area.' The MI5 agent acknowledged the ACC's kindness by way of a silently mouthed 'thank you' before Perrin continued. They were playing each other, thought Faraday. 'The driver's licence found in his wallet is also in this name and his current address.'

He stretched forward and picked up his cup and saucer again as Mark placed his leather briefing file at the side of his chair and picked up the plate of biscuits, handing them to Helen, Kay and the ACC in turn. Both women took a shortbread biscuit. Perrin declined. As Helen Cave began to eat her biscuit, Perrin continued. 'Found in an overnight bag was a French passport in the name of Edouard Melies, date of birth and photograph as Harvey's driver's licence. Mark stopped what would have been the routine notification to the French embassy and blocked any publicity. Late Friday morning, Mark and Kay gained entry to Harvey's apartment and discovered a UK passport in the name of Harvey.' Perrin looked across towards the chief inspector. 'Kay, you are able to update us I think?'

'Yes, sir. Thank you,' she said. 'Documentation in the apartment shows that Harvey worked with Research Group AT12 at Abbeywood. He was married to an Annette Goodman but they were divorced about four years ago. I interviewed Annette yesterday. We are analysing his computer, a pocket voice recorder and a mobile phone found in his apartment, as well as bundles of correspondence, bank statements and accounts. We have asked for bank records under the money laundering provisions. The bank is being co-operative and we are accessing landline and mobile phone records.'

'And you, Helen,' asked Perrin almost casually, 'your people would have been aware that Harvey worked at Abbeywood?'

‘Oh yes,’ replied the MI5 agent picking up her coffee cup from the table. She sipped the coffee, then added: ‘Harvey worked there as a researcher.’

‘Researching what exactly?’ probed Faraday gently.

‘He originally worked at the Hydrographic Office at Taunton but was moved to Abbeywood in 2009 or 2010.’

‘Why was that?’ Faraday asked.

‘Harvey had been researching the Scotia Ridge. Later, his duties included research in connection with the South Shetland Trough,’ she replied unhelpfully, adding unnecessarily, ‘that is all,’ hoping that this explanation would forestall any further enquiry. It didn’t.

‘And that is where?’ asked Kay Yin, although she had a vague idea of its general location.

‘Oh, it’s an area near the Antarctic Peninsular,’ replied Helen Cave as if this fact was of no consequence.

‘But Harvey had been removing MoD files, hadn’t he Helen?’ challenged Faraday, his voice soft but all business.

For a moment, Perrin was caught unawares, but did not show it, merely leaning forward with raised eyebrows as if to ask the MI5 agent to confirm Faraday’s suspicions.

Helen Cave hesitated so as to gather her thoughts and for effect. ‘This is rather embarrassing, Mr Perrin,’ she added.

‘Come, come, you are amongst friends here, Helen,’ he ventured, confident that Faraday was on to something.

‘We knew that some of Harvey’s research material was being passed on to the Argentineans,’ she said in an easy manner. ‘The value of the information was low grade, but it suited us that this information was being leaked. We hoped to exploit this conduit. However, we were not originally sure of the source, although we believed that it was probably Harvey. As accommodation at Taunton was at a premium, it was very convenient and logical for us to relocate Harvey nearer his home in Bristol which provided us with the opportunity to monitor him more closely. As a result we were able to confirm Harvey as the source and ensure that he had access to information we were confident he would pass on. And he did. With Harvey’s phase of the Antarctic work completed about four years ago, he was reassigned to work connected with the Strait of Gibraltar.’

‘And that was in connection with what?’ asked Perrin feigning Mr Plod-like ignorance.

‘The continental shelf there and all the fuss the Spanish continue to make about fishing and territorial rights.’

‘And no doubt,’ Perrin suggested, ‘that research information has been fed to the Spanish via the Argentineans?’

‘Oh, yes. The Spanish and Argentineans were close before, during and after the Falklands War, and continue to be so.

As I said, this suited us very well,' she replied, then adding as if confiding in the police officers: 'Some of this information included dis-information and mis-information of course,' knowing that she would never be permitted to elaborate and that Perrin would not probe this aspect further.

Perrin turned to Faraday. 'And your next step, Mark?'

Mark knew how the ACC's mind worked. They needed more time. 'This is an on-going investigation,' he replied, 'into the, as yet, unexplained death of Harvey. We are still awaiting the results of a full PM and the tox screen. Kay and I have a meeting scheduled for this afternoon. I will continue to go through Harvey's diary, telephone logs and so on whilst Kay will be picking up Mrs Harvey and taking her to formally identify her late husband and, of course, some pressing District duties.'

'Good, so some progress then,' concluded the ACC. 'Incidentally, Kay, I spoke with your District Commander earlier. I don't think he was keen to have his cooked breakfast interrupted by a long conversation with me and so he was most co-operative and readily agreed to you working with Mr Faraday.' The ACC beamed. 'With both of you on the case, I'm hoping that we can wrap this up quickly.' Although that likelihood he knew was unlikely.

'Thank you, sir,' Kay acknowledged.

‘I have some of my own enquiries to make,’ interjected Helen Cave, ‘but I could link up with Mark later on and compare notes. Is that alright with you, Mr Perrin?’

The ACC was tempted to remark that he was sure that Helen Cave would very much like to compare notes but simply looked across towards Mark Faraday. ‘Let’s say at four-thirty,’ responded Mark, a time-frame that would allow him to go through more of Harvey’s documents with Chief Inspector Yin alone.

Helen Cave smiled her perfect smile. ‘Four-thirty would be perfect, Mark.’

‘Okay,’ agreed Perrin sensing a change of atmosphere in his office. ‘Helen will be staying at the Marriott, Victoria Street. I suggest that the three of you meet up again tomorrow at The Grove,’ he recommended, referring to the location of the Bristol Central Police Headquarters, just a half-mile from the Marriott Hotel, where Detective Chief Inspector Yin was based and thus steering the MI5 agent well away from the offices of the Special Branch at Force Headquarters. ‘By then the PM and tox results will be in. Are we agreed?’

Perrin looked at each in turn. They each nodded their agreement. ‘Okay,’ said Perrin, ‘teleconference tomorrow at ten-thirty, no, make it eleven. I hope by then that we can wrap this traffic accident up,’ although he was quite sure that this was only the beginning of a more intriguing and significant investigation.

‘If you, Kay, would like to walk Helen to reception, I just need a few moments with Mr Faraday.’ Perrin waited until Chief Inspector Kay Yin and Agent Helen Cave had left the office before turning to Faraday. ‘Take a seat, Mark.’ Both men sat down. Perrin was the first to speak. ‘How did you know about the MoD papers?’

‘I didn’t, sir,’ replied Faraday, then he explained. ‘Well, not for sure, anyway. You see, Harvey is all into the environment and recycling. He only uses roll-on deodorants and uses both sides of small note pads, that sort of thing. In his bureau drop-files, one group of files, the maroon ones, was empty. It appeared that the little card name tags had been used before and so I removed them, turned them inside-out only to find,’ he paused to open his briefing file and scanned his notes. ‘Yes, here we are. “Hudson Bay”, “Inuits”, “Nunavut”, “Frobisher”, “Oviedo”, “Mi’kmaq”, whatever or whoever that is, and so on, written on them. Harvey had been researching something, maybe something about the Hudson Bay, but the files are now empty.’

‘But Cave was talking about the Antarctic wasn’t she. The Hudson Bay is near, or in, the Arctic isn’t it?’

‘Well, yes. Just below,’ he said, then realised that that may have sounded patronising. He moved quickly on. ‘But, as you say, she did seem to concentrate on the Southern Hemisphere, didn’t she?’ he said rhetorically, ‘and I just wonder why, particularly as one of the name tags had the name “Arctic Islands” written on it,’ Faraday continued, conscious of his rule never to mislead his superiors.

'However, I only had time to quickly check the index of my atlas at home and I couldn't find an Arctic Island, although there is an Arctic Ocean and a town called Arctic Bay.'

'Okay, but the missing files, *if* they are actually missing, are not necessarily MoD files. They could have simply been another bunch of research in connection with some hobby he was pursuing or another piece of academic study.'

Faraday remained silent and said nothing for a short moment. 'That could be the case, sir, but if that were so, where were the lever-arch files full of notes? Where were the drafts? I just feel uncomfortable with how this is settling down.'

'The real problem is that you don't trust 'em, the Security Services, do you, Mark?'

The response of the Head of Special Branch was immediate. 'By the very nature of their job, sir, the Security Services are never open. To operate effectively they have to deceive. On a daily basis they tell lies and purport to be what they are not.' Faraday picked up his cup and drank the now lukewarm coffee. It was still good coffee. He replaced the cup in the saucer and spoke again explaining his reasoning. 'I have a neighbour who is a car salesman. If I meet him he can't resist giving me a sales pitch. He's a really nice guy and a good neighbour but he's hard-wired into the sales pitch. It's second nature to him. He can't resist telling me in great detail how marvellous his new TV is, or describing how wonderful his latest holiday was and how brilliantly his children are doing at their superb school. Cops are the same. We act out of habit. We enter a pub and look around, the non-police officer would just head straight for the bar. If I go to a restaurant, I like to have a table that allows me to see the entrance and toilet doors. I don't like to sit with my back to a window or door. We tend to be mistrusting. It's what we do. It's what we are.' Faraday re-crossed his legs, adjusted his jacket and fiddled with his papers, thinking as he did so.

'But you in Special Branch can't be completely open,' the ACC challenged gently. 'You and your staff often purport to be someone whom you are not?'

'True, but the difference is that there are mechanisms in place that make me, that is us, accountable. The reality of the situation is that we, and the public, haven't a clue who the Security Services are and what they are up to. They operate in the darkest of shadows. If challenged they will hide under the national security shroud. My experience is that, in a case like the one we are dealing with now, they will, if they think it's necessary, deceive their superiors, their political masters, the public and the police without a thought.

Perrin stood and smiled. 'It may be wise for us to remember that in the weeks to come.' He returned to his desk and sat down with a sigh. 'I'll leave it to you, Mark. Follow your instincts. If something important crops up, be certain to tell me about it – before we get into an unpleasant turf war.

Faraday left the ACC's office and walked through the empty conference room and down the stairs to the entrance foyer. Kay was there chatting to the female receptionists. She turned as he was half-way down the stairs and smiled, a smile more radiant than the late afternoon sun over the far-off hills. The two police officers wished the receptionists good day, they smiled in return, Faraday oblivious to the effect that he had on women. They walked to the almost empty visitors' car park at the front of the headquarters and Faraday opened the passenger door of his Audi A5 for Kay. She slid gracefully into the passenger seat and pulled the door closed. Perrin looked down from his office window as Faraday walked around the rear of his car and got into the driver's seat. Faraday started the 2.7 litre engine. There was a powerful purr in response and they drove along the gentle twists of the drive and through the gates leaving the headquarters at top of the hill.

Faraday was the first to speak. 'You don't like her too much, do you?'

Kay didn't answer immediately, then turned her beautiful Oriental face towards her lover and asked: 'Do you?'

'I *liked* her once. For a very short while she was an important part of my life. It would be silly to suggest that it all meant nothing.'

'And now?'

Faraday found it impossible to lie to her. 'For a moment there was something, the something that had attracted me before but … 'he paused as he searched for the words, ' … it was just a fleeting memory, Kay, that was all.' He put his hand on her thigh. 'You are my only love. You know that I am completely committed to you.'

Kay responded, covering his strong hand with her beautiful fingers. 'I know. And I to you, but I don't trust her at all.'

He asked: 'Is that simply because you believe that she wasn't straightforward and open with us?'

'Not entirely,' she replied, adding: 'although the Security Services are never straightforward and open with us. They reap the rewards of our work and dump on us when they foul-up.'

They drove along the Portbury Hundreds then slowed at the intersection with the M5 motorway. Once on the M5, Faraday gently accelerated towards the Avon Bridge. As the traffic settled, Kay continued. 'Helen dropped her guard when she accepted the biscuit, as no doubt you and the ACC knew she would. When he mentioned the French passport she was concentrating on making sure crumbs didn't fall on her skirt. Beautiful timing.' She smiled. 'Just for a moment the biscuit hovered in her mouth. She recovered quickly, but the information about a French passport took her by surprise. She didn't know anything about Harvey's other identity.' Kay looked at Mark who glanced at her as he drove. Even the quickest glimpses of her excited him.

'Will you be calling the ACC later today?' she asked.

It was his turn to smile. 'I think he's expecting my call.'

***

Kay entered Mark Faraday's apartment at Avon View Court at ten minutes to seven. He had prepared tuna salads for them both and a bottle of Chardonnay was chilling in the fridge. They spoke again of her interview with Annette Harvey, her suspicions of his sexual activities and holidays, most likely, in Dorset. He spoke of what he had gleaned from Harvey's bank account, Harvey's diary and mobile phone. Harvey's computer would have to be accessed and his phone records and bank transactions examined with forensic attention but, already, patterns were emerging. As they ate, their discussion shifted to Adrian Harvey's water-front apartment, the painting hanging over the lounge fireplace, model sailboats and shelves of books.

'His choice of books might help us,' mused Faraday, typically dyslexic, his mind a kaleidoscope of thoughts, reflections and vivid memories. He checked his A4 leather folder containing his sheets of lined paper filled with scribbled notes, some in red ink, some in blue, some circled and linked to other groups of words by sweeping lines. Blobs of orange highlighter adorned the pages indicating significant points and data whereas yellow highlighter indicated actions to be taken, although some had already had little ticks inserted. He turned a page and found the note he sought.

'Here we are. Six hundred and twenty-four books.' He laughed. 'I counted them all. What a gripping life a detective has.' He looked at his notes again. 'But what does all of this tell us about Mr Harvey?' he posed rhetorically. 'One hundred and eighty-six books were concerned with French history, geography and literature. Eight were about General de Gaulle including: *L'Unite* by de Gaulle himself; *The Last Great Frenchman* by Williams; *The Last of the Giants* by Sulzberger and Kersaudy's *de Gaulle et Churchill*, with fourteen about Quebec and its history. There are quite a few about Napoleon: *Napoleon – His Wives and Women* by Hibberts; *Nelson and Napoleon* by Lee and *Bonaparte* by Barnett, seventeen in total. There was even a complete set of Thomas Hardy's novels. Also a beautifully bound and illustrated 1932 edition of *L'oiseau et la Revue Francaise d'Ornothologie* by Delacour. But, more interestingly, a 1936 edition of *Birds of Dorset* by Arnold and *Birds and Habitat: Relationships in Changing Landscapes* by Fuller – and, a landscape that is constantly changing is the coastline of Dorset.'

Faraday relaxed back into his chair, his gaze apparently fixed on some far-off object a million miles away, deep in thought.

'You are not happy with this case, are you?' Kay asked as she cleared the dishes and put the plates and cutlery in the dishwasher.

'I don't like loose ends,' he replied seemingly deep in thought again, but only for a few minutes. 'I'm not comfortable with MI5. Helen should have asked why we thought that Harvey was stealing files. She should have been keen to search his home address to discover if he did have any MoD files. She knew what files were missing, but made no mention of the Arctic but instead gave us a load of misinformation about the Antarctic. Helen seemed content to let this Harvey business just go away, to let matters rest and forget all about it. That doesn't sit comfortably with me at all.'

'Maybe it is all about the Antarctic,' ventured Kay as Mark prepared gin and tonics. 'We have the British Antarctic Territory down there, most of which is claimed by Argentina and there is supposed to be huge reserves of oil and gas under the ice.'

'True,' conceded Mark. 'Maybe that's it. It could be all about oil and gas and the Security Services are making light of it so as not to draw attention to it.'

'Or draw attention to their blunders and rogue agents, well, not until thirty or forty years later,' she said, adding: 'They love to give the appearance of being very efficient and super-human.'

'Oh dear,' remarked Faraday feigning astonishment, placing the drinks on the low table, then pulled her closer into his arms, 'and I thought they were super-human. Clearly, I was misinformed.' Then added more seriously: 'And she showed no apparent interest in Harvey's second passport. When we met up, she spent most of the time drinking coffee and talking about her secondment to the United States.'

‘The passport will be an embarrassment for them,’ suggested Kay, ‘but they will sweep that under the carpet.’ They clinked glasses.

‘That’s true, but how does a mid-ranking researcher afford a second home, a decent car, reasonably priced clothing and hundreds of books, and also be able to give his ex-wife £3,000 every year and a hooker a few hundred pounds every other week? No. I’m not comfortable with MI5’s approach to this.’

‘And what about her, did she make an *approach* to you whilst drinking hotel coffee?’ asked Kay more quietly.

‘Oh yes,’ replied Mark quite openly. ‘A bit embarrassing really. She actually apologised saying that it was a misunderstanding.’

‘Does she really think that that makes it any better?’ she questioned, an edge to her voice.

‘I think she thought it did,’ replied Mark, then added in a matter-of-fact way: ‘but we know that she wasn’t really apologising at all.’

‘Hum, well,’ Kay said as if referring to a suspect, ‘I don’t trust her one inch, and she will try it again.’

Mark kissed her head. She looked up at him and smiled, her pearl-white teeth and dark eyes intense against her olive-brown skin. He put his glass down on the little table, sank to his knees in front of her and buried his head into her body as he often did. He felt safe here as his lips followed the course of her ribs and he kissed her through the delicate silk of her blouse. 'You know that I would never betray you. You know that I worship you,' he said. Kay dropped to her knees too and wrapped her arms around his legs, the aroma of her *Amor Amor* perfume intoxicating his mind.

'And you know that I couldn't go on without you,' she said, tears stinging her eyes.

He gently pulled her up in his strong arms and kissed her salty tears that tasted like an irresistible drug. 'I know that it wasn't a misunderstanding … .' As he spoke, Kay suddenly pulled away, her facial expression changing, an expression of deep concentration and perception, her hand to her mouth.

'What is it?' asked Faraday as Kay stood back, turned and walked through the lounge and into the study, her little naked feet making delicate footprints in the thick pile carpet.

'The Valentine's card in Harvey's Hotwells' apartment,' she said as Faraday followed her. 'You thought it was French and … what did you say was written inside, something about a spelling error, a grammatical error?'

The exhibit bags were on the desk. Faraday selected a clear A4 envelope containing the Valentine's Day card folded open, showing the front, back and the insides. 'Here it is: *"There will always be a misunderstanding for you",*' said

Faraday as Kay began to search amongst the legal text books on the bookshelves.

‘There was a trial a few years ago, in South Wales I think,’ Kay said as she thumbed through a blue-coloured volume, ‘about a porn shop with a woman’s name – “Miss somebody”, something like that.’

Mark closed his eyes, his mind whirling. ‘It wasn’t Wales ... not Wales,’ he said to himself. ‘No, not Scotland ... it ... it was Northern Ireland. I’m sure it was Northern Ireland.’ He went to his laptop on the desk and booted it up. It took less than a minute. But not quick enough.

‘Here it is,’ said Kay. ‘Belfast City Council v Miss Behavin’ Ltd., 2007.’ She replaced the book, speaking as she did so. ‘Harvey’s ATM transactions were either before long weekend breaks or on every other Thursday, and his diary was endorsed: *“Miss U”* on those Thursdays. Annette Harvey kept telling me again and again that her husband said that she didn’t understand him or his sexual needs.’ She looked at Faraday, her triumphant smile captivating. ‘What do you think? Do you think that *“Miss U”* could mean *“Miss Understanding”* and that Miss Understanding is a hooker, an expensive Chinese hooker?’

Chapter 6

Monday, 2nd May.

Bristol, England.

AT TWENTY PAST SEVEN, Detective Superintendent Mark Faraday and Detective Chief Inspector Kay Yin opened up the windowless and totally secure **Re**stricted **D**esignated Centre Number **One**, code name **Red One**, one of three stand-by command centres in a bunker-style complex at the Severnside Police Headquarters, Portishead Down on the outskirts of Bristol, that could be brought into use in the event of the failure of the Force Communication Centre or one of the Area Control Centres or for use in connection with a delicate or major operation.

He had called ACC Robert Perrin the previous evening requesting that, as a result of enquiries and the sensitive nature of the enquiries to come, that Red One be placed at his disposal. Perrin readily agreed, as he did to the secondment of Sergeant Purchell to the enquiry.

His second call that evening had been to the wife of Lord Chelwood, Detective Sergeant Pippa Blanchard of Special Branch.

Gribble, the butler, had put him through. 'Good evening, Pippa,' said Faraday. 'Apologies for calling you at home, but I was wondering if you could recommend to me anyone at all who was very discrete, remarkably intelligent and fantastically good at research?'

'That's a difficult one,' she mocked. 'Where and when would you like me to start?'

'Don't report to the office tomorrow, report to Red One as soon as you get in please,'

'Of course, sir. Will eight o'clock be okay?' she asked.

'Eight will be fine. See you then and regards to Charles.'

Faraday's final call the previous evening had been a courtesy call to Superintendent Geoff Fowler at Ops Planning confirming the request for the services of the multi-lingual Sergeant Purchell, an able and resourceful officer with whom Faraday had previously worked.

A little after eight the research parameters were outlined to DS Blanchard so that Mark and Kay could prepare Red One in advance of the meeting. They both worked silently, Mark selecting the street plans from the map cabinet, activating the CCTV monitors and DVD players, as Kay placed in order the documents they had accumulated on the vast central table and displayed copies of the key pages of the passports belonging to Adrian Harvey and Edouard Melies; photographs of Harvey's car and estate agent-style photographs and floor plans of his apartment; hard copy bank statements and phone records. They worked in completely instinctive harmony. Kay walked towards the street map and listed times and locations of mobile phone calls as Mark selected blue-coloured magnets. As Kay leaned in and offered him the box of red magnets, she detailed the times and locations of relevant credit card transactions, marking these on a calendar matrix displayed on a magnetic dry-wipe board.

Kay understood her lover like no other; his moods, his need to be uninterrupted and thoughtful. She recognised his great imagination and intuition; his integrity, rock-like strength of character and his need to be protective towards her, whilst she was well aware of her more acute, perceptive instincts, her razor-sharp intelligence and her own vulnerabilities.

At nine o'clock, Faraday returned to his own department two floors above Red One and chaired 'morning prayers', the routine briefing of his senior team when the events of the previous twenty-four hours were reviewed and the following fifty-six hours considered and assessed. He returned to Red One, together with Sergeant Peter Jean Purchell, usually referred to as 'PP'.

One and a half hours later Kay, alerted by security at the main gates, went to the entrance foyer, met Helen Cave and escorted her to Red One.

'Ah, Helen,' said Mark Faraday. 'Let me introduce you to Detective Sergeant Pippa Blanchard.' Helen walked forward confidently, after all, she thought, this young woman was only a sergeant. They shook hands but the young detective's sparkling, yet intense ice-blue eyes unnerved her. 'And this is Sergeant Peter Purchell from Ops

Planning,' said Faraday, introducing the thirty-two year old officer, whose Mediterranean appearance was the result of the marriage between his English father and French mother.

Whilst Faraday appeared to busying himself with making coffee, he was observing Agent Cave, noting what attracted her attention on the displays and on the large table – and what did not. Coffees in hand, the four stood, gathered between the central table and map wall exchanging pleasantries before they focused upon the case.

Faraday tapped the side of his coffee cup with his spoon. The noise seemed to echo before the room fell silent. 'I think you have all had an opportunity to read the bullet-point briefing sheet,' he said, 'and review the information on the boards?' All those present nodded. 'That's good. Let's start with Mrs Harvey. Kay, maybe you could kick-off,' suggested Mark formally.

Kay spoke of their meeting, Adrian Harvey's home background and education; his brilliance and frustrations; their marriage and her late husband's sexual peccadilloes. 'He would big himself up,' she related, 'exaggerating the model of the car he drove. He would allow people to believe that he was a member of the Harvey family,' she said, referring to John Harvey & Son of Bristol, the famous wine merchants that had been established in the city in 1796. 'Harmless in isolation, although he wasn't even a distant relative. Their marriage drifted towards the rocks about six years ago, in fact, Annette can be reasonably precise. It was just after her husband's new female boss arrived. He moved out of their Stoke Bishop home about four years ago.'

'Is any of this significant, Mark?' asked Helen Cave in a rather dismissive tone. Mistake. Before Mark could respond, Kay spoke. The inevitable stand-off had come and this was the moment.

'You can ask me the questions, Helen, *if* you don't mind.'

For a moment there was silence – utter silence. 'I wasn't in any way being disrespectful, Kay. I ... I wasn't too sure of the protocol.'

Kay raised her right hand as if to say: 'Don't dismiss me and don't justify your dismissive remark with that puny excuse,' but continued calmly. 'Every action a person takes is triggered by something and is of some significance. It may be easily explained: a daily job-related routine, an automatic reaction to a deceitful family member, a very reasonable habit or an unattractive trait. In this case ATM transactions and mobile phone patterns have emerged,' she said as she walked the few steps towards the calendar matrix and street plan. She pointed to a cluster of blue and red markers. 'You will see that phone calls have been regularly made by Harvey to a particular unregistered mobile phone in this area.' Kay circled an area around the prestigious Trans-European Hotel on the waterfront. 'ATM transactions are clustered around this area too. Initially from machines in a variety of locations but, as I suspect he became more confident and careless, he used only one

ATM – here in Baldwin Street. And the numbers are constant: £300, £400 or £600.'

'Any conclusions, Kay?' asked Faraday, although he knew the answer perfectly well.

'My supposition would be, supported by Annette, that Harvey was paying cash to a prostitute, a high-end prostitute. There is no evidence that he took girls back to his apartment and you don't pay a sex worker £300 plus for a quick leg-over in a flop house or in the back of a steamy car.' Kay moved with feline grace to the left of the board and continued. 'No, he went somewhere more comfortable, but the question is – where? All the buildings here,' she said, pointing her beautiful finger at the map, 'across the river from the old castle, are occupied by law firms, accountants and insurance companies, with a Starbucks in the mix.' This throw-away remark was greeted with smiles – but not from MI5. 'There's only one place it is likely to be and that's here,' she asserted tapping the street plan, 'the Trans-European Hotel'.

'You are very positive, Kay?' asked Agent Cave - but carefully.

'It is the reasonable assumption supported by the fact that he had screwed up in his jacket pocket a parking meter ticket for three hours on the evening of the 28th and the ticket was issued from the machine in the near-by Counterslip,' she explained, referring to the road that leads from Victoria Street towards Narrow Plain. 'We have other avenues of enquiry with the hotel, but I'm reasonably certain that we are talking here about the Trans-European.' She paused as she placed her cup and saucer on the table. 'Some of the cash withdrawals were a day or two before he took short or long weekends. Those are the £400 and £600 amounts, and I'm guessing that the £300s are for the sex worker,' replied Kay in a level and considered tone. 'The Trans-European would be attractive to him.'

'Why?' Helen Cave asked, apparently unconvinced.

'It's a French-owned hotel,' interjected Sergeant Purchell, adding quickly: 'Sorry, ma'am, I've interrupted you.'

'No, gone on, Peter,' encouraged Kay.

'Harvey's father was English and his mother French,' said PS Purchell, 'like my parents, in fact. Harvey spoke French fluently. He would have been comfortable there, and, to a large extent anonymous – particularly with his French passport.'

'I think that you are absolutely right, Peter,' Kay said, but her look towards Helen Cave wasn't at all warm as she asked: 'What do you know about the French side of the family?'

'What do *you* mean?' she questioned defensively.

'What *I* mean, Helen, is that's not the helpful response we were hoping for,' Kay responded sharply, then added as if exasperated: '*You* are making this unnecessarily hard work. *You* are not being very open with us.' Before Helen Cave could reply, Kay continued in a condemning tone. 'Your people must know something about his family background, even if you weren't aware of his *double identity* and dalliances with, oh yes, *hookers*.' There was tense silence. Detective Chief Inspector Yin continued. 'Look here, Helen, the Security Services have screwed up. The police are not here to point-score. You know and I know that none of this is going to get out. Harvey will be buried along with his grubby little secrets, but we are wasting time and we need to clear this mess up before Harvey is supposed to return to work, when was it, by the 16th.'

'Harvey's grandfather was killed at Oran, wasn't he?' questioned Detective Sergeant Blanchard.

Helen Cave cleared her throat at the revelations already unearthed by Pippa Blanchard. 'Yes, that's absolutely true. Harvey's maternal grand-father was a lieutenant in the French navy in 1940. Winston Churchill, afraid that the ships of the French Atlantic Squadron based at Mers-el-Kebir would fall into the hands of the Germans, ordered their sinking by the Royal Navy. Harvey's grand-father was killed aboard the *Bretagne*.'

'And his family, they had been extremely wealthy. Had they not?' pressed DS Blanchard.

'Yes, yes,' replied Cave, unnerved by the knowledge gained by the police. 'His family *were* very prosperous and,' adding as if helpfully concluding this part of the meeting: 'they were originally from somewhere in Alsace.'

‘The area in France that was occupied at one time by the Prussians and later the Nazis,’ observed Sergeant Purchell, ‘who chose to rename the area Elsass.’

‘I think that is correct,’ replied Helen Cave.

Kay was about to say: ‘you don’t need to *think* about it’ but responded with restrained calm: ‘It is Mrs Harvey’s view that these facts have helped to fuel Adrian Harvey’s bitterness, confirming in his mind how he and his family had been constantly, to use her husband’s words, “robbed of position, privilege and advancement”. Her husband, so she says, would always delight in basking in the glow of French culture, national pride and dignity which he would compare contemptuously with what he saw as the shallowness of the British and the diminishing standards of the UK.’

‘Is that how your people saw him, Helen?’ asked Faraday.

‘We knew about the Battle of Oran, of course,’ she replied, although with little conviction, ‘but Harvey was seen by his managers, wrongly, as merely academically arrogant, not particularly sociable, something of a research nerd, without the inter-personal and managerial skills to ensure promotion. We knew that he was a traitor but believed that we had him under control. We didn’t,’ she admitted, then changed tact. ‘He was a very intelligent man. At Cambridge he gained a first in Geography, then some sort of degree in French and German from Paris, a master’s in Oceanography from, I think it was Southampton, and a PhD about sub-glacial lakes, or something like that, from Bristol. But he was arrogant and boorish. He managed to upset his co-workers and managers alike and, whilst he received two promotions, the coveted jobs went to others and then to a female. He received advice regarding his unreciprocated attentions towards a slightly older female colleague and was subject to a training course because of inappropriate comments he made about female staff at a meeting.' Helen Cave paused, walked towards the kitchenette area and placed her coffee cup down. When she returned she suggested in a softer tone: 'Could we sit do you think, Mark?'

They all moved to easy chairs grouped around a partitioned section in the far corner of the room. She didn't speak immediately as if she was weighing what she could or could not say.

'We know that we,' said Helen Cave, 'the United States and Chile, the Argentinians and the Russians, in fact everyone engaged in intelligence and the search for potential oil reserves, are primarily focusing upon the Antarctic. But, who Harvey's contacts actually were, we don't know.'

'And the significance of his French passport?' asked Faraday.

'We knew nothing about a second passport and so I am not sure,' replied Cave thinking on her feet and clearly embarrassed. 'He would travel on odd occasions to and from France, St Lô to be precise, where he has, had, family. Distant cousins I believe. But his applications for annual leave were usually endorsed "travelling south coast", "travelling East Anglia", something like that. But very little indication of travelling overseas, and, we would be automatically informed of these things, particularly as he always seemed to use his British passport.'

'The Border Agency would inform you?' asked DS Blanchard.

Helen Cave smiled, relieved that she could indicate another agency's imperfections. 'They are required to inform us, but we all know that they don't keep comprehensive records of people entering or leaving the UK. Our borders are like a sieve.'

'Well,' suggested Faraday deep in wandering thought, his eyes focused on a bare wall, 'the French passport must be either to facilitate movement across borders or to support a "legend",' he said, referring to a false but coherent and plausible account of an individual's background, daily activities and family to confuse any enquiry, 'or to provide proof of his standing, his origins, his authenticity in order to perpetuate his French antecedents. This is reinforced by the discovery by forensics of a mobile phone concealed under a sock in one of the hiking boots found in Harvey's car, along with a charger in the other boot. They are still working through his messages, but, you might think significantly, they are all in French.'

'And the hotel?' asked the MI5 agent.

'When I was with the Vice Squad in Hong Kong,' remarked Kay, 'the gangs that ran the prostitutes also owned numerous bordellos, one masquerading as a hotel called the *Golden Oasis*. The hotel was prestigious and attracted the great and the good, foreign diplomats, visiting scientists and top business men, all of whom were monitored by the staff and ripe for blackmail.'

'Are you really saying that the Trans-European is an English version of the *Golden Oasis*? asked an incredulous Helen Cave.

'What *we* are really saying, Helen, is that it could easily be so,' suggested Faraday thoughtfully. 'Before I joined the local Vice Squad, they sent me off to Scotland Yard. I can remember one of the more colourful lecturers there describe in considerable detail the activities of *The Green House*, a brothel established in Berlin, I think it was during the Franco-Prussian War, staffed by undercover agents who very successfully blackmailed the clientele. This success was imitated by the Gestapo during the Second World War who established a high-class brothel in Berlin called the *Salon Kitty*.'

'Look, I'm not an expert on this,' Helen Cave said, 'but do you both really think that the Trans-European is operating a brothel?'

'I don't know, nor does Kay,' replied Faraday. 'I doubt it, but, the Trans-European is part of a French-owned group of companies and you would know, Helen, that our Security Services have a vast network of people who are useful to them. These sub-agents can be found throughout the banking and aviation industries, within universities and trade unions, in fact, in every walk of life from North Sea oil platforms and the Cornish fishing fleets to the road haulage business and the tourist industry, and from motoring organisations to flying clubs. The French would be remiss if they were alone in operating differently. As far as the Trans-European is concerned, it may be just a hotel, but I really don't know. And I exclude nothing at this stage. I have been to the hotel a few times on walk-abouts prior to VIP visits. The Home Secretary has stayed there as have the Prince and Princess Michael of Kent, the Duchess of York and the Bulgarian Minister of the Interior,' he paused and shook his head from side to side, adding: 'dreadful man. Anyway, the hotel has an excellent reputation; its cuisine is mentioned in all the glossy magazines and never a hint of trouble by guests or staff – many of whom are French.'

'Okay, so are you suggesting that Adrian Harvey could have gone to this hotel for, what, erotic and noisy sex?' asked the MI5 agent.

'Well,' suggested Kay casually but with a mischievous grin, 'erotic sex doesn't have to be noisy... but ... more importantly, we need to speak with Miss Understanding and just see how understanding she really wants to be?'

'Do you have a plan in mind?'

'Pretty much,' Kay Yin confirmed. 'I think you could leave that with Pippa and me, sir.'

***

The Bentley Continental GT was almost silent as it approached the Trans-European Hotel, save for the slightest of reassuring murmurs from the 521bhp V8 engine and the gentle grumble from the 20" tyres as they rolled over the cobble stones. The beautiful Beluga-styled Ghost White coupé glided effortlessly up the slight gradient towards the grey frock-coated doorman resplendent in silk top hat. The doorman timed his steps perfectly. As the Bentley came to a gentle halt, the doorman's white-gloved left hand was at the passenger door handle, his right hand smartly at the brim of his hat.

Detective Sergeant Pippa Blanchard kissed her husband, Charles, on the cheek and gracefully stepped from the Piano Black leather interior. 'Lady Chelwood, how good to see you again,' said the doorman, admiring the pale blue Claude Pierlot suit she wore.

'Thank you, Howard,' she replied. 'I'm just stopping for tea.'

'Of course, my lady,' he said as he choreographed her arrival. 'Would it be the Blue Room as usual?'

'No, Howard. Not today. The entrance lounge would be fine. I'm hoping to meet an acquaintance on the off-chance.'

The entrance hall was modern, light and refined, with beautiful displays of flowers arranged on a large oval table and upon numerous Ionic pedestals, their scent pervading everywhere. Howard escorted Lady Chelwood to a button-backed chair and a small table. She declined. 'Just here will be fine, Howard. Thank you,' she remarked as she moved to another identical pale-green chair and circular table, but one that gave her a perfect view of the entrance doors, reception desk and lifts.

'Of course, my lady,' acknowledged Howard, 'a much more agreeable table. I will arrange for Golden Darjeeling tea, ma'am, and Caffe Terzi biscuits, if you wish?'

'That would be perfect, Howard.'

At 3.20pm precisely, Detective Chief Inspector Kay Yin entered the hotel wearing a beautifully tailored orange, Marlene Birger suit. She walked like a mannequin to the desk. Eyes turned. Men glanced. Interested if not aroused. Woman glanced, dismissively if not enviously, as she glided across the pale marble floor. Two male reception staff smiled at her approach. She waited for a short moment then simply passed an envelope to the older male member of staff who seemed to have a more knowing smile. Kay winked very slowly, just once, and simply walked out, equally slowly. The wide eyes of the two men followed her exit, their imaginings for a moment incapacitating them.

Once Kay was lost to sight, the older man, with the silly smirk and raised eyebrow, read the words written on the envelope:

'VERY URGENT. For Miss Understanding'.

He tapped the envelope knowingly in the palm of his hand and smugly left the reception area. Lady Chelwood followed, with unhurried elegance. The lift doors opened and the receptionist with the silly smirk entered the empty lift and pressed the button for the fifth floor. The lift doors began to close as Lady Chelwood reached them, her remarkably soft yet intense blue eyes ensured that Mr Silly Smirk pressed the button and the doors stopped closing and opened again.

'Which floor would you like, madam?' he asked.

Pippa glanced at the row of lights. 'I'm for the fifth too, thank you,' said Lady Chelwood as she removed her mobile from her handbag and pretended to speak. 'Hi, darling.' She paused and then spoke to Mr Silly Smirk. 'No reception in the lift I suppose?' Sensibly, Pippa did not pretend to speak when she wasn't sure that there would have been reception.

'No madam, but on the floor it will be fine.'

The lift stopped at the fifth and Pippa nodded a thank you to Mr Silly Smirk before speaking again into a mute phone, stopping to allow Mr Silly Smirk to walk along the corridor. 'Darling, I will be a little late,' she said and carried on her one-sided conversation until she was certain as to the door in which Mr Silly Smirk posted the letter. 'I am really juggling with appointments today and have already missed Suzi,' she continued until Mr Silly Smirk had returned to the lift and pressed the button. He had been tempted to ask if madam required the lift, but madam's preoccupation with her telephone call was such that he entered the lift alone. The doors closed. The lift began its descent and Pippa quickly checked the number of Miss Understanding's suite. Number 511.

***

At 3.27pm Edouard Melies' mobile phone bleeped. The text message read, in French: 'What the hell you doing?'

DS Pippa Blanchard smiled at DCI Yin. 'Better than we hoped, ma'am,' acknowledged Pippa as she typed in a reply, also in French: 'I have to see you. Very urgent and it's in your interest too.' She showed the screen to Kay who nodded in agreement. Pippa pressed the send key.

Almost immediately Miss Understanding texted again in French: 'I see you Ladies Mile. NOW.' That was all.

Chief Inspector Yin turned on the ignition of the 2.2 litre unmarked grey-coloured police saloon and waited for Miss Understanding to emerge from either the hotel's car park or front entrance. Seven minutes later it was the front entrance. Howard hailed a Bristol Blue-coloured taxi from the rank. Within moments a flustered Miss Understanding was being driven across Bristol Bridge into the slow moving traffic of Baldwin Street, through the City Centre and up Park Street towards the university's imposing Wills Memorial Tower and the city's Durdham Downs. Kay had been able to keep the taxi in discreet view without drawing attention to her police vehicle as she negotiated wandering pedestrians crossing the roads, slow moving buses and aimless motorists. Soon they passed through the traffic lights on the brow of Black Boy Hill with Upper Belgrave Road. The taxi drove along Stoke Road a short distance, indicated left and began a slow turn into the long straight road that was Ladies Mile, ironically named in recognition of the road's use by prostitutes during the reign of Queen Victoria.

'Let's say hello,' said Kay. Pippa activated the blue strobe lights hidden behind the black radiator grill and pressed, just once, the two-tone horns, at the same time holding her left forearm against the windscreen directing the taxi to pull over to the parking bays on the right. The taxi complied and slowed to a stop as did the police vehicle some fifteen feet behind.

Both officers got out of their car and approached the taxi, Kay to the driver's side, Pippa at the off-side passenger door. Kay produced her warrant card and spoke to the driver: 'Thank you for stopping, driver. I am Detective Chief Inspector Yin and this is my colleague, Detective Sergeant Blanchard. Your passenger will be leaving you *now*.' The driver seemed confused, looking from one extremely attractive and beautifully dressed officer to the other. 'Keep the change,' Kay said as she passed him a £10 note. As he fingered the crisp bank note, his confusion seemed to miraculously desert him.

'Driver,' ordered Miss Understanding, 'these aren't police officers, they bad people, criminals. Drive on,' her accent tinged more with French than Chinese.

'Sorry, miss. Can't dooz that or I's looz me licence.'

Miss Understanding was tall for a Chinese female. About 130 pounds and in her early thirties. She worked-out constantly to keep her body in fine shape for her clients but she was not muscular in the athletic sense. She studied both officers. She was taken aback by Pippa's ice-blue eyes that seemed to penetrate her thoughts. She took account of the firmness of Kay's jaw and the determination etched into her eyes. Yes, she concluded, the Chinese officer might be slight of build but she would be a fighter, and she noticed both officers' well-manicured but short finger nails. Those nails were not for the cat-walk, they were for gutter fighting if necessary. And, she reasoned, they would both fight. She decided to be compliant and wait for them to act.

'Step out of the vehicle and take a seat in the police car parked behind,' said Kay and, after a deliberate pause added: 'And do it right now.'

Miss Understanding stepped elegantly from the taxi and looked towards the blue strobe lights still pulsating behind the police car's radiator grill. She said nothing but walked towards the grey-coloured car. Pippa opened the rear, off-side door. Miss Understanding was boxed in. There was no escape.

'Slide right across behind the front passenger seat,' said the sergeant, ensuring that Miss Understanding would be less able to attack the driver. Then Sergeant Blanchard got into the rear compartment behind the driver's seat.

‘Belt up,’ said Kay as she got behind the steering wheel, ‘we are going for a little ride.’

‘Am I under arrest?’ asked Miss Understanding as a gap in the on-coming traffic allowed the car to accelerate across to the near-side of the road.

‘Not at the moment’, replied Pippa. ‘That might come later.’

‘What do you want with me?’ she asked as the police vehicle continued along Ladies Mile and across the junction to descend the winding Bridge Valley Road.

‘It’s more a matter of what you know about Edouard Melies?’ asked Kay as she drove purposefully and easily through the city’s heavy traffic along the Hotwells Road. There was no need for blues and twos, but her driving was all theatre. By means of observing, positioning, timing and speed, DCI Yin was able to dominate the road without sharp breaking or aggressive acceleration. It was a deliberate statement for the benefit of Miss Understanding that the police had a task to perform, the police were in control and the police intended to succeed.

‘What should I know about him?’ she asked, staring at Kay in the interior rear-view mirror.

Pippa turned towards Miss Understanding. ‘For a start,’ said Pippa in a no-nonsense manner, ‘why didn’t Edouard Melies turn up at his home last Friday morning?’

The question had an ominous tone to it. She was caught off-guard for a long moment. She hesitated. She dropped her hard gaze and thought quickly. 'I expect he went to his country cottage,' she replied.

'Then … why hasn't he arrived at his country cottage?' asked Pippa.

'How should I know?' she snapped as she sought to control the situation, as she always did with her clients.

'Because,' said Kay slowly and deliberately, 'you seem to be the last person to have seen him.'

'The last time I saw him was just after one on Friday morning.'

The officers had sown the worrying seeds. They neither answered her nor questioned her further. They drove the last two miles to The Grove in silence and allowed Miss Understanding to reflect upon the situation she now found herself, a woman with weak admirers but no one in whom she could place her trust; a woman who had always relied upon her own skills but conscious that those very skills may no longer be useful; a woman vulnerable and alone.

They drove along The Grove from Prince Street towards the Bristol Central Police Headquarters. There was no disguising the building. In addition to the flag flying proudly from its mast atop the three-storey building, it was the design and construction of the building that proclaimed its function. The first six foot of the lower part of the ground floor consisted of honey-coloured Cotswold stone, immediately above which was a thin course of grey granite, followed by three rows of perfectly square Cotswold stone blocks interspersed by identically-sized empty gaps. A thin course of granite was immediately above this chequered pattern which was topped off by another six foot of Cotswold stone, an arrangement which replicated the police chequered cap band, a feature that also allowed for ample through-ventilation for the ground floor police car park. DCI Yin halted the police car at the steel-grilled entry barrier, wound down her window and inserted her card in the barrier control. She looked straight ahead and waited whilst her profile was scanned, then the barrier trundled sideways and allowed her to drive through, the security camera remaining vigilant as the barrier trundled closed again. Once parked the three women alighted from the car and mounted the steps to the station entrance where Kay used her card again, as well as keyed a digital pad, to gain access.

CID was accommodated on the first floor. They walked up the stairs then along a carpeted corridor, the DCI to her office further along this corridor, DS Blanchard and Miss Understanding to the interview suites. Suites One, Three and Four were unoccupied. They entered Suite Four. Pippa switch on the ceiling lights that flickered then shone brightly. The door was then pulled closed. DS Blanchard pointed Miss Understanding to a single chair at the far side of the grey-topped desk. She sat down, her eyes examining the bare, mid-grey painted walls, the CCTV camera, the ceiling with its concealed lighting and every move the officer made. Moments later DCI Yin entered the interview room with three buff-coloured files under her arm. The two officers occupied the two remaining seats, their backs against the only door.

Kay pressed two buttons, one controlling the red-coloured 'engaged' light outside the door, the other activating the recording system. Then she spoke.

'You are, at the moment, a helpful member of the public, maybe a witness - whatever. That status can, of course, change instantly.' She shuffled the police files on the desk in front of her, none of which pertained to Miss Understanding at all, and removed a pad of paper from one. Then she removed a black and silver Mont Blanc ball-point pen from inside her jacket, thumbed the top and allowed the tip to hover over the paper.

'Your full name, please?'

'Why should I give you my details?'

'Here's the thing,' answered Kay in a matter-of-fact way, 'once the general manager of your hotel is made aware of our interest in your, ah, *activities*, he will certainly not allow you to use Suite 511 again. Co-operate with us now and your clients will continue to enjoy your services at the five-star Trans-European, as opposed to a no-star bed and breakfast in Stokes Croft. And so ... your full name please?'

The ambience and the business benefits of a five-star hotel compared to those offered by a no-star B&B were not lost on Miss Understanding. 'My name is Sun Bo Nguyen.'

Kay pondered the origins of her name. ‘Ah, your family must have originated from French Indo-China, from Vietnam. Is that correct?’

‘Yes,’ she replied, bitter memories flooding back of the photographs of her dirt-poor grand-parents from Quang Ngai. ‘Yes, they did.’

‘But you were born in France?’

‘Allauch.’

‘And where is that exactly?’

‘Near,’ she replied, waving her hand as if the thought was distasteful, ‘a little east of Marseille.’

‘And your date of birth?’

‘April 9th, 1982.’

‘And how long have you been living at the hotel?’

‘Three years.’

‘You said that you last saw Edouard Melies a little after one o’clock on Friday morning last?’

‘Yes.’

‘Can you recall what he was wearing?’ asked Kay, a question common to a routine missing person enquiry.

Sun Bo described Harvey’s clothing accurately, a description matching those that the DCI had last seen in the mortuary.

‘Did he say where he was going after he left you?’

‘No.’

‘Did he seem to have any worries on his mind?’

‘No.’

‘Did he seem anxious at all?’

‘No,’ replied Miss Understanding who was now beginning to warm to these questions. Maybe these officers did see her as a helpful witness in a missing person enquiry she thought. She considered her options and concluded that being a helpful witness would be advantageous to her – for the present.

‘How long has Edouard been a client of yours?’

‘About two years.’

‘How often do you see him?’

‘Every other week,’ she replied, then offered helpfully: ‘Usually on a Thursday.’

'How much are your fees?'

'For him, £300.'

'And what service do you offer him in particular?'

'He likes bondage, but also straight sex.'

'I sense there is more?'

'Not really,' she replied with a shrug. 'Sometimes he just likes to talk.'

DCI Yin wanted to know what Harvey liked to talk about, but it was too early to ask those questions. 'How did you meet?'

She was more relaxed now. 'We met at the hotel. He was alone. He looked lonely. I made him feel less lonely.'

'What is he like as a person?' she asked, constantly careful not to refer to Harvey in the past tense.

'He is like most men,' she replied with the knowing smile of her profession.

'Enlighten me?' asked Kay coldly.

'I think you know what most men are like?' she said, still with a conspiratorial smile, hoping to gain some control over the interview.

'I probably do,' replied Kay confidently, seeking a possible useful future meeting of minds, 'but I'm interested in *your* perceptions of Edouard Melies?'

'He craved affection ... and attention. He was weak,' she replied, without contempt. For a moment she lost her smile as she thought further. 'He was arrogant, well, arrogant at first. But behind that façade of arrogance was a lack of confidence. I gave him his confidence back, at least for the time he was with me.'

'And so, he needed to return to you on a regular basis?'

'Of course.' That smile again.

'In what areas did he lack confidence?'

Sun Bo considered her reply for a moment as she wrestled with the most appropriate words. Both officers were patient. 'Confidence is probably the wrong word, she said. 'Maybe it is self-esteem. In France you would say *amour-propre*.'

Kay wanted to know what Sun Bo knew of him and so she casually probed. 'And why should he lack *amour-propre*?'

'He was needy, something not recognised by his wife. And he was very intelligent and this was not recognised by his colleagues either.'

Kay picked up one of the files and pretended to scan its contents. She frowned as she asked: 'And where would his colleagues work?'

'I wouldn't know,' she replied a little too quickly thought Kay Yin.

'*I* know,' responded Kay, 'and *I* don't do bondage with him. You must know where he works?'

'I think it may have been at a university or a college, here or in Bath.'

'And why do you think that?'

'I think he taught French, something like that. He would talk romantically of France, of French geography and of French history.'

'In what way?'

'When he talked about France, he … I don't know … ,' she paused as she examined her beautifully painted finger nails,' he changed. 'He delighted to talk of the glories of France. It wasn't all sex. We would sometimes watch TV together or he would talk about an article he had read in a paper. If he saw the French president at the Élysée Palace surrounded by ceremonial soldiers, he gloated and compared the scene of your Prime Minister outside of Number 10 with only a scruffy policeman on duty. If we drank wine, and we usually did, a little that is, we always had to have a fine French wine which he considered superior to all others.'

'You said that he would speak of French geography. In what context?'

'Not just about France. He would ramble on about the vastness of Russia and culture within its borders. About America, its history, its complexities. He would romanticise about the history of the Wild West and America's struggle against the British. He would talk affectionately about Canada. But, recently, he would talk about the French and how something, I don't know what, would destroy Britain's smugness.'

'Oh,' she said as if confused. 'And this something, what was that?'

'I think that it was some sort of discovery that would embarrass Britain.'

'I'm not sure I follow,' she said, fiddling with pages in one of the files. 'Discovery of what do you think?'

'I really don't know.'

'Okay. I'm not sure that this is going to help us find out what has happened to Edouard Melies,' said Kay not wishing to concentrate, for the moment, on Harvey's perceptions of Britain, although everything was telling her that his perceptions of Britain and of France were the key to this enquiry. Kay thought it a good time to change tack. 'Your services are expensive?'

'My clients believe that I provide good value for money,' she replied with that smile again.

'Where do you think Edouard got his money from? A university lecturer wouldn't be that well paid?'

'I think he was connected with a wine company or vineyards.'

Kay made the pretence of studying her file again. 'Do you know which company, which vineyards?'

'No.'

Kay reflected for a second. It would appear that Harvey had maintained his 'legend' as a Frenchman and some vague connection with the wine trade, but she continued with this theme for appearance sake. 'Was it a French or British company, Australian maybe?'

'I don't know.'

Kay knew that she needed to return to the main thrust of her enquiry. 'You mentioned a discovery. I am wondering whether this discovery has taken him off somewhere?' asked the DCI, maintaining the missing person theme. 'When did he first discuss this?'

‘I don’t discuss,’ replied Miss Understanding, almost offended by the suggestion. ‘I *allow* my clients to talk if that is what they wish to do.’

‘You are good listener?’

‘Of course,’ she replied, adding as if referring to her CV. ‘As I said, it’s not all about sex.’

DCI Yin continued to probe, suggesting that she needed to know more about Edouard Melies. She asked about any friends and hobbies Edouard might have, any religious beliefs she knew of or any vacations he might take. She asked about the bars, restaurants and cafés he might frequent; sporting and musical interests he had; cinemas and theatres he visited, even the supermarkets he might favour and the foods he ate.

Kay looked at her Tag watch. ‘Let’s have a cup of coffee, Sun Bo,’ suggested Kay Yin. ‘Let’s go to my office – more comfortable chairs and a much better view. Then we can come back her for a little longer.’

DCI Yin’s office gave a pleasant view over the city docks, now devoid of tramp steamers and coastal freighters, but filled with bobbing yachts and small cabin cruisers, making their unhurried way across the sparkling, late afternoon water. The grime of the dock-side buildings had gone many years before to be replaced by converted and expensive homes, cafés and bars. The coffee, Douwe Egberts, was good and the chairs were comfortable, a reminder to Miss Understanding that comfort came at a price, and that price was her co-operation. The alternatives were only too clear in her mind. At best an interview room. At worst a prison cell on remand.

After coffee, both officers and Miss Understanding returned to the interview suite, Kay Yin reverting to a previous theme and asking, apparently absent-mindedly: 'I want to ask you about any vehicles Edouard had access to, but,' Kay scanned her notes as if to recall a thought, 'before I forget, what were you previously saying about some sort of discovery, what was that all about?' she asked as if bemused.

'He seemed to delight in his knowledge of something that would cause … I don't know, embarrassment to your government, I guess.'

'How intriguing,' remarked Kay. 'I wonder what would cause this embarrassment? Maybe a minister with a mistress, a cabinet minister fiddling expenses, a minister's indiscretion with another government? Although I'm not sure anything like that would destroy Britain's smugness, as you say.'

'I did not say. It is what Edouard said. You must ask him when you find him.'

'But you mentioned France?'

'Yes, Edouard said that some … I think he said "miserable" pieces of paper would embarrass Britain and affect its standing in the world and with the, what is it … yes, your Commonwealth.'

'When did you first hear of this discovery?' she asked as if her interest was more an amusing distraction than an essential part of a missing person enquiry.

'Probably a year ago. More so since.'

'How did the subject crop up?'

'Sometimes he would see something on TV or hear something on the news that would prompt some comment.' She pondered for a moment. 'This would be particularly if it was something about the British parliament or the monarchy, who he considered, as he put it: "a bunch of Germans". He would say something like: "the French people will soon wipe that smug look off their faces".'

'And what do you think he meant by that?'

'I don't know. Geography and politics are not really my area of expertise.'

DCI Yin decided to change tact again and asked her about her clients, particularly whether clients knew the identities of her other clients. Miss Understanding insisted that one of the reasons why she was able to confine her clientele to a carefully selected group of fifteen loyal followers was because she was scrupulously careful to protect their identities. Yet, when DCI Yin and DS Blanchard accompanied Miss Understanding discreetly back to Suite

511, she had no reservation about cynically confirming the details of those clients.

The officers maintained the missing person theme whilst at the hotel when Miss Understanding was told to be certain to call them immediately should she hear from Edouard Milies. What was also certain was that Miss Understanding had a very clear understanding of her precarious commercial position.

At 6.35pm the two officers arrived at Detective Superintendent Faraday's office at Force Headquarters where he had been seated at his computer screen reviewing the interview of Miss Understanding. They discussed the interview, particularly Miss Understanding's clients. The clients were an interesting collection of a former mayor, an orthodontist, a shipping agent who was also the French Consul, a Deputy Lord Lieutenant, seven company directors, a vice-chancellor of a university, an eye surgeon and an Assistant Chief Constable.

Chapter 7

Tuesday, 3rd May.

London and Police Headquarters, Portishead Down, Bristol, England.

IT WAS ONLY LIGHT DRIZZLE as the two Americans turned left out of the Oxford Circus subway and walked along Regent Street towards Garfunkel's restaurant. When they wanted to talk alone, they often met here, Commander Walt Bergman and one of his junior assistants, Lieutenant Janet Lightfoot. He liked walking with her – walking with her did his ego a power of good. They hung their coats on the pegs and sat at a window table, not in a booth. From here they would not be overheard and this vantage point allowed them a panoramic view of the entrance and road beyond. The restaurant was cool, clean and bright. The cuisine pure Uncle Sam American. The waitress, in black blouse and trousers with maroon-coloured apron, was friendly, efficient and wore a *'hi guys'* smile. They both ordered the Classic Burgers on toasted brioche buns with fries and coleslaw. Walt had additional Applewood cheese and a Samuel Adams Boston Lager, whilst Janet had cranberry juice. They talked in generalities, then in code as if architects or surveyors.

'I guess I'm a little uneasy about the next project,' asked Janet from the Office of Naval Intelligence. 'How about you?'

‘It’s what we do,’ replied Walt as he took another bite of his burger.

The young American looked about the restaurant to ensure that they could not be overheard then spoke quietly. ‘I don’t understand why the Brits are not involved here. GCHQ must be picking up the intel and I thought *Five Eyes* shared all this stuff?’ Janet questioned, referring to the defence intelligence agencies of the United States, Canada, the UK, Australia and New Zealand.

Walt finished his burger and picked at his fries before wiping his mouth with the cotton napkin. ‘Of course we share,’ he said as he picked up his lager, held it to his mouth, his eyes peering over the glass rim towards his much more junior colleague, ‘when it’s in the interests of Uncle Sam.’

Lieutenant Lightfoot had made a lot of English friends whilst reading law at Oxford and felt uncomfortable. The older officer tried reassurance. ‘Look, the Brits don’t share everything with us. Anyway, we don’t know what the package contains. Once we have collected, the specialists will take over and examine. Then we think again about sharing,’ he said replacing the glass on the table, ‘but that decision is way, way above my pay grade and certainly above yours.’

‘Okay,’ came the resigned response. They drank their drinks some more before Janet spoke again, worried that their boss, Captain Martin Turner USN, appeared to be unconcerned about them taking automatic weapons on the operation. 'The main man said that when we have a "site meeting" we should take our own "equipment" with us?'

Walt considered this prospect for a moment before replying. 'I think we are good, Janet. We are all looking on this as a field training exercise just for you. There's no problem. We are just like a couple of regular UPS guys, that's all. We pick up a parcel. We deliver a parcel. And the "equipment",' he continued with a shrug, 'isn't ours, it's only on loan,' adding: 'and I'm told that the south coast of England is a real relaxing place to be.'

He thought for a while longer as he beckoned the *'hi guys'* waitress. He looked at Janet. She was young and she was nice to have around. Thirteen years younger than Walt. He knew that. He knew that because he had double-checked her file. He studied her features again. She wasn't beautiful or pretty he thought, but, back some ways was Native American blood and she was sure handsome. Maybe her long legs were a little skinny for Walt's tastes, but he considered her more than well-proportioned on the upper deck. He smiled at the naval analogy, reminding himself that she had been responsive to his interest in developing her career and, he reasoned, the south coast of Merry England could hold some unexpected attractions. He could see that there were opportunities presenting themselves here which should not be wasted. He would tread carefully, of course, but he was sure that those opportunities were there to be grasped. Then, gentleman as he considered himself to be, he ordered two cappuccinos for them both.

Detective Superintendent Faraday and Detective Chief Inspector Yin waited, comfortably seated, but warily, outside the office of the Assistant Chief Constable (Crime). Faraday, wearing a blue blazer, pink-striped shirt and grey trousers, glanced up at the wall-mounted clock. It was 4.43pm. Their appointment had been scheduled for 4.30 and they had arrived at 4.15. The polished pine doors had remained closed throughout. Sometimes laughter could be heard from within. But, mostly, there was silence, other than the ACC's secretary answering innumerable calls, stating that 'Mr Perrin will be engaged until at least six o'clock' or 'the ACC will be engaged for some while yet' or 'let me take your number and I will ask him call you'.

At 4.44pm the buzzer sounded on the secretary's desk. She looked up. 'Mr Perrin will see you now, Mr Faraday. Miss Yin.'

The two officers stood up, Kay adjusting her black trouser suit. They both approached the doors which suddenly opened. The ACC dressed, as usual, in a beautifully tailored, light-grey, double-breasted suit, greeted them both with his Berlusconi smile and outstretched arms. 'I'm so, so sorry to have kept you both waiting. Come in. Come in.'

Helen Cave was seated at the low coffee table posing, in a dark-grey business suit, as if waiting for her publicist to arrive. Pleasantries were exchanged, then the three police officers sat down at the table too. 'Well, let's get on with this,' suggested Perrin, eager to get the meeting underway. Faraday began his briefing of the little group. As usual, it was crisp, sharp and to the point – a stage performance. He explained that the post-mortem carried out upon Adrian Harvey very clearly established that the cause of death was due to a heart attack as the result of a hitherto undetected defect in the left ventricle. There was a small trace of alcohol consistent with the consumption of one large glass of wine, but the tox screen had proved absolutely clear and, consequently, death was determined to be as a result of natural causes. Faraday looked across at DCI Yin, the cue for her to speak.

Kay Yin spoke of her interview with Miss Understanding, her true identity and family background. She spoke of Harvey's sexual liaisons every other Thursday night at a cost of £300. She spoke of Miss Understanding's clients, although she omitted to mention an assistant chief constable, but did mention the shipping agent who happened to be the French Consul in the city. Kay referred to Harvey's UK passport which she removed from her leather file on her lap and deliberately placed on the table in front of her, and his visits to France, apparently to see his very distant cousins in St Lô, which coincided with some of his authorised periods of annual leave. Then she moved on to the French passport. She produced this from her file too and laid it on the table alongside the other. Perrin reached forward and picked up both passports and examined and compared each. Kay remained silent whilst he did so. Perrin replaced the documents on the table and nodded for Kay to continue. She said that the French authorities had been helpful and provided her with details of Harvey's or, more accurately, Edouard Melies' journeys, not just to St Lô but across the French border into Spain.

‘How often did he make those sorts of journeys, Kay?’ probed Perrin.

‘On four occasions as far as the French authorities are aware … ,‘ the ACC was about to interrupt, but Kay had anticipated his question, ‘… all of which coincide with the larger financial withdraws, usually between £400 and £600.’

The ACC directed his question to Faraday. ‘You’ve kept Helen in the loop?’

‘Yes, sir. We e-mailed the details earlier this morning.’

‘So, Helen,’ Perrin asked. ‘Why these visits and where did he go once he crossed into Spain?’

No thought was given to her reply which was immediate. Rehearsed. ‘We assume that this would have been to facilitate his contact directly with the Spanish or with the Argentinians via the Spanish,’ she replied, adding: ‘I spoke with MI6 this morning and they will be following this up.’

There was silence for a few moments. As Helen Cave made no further comment Faraday continued the briefing. He spoke of the possibility of a second property owned by Harvey. He was certain there was one, he said, but where, he had no idea – which was true to a point. He then turned to the service log of Harvey’s vehicle, Harvey’s duty log listing mileage covered in respect of his official duties and bank accounts listing fuel purchases. These, he said, had been examined and the data extrapolated to provide a potential radius in which a second home might fall. Faraday estimated that this could be between 140 and 170 miles from Bristol.

'And no fuel or other purchases that would give us a likely location?' asked Perrin.

'No, sir,' answered Faraday. 'It seems that Harvey did not use his mobile phone, nor did he use a cash point, but withdrew cash and filled up with fuel in Bristol prior to his short and long weekends or short breaks away. As a result, we don't know where he went.'

'And so, he had something to hide?'

'Yes he did,' replied Faraday firmly, 'but what, we don't know.'

'Does MI5 know, Helen?'

'No. In the light of what Mark has discovered, it is our assumption that he was seeking to conceal his second home, the existence of which would have drawn attention to his healthy financial position.' Faraday thought that this seemingly plausible explanation was complete nonsense, but remained silent.

'And MI5 is not concerned about this?' asked Perrin with an incredulous Jeremy Paxman-type frown.

'We aren't being complacent,' she countered, 'but we were aware of his treachery, mild and convenient as it was to us. Mark has reminded me that Harvey's liaison with a prostitute is not, in itself, an offence, nor is prostitution itself unless either party is soliciting on the streets or Miss Understanding was operating in a brothel. In this regard, from a criminal perspective, there is no crime or criminal to pursue. It has been established that the death of Harvey was due to natural causes, and with his death dies our useful, although not critical, contact with the Spanish and the Argentinians. As far as the Security Services are concerned, this matter appears to be closed, unless you have something else for us, Mark?'

'I don't think so,' replied Mark with a facial expression of apparent disinterest, even less convinced by Helen Cave's cavalier and seemingly rehearsed explanation. 'We can release the body and his work colleagues can be informed.'

Kay made a silent and discreet gesture to Perrin indicating that there was no need for urgency. Perrin took the hint. 'How long will the paper work take, Kay?' asked the ACC.

'There's no real rush, sir. I understand that the coroner is happy to place this case amongst a batch of other similar deaths.'

'Could I suggest, Mr Perrin,' offered Helen Cave, 'that the MoD are informed on the 16th when Harvey was scheduled to return to work. There is no need for any press statement and this will allow this rather embarrassing and seedy episode to be quietly forgotten?'
'Mark?' asked the ACC.

'I'm easy, sir. The 16th seems eminently sound.'

Helen Cave made an exaggerated point of looking at her Omega wrist watch. 'Well, that's perfect timing, Mr Perrin,' she said as she stood and collected up her brief case. 'If I leave now, I will avoid the capital's commuter traffic and get to my flat in time for bed.' She turned as the three police officers stood and she shook hands with the Assistant Chief Constable. 'Thank you so much for your hospitality,' she said with a beaming smile then turned to Mark in one seamless movement. 'And thank you too, Mark. It was really good to work with you again.' Then the seamless flow again as she turned finally to Kay Yin, remarking more formally: 'And with you too, Chief Inspector.'

Perrin showed Helen Cave to the door where his secretary took charge and led the MI5 agent across the carpeted floor and onward towards reception and an awaiting car.

The ACC resumed his seat at the coffee table. 'Sit down, people, I don't think we have finished, have we?'

'I think we are just about to get started, sir,' observed the Head of Special Branch as they all took their seats around the table.

'Go on, Mark.'

'MI5 might want to do a Pontius Pilate and wash their hands of this, but I'm pretty uncomfortable with it all.'
'Why?' he asked, neither encouraging or discouraging an answer, as if discussing the choice of a holiday destination.

‘If I had been MI5 I would want to know where Harvey’s other property was. This apartment, cottage, whatever, might be an Aladdin’s cave, a treasure trove full of useful information. I would want to explore any connection between the French Consul and Harvey. I would be worried that Miss Understanding would not keep her mouth shut. I would … .’

Perrin interrupted. ‘It’s a concern I have. Can we really rely upon her?’

‘No,’ came his simple reply.

‘Miss Understanding doesn’t know that Harvey is dead, at least, not yet,’ interjected Kay. ‘We will have to be careful when the news comes out, sir, but I would suggest that we can leave that problem for a little later. Whether she talks to her clients, we can’t be certain, but she won’t really have a great deal to say. We will have to hope that she will see that it’s in her *business* interests to play ball with us and keep her mouth shut.’

‘But she might talk,’ said Perrin to no one in particular.

‘Of course,’ responded Faraday.

‘And there are the passports,’ Kay Yin said, seeking to return the conversation back to Mark’s theme of MI5’s apparent lack of interest in Harvey. Mark took the hint.
‘Yes, that’s true. If I had been MI5 I would have at least picked up Harvey’s French passport and glanced at the photograph of Edouard Melies, if nothing else, out of simple

curiosity. You, sir, looked at both. Helen looked at neither. Some of her responses were too scripted and I suspect that she had been briefed yesterday not to urge us to pursue this.'

'Is there anything to pursue?'

'There must be another bank account somewhere,' suggested Kay. 'The numbers don't add up. Harvey's apartment must be worth 800K. How is he able to afford that? He's on the absolute limit of the bank account we know of and he must be sourced from elsewhere.'

'From the Spanish or Argentinians?' proposed the ACC.

'I think we have to assume that to be so, although, I think that Harvey's main driver is pride and resentfulness,' reflected Mark.

'And there is the research he is apparently undertaking,' prompted Kay.

'You think there's a French connection somewhere?' the ACC asked Kay as she crossed her legs.

'I missed it,' she replied, 'but Mar … Mr Faraday … has been pouring over the interview tapes and spotted something.'

'You didn't miss it, Kay,' said Faraday, not so much in defence of his lover but more because he detested negativity which he always believed hampered thought and action. 'I had the advantage of being a detached observer and had the luxury of time to think.' He looked across at her, the evening sun light enhancing even more her beautiful olive-brown complexion. For a quick brief moment he was lost in admiration of her, then checked himself. 'Go on, Kay, you know what it's all about.' He moved in his chair and re-crossed his legs. As he did so, Perrin noticed the officers' shoes. They both wore identical American-style black tasselled loafers.

'When I was interviewing Miss Understanding, she said that she and Harvey would often just talk. Harvey would apparently become quite animated when the topic of the conversation turned to France. Harvey had mentioned, so she said and I don't disbelieve her, that he had been privy to some sort of discovery during the last month or so,' she paused as she checked her transcript, the relevant text already highlighted. 'Yes, here we are. She said that Harvey had mentioned a "miserable piece of paper that would embarrass Britain and affect its standing in the world and the Commonwealth". The bit I overlooked was that Harvey would refer to America or Britain, France or Canada, but, in the particular context of this "piece of paper" he said that … ' she referred to her notes again: '"the *French people* will soon wipe that smug look off their faces".'

'The significance is lost on me, Mark.'

There was a long silence as Faraday appeared to contemplate his response before replying. 'I just thought it strange that, in *this* particular context, Harvey refers to the *French people* and not to *France*.'

'And?'

'Well, I can't imagine an uprising in France against the English, nor in any of the French colonies. But,' and now the pause was much, much longer before he continued in a quieter tone, looking directly at Perrin with those piercing brown eyes, 'there could be an uprising in Quebec.'

Perrin slowly leaned back in his chair. He considered the enormity of what Faraday had said and concern etched his face. 'Go on.'

'If a popular rebellion was timed,' suggested Faraday, 'say, to coincide with the death of, Heaven forbid, or the abdication of, Her Majesty, a sensitive or embarrassing document might be a very convenient and emotive trigger for the Quebec Separatists to act.'

'That's a bit of a stretch, Mark,' said Perrin, his initial shock giving way to practical implications.

Mark was about to say that the Indian Mutiny had been triggered, not by fact but by inaccurate and unsubstantiated rumour, but thought the better of it.

'And?' probed Perrin.

'Helen Cave knows that I don't like loose ends, and the Security Services shouldn't either. If we find something, they will take the credit. If we don't, then no harm done. That was my initial view anyway, but now I'm thinking that they may want us to pursue our enquiries.'

‘Why?’

‘Any internal problems within the Quebec province would not remain internal and would be of understandable interest to, and impact upon, the security of the United States.’

Faraday glanced out of the window across the Gordano Valley towards the far-off hills where King Arthur was said to have established a stronghold at Cadbury Camp. He sat there mentally pulling threads together, gathering his thoughts. Both the ACC and Kay Yin knew how he reasoned, both were aware of his dyslexia and its value, now recognised by the recruiters at GCHQ. They waited until he spoke again.

‘Since the Second World War, sir, MI5, MI6 and GCHQ have been in bed with the CIA and all the other sixteen or seventeen American agencies. We know that GCHQ shares pretty much all intelligence and communications with NSA. In fact, it would probably be difficult for MI5 to have an unscheduled coffee break without the Americans being alerted.’ He paused again. ‘Most of the mobile phone communication satellites and all GPS satellites are owned and run by the US military and, I suspect that, it would be inconceivable for MI5 to mount a thorough enquiry into Harvey’s activities without the Americans picking up on it.’ He paused before speaking again. ‘I think that MI5 want us to continue our enquiries. Maybe MI5 assume that the American agencies wouldn’t be too interested in any enquiries carried out by the bumbling British Bobby.’

Like most police officers, they are at their best when responding spontaneously to urgent or unpredictable demands. It's in their DNA. It's what they do. The Assistant Chief Constable (Crime) was no different. Perrin had decided. 'What do you want to do, Mark?'

'I thought we might have a poke about in the darkest of shadows, sir.'

'And you want two weeks?'

'I think if anything is likely to happen, I think it will be within the next *few* weeks.'

'I will give you *two* weeks, Mark.'

'Thank you, sir. And I will require absolute secrecy.'

He paused but only for three seconds. 'Approved, but I will inform the chief constable. And he will need to know if any of these darkest of shadows fall over another force area too.'

'Understood, sir. And it would be a great help to me if I could keep Sergeant Peter Purchell from Ops Planning for the duration of the enquiry.'

'Ah, yes. He's half French isn't he? Doesn't he have a middle French name or something?'

'Yes, sir. Jean. He looks Mediterranean and speaks French with a perfect French accent.'

‘Okay. Agreed,’ said Perrin with a smile, adding: ‘Maybe if you want someone on your team who looks like an Italian but has an English middle name you will give me a call.’

‘You never now, sir, we may need just such a person. I will, of course, bear you in mind for such an exacting and demanding role,’ he replied as he unsuccessfully attempted to control a huge grin, adding: ‘And I may need, in fact, certainly will, require extra boots on the ground.’

‘As and when,’ agreed Perrin, knowing that Faraday would never abuse a requirement or an agreement.

‘Thank you, sir, for your support,’ then added in a serious tone. ‘But there is just one other matter.’

‘I had a feeling there would be. Go on,’ said a very perceptive Perrin warily.

‘We will need a Code 3 budget.’

‘Why?’ asked Perrin, realising that what Faraday was about to say was likely to unlock a Pandora’s Box.

‘Because one of Miss Understanding’s clients is, as she describes him, an assistant chief constable.’
The revelation stopped Perrin in his tracks. ‘Which one?’ he asked sharply.

‘Colonel Michael Thorne, sir, our civilian Assistant Chief Officer (Administration and Finance).’

Chapter 8

Wednesday, 6th May.

38° 37' N 10° 04' W, Bay of Biscay and Bristol, England.

PAUL DELISILE HAD SAILED ON AUTO-PILOT throughout the night, the *Angeline's* course constantly changing so as to compensate for the currents and the prevailing winds. For the most part Paul had slept soundly enough. He had complete confidence in the Neco auto-pilot and the Garmin radar that would provide him with a distinctive audible alarm warning him of the distance, course and speed of any nearby vessel that might impede his passage.

At day-break he had stirred, as a black star-lit night gave way to a fair dawn, and gone on deck and checked all lashings and gear. He was 6' 2" and bronzed, his fair, sun-bleached, tasselled hair blowing in the wind as he studied with seasoned care the state of the sea and the patterns of the clouds, gauging the weather as he did so. He checked the touch-screen of the Raymarine plotter in the deckhouse, the overlays confirming his assessment of the weather to come. Satisfied, he went below to the galley and prepared a breakfast of ham, eggs and beans, then returned to the deck house with his favourite tin mug filled with black coffee. The sun had now shown through proclaiming its dominance of the sky. It was warm with little breeze, nevertheless, Delisile braced himself on the port side against the varnished mahogany of the deckhouse, as he tripped-off the auto-pilot and took the con, both hands firmly on the traditional wooden eight-spoked wheel. He stood legs apart, his Quayside Sydney shoes gripping the deck as his eyes flitted across the plotter and compass. He adjusted his course by a few points to port, compensating for the moderate sea running at her stern that made the steering a little more demanding. The 30-tons *Angeline* responded to his touch and drove her bow into the dark-blue sea, white water foaming along her sides and a gentle drizzling salty spray falling gracefully upon her varnished teak deck. With each wave her bow rode up smoothly and seemed to hesitate for a moment as if preparing herself for the next wave. But it was an illusion. The fifty-nine foot Ormidale motor yacht was a sound vessel and simply ploughed on, neither she nor her helmsman concerned as the westerlies complimented the power of the twin Gardner diesels, driving her forward at a little over thirteen knots.

The *Angeline*, a winner of the Pavilion D'or Boat Race, was built by J N Miller and Son, and had recently undergone an extensive refit at the fabled classic yacht yard of Cantiere del Argentario in Santo Stefano, Italy. With *Angeline's* timeless, classical good looks and accommodation for four in two beautifully fitted double cabins, each with their own shower, and an owner's double suite aft, Paul Delisle made an enjoyable and care-free living providing bespoke cruising holidays for discerning couples around the Aegean and Balearic Islands and the Adriatic and Tyrrhenian Seas. Although, often finding his guests both boring and boorish, Delisle was able to add spice to his life, and considerable cash to his bank account, by way of smuggling. Never firearms, drugs or people, but, anything else was good. He saw nothing wrong in this illegal enterprise. Like many of his rich and spoilt guests he viewed his activities as those of any entrepreneur. Yes, he reasoned, he avoided taxes, but so did the bankers who came on board as passengers. He thought of some of his passengers and recalled that during aft deck barbecues under the sun awning, these passengers would regularly boast of their skill at avoiding the attentions of HM Revenue and Customs for themselves and their clients; shifting money and bonds around the world; brokering commodity deals with the corrupt and exploiting the poor. He smiled at the thought that he knew very little of the package that he had been asked to smuggle, but with so many of his passengers being bankers, it was ironic that he knew that the package had something to do with an obscure Italian banker from Milan.

On one occasion around the Greek islands his passengers had been a British cabinet minister, his beautiful wife and two daughters. They were pleasant enough people, but Delisle's view of all politicians was that the vast majority were guided by self-interest and short-term advantage. Gibraltar was particularly in his mind and provided a clear example of the duplicity of politicians. The British he had encountered in ports had always been friendly, the Gibraltarians particularly so, with Gibraltar's cosmopolitan blend of its inhabitants cemented by the unity of the besieged and the mutual determination to resist the Spanish. Yet, a recent British Labour minister had been prepared to concede the sovereignty of Gibraltar to Spain, a Spain that conveniently overlooked the fact that they determinedly held on to the much larger enclaves of Ceuta and Melilla on the northern coast of Morocco. Politicians, he concluded, could not be trusted. They spoke of democracy and freedom but, for Delisle, the only freedom was that of the sea.

He looked for'ard towards a clear horizon and aft towards the effervescent wake and the gulls that followed his passage. He was pleased. The winds, particularly the currents, had helped him make up time after an anxious, enforced stay in Gibraltar. The *Angeline* had taken on one hundred and twenty litres of drinking water and one thousand, four hundred litres of fuel, not the maximum her tanks could hold by any means but, at normal cruising speed and fuel consumption, ample for this journey, and well short of *Angeline's* maximum cruising range. He had stored too with some extra provisions of fruit, eggs, basmati rice, whole wheat penne, jars of tomato and mascarpone, tomato and basil sauces, chicken breasts, wine, cheese and tins of soup. All of this made necessary because the planned one-day stop-over in Gibraltar had been extended to three days as a result of the essential repairs to the Kohler generator. Now he would not proceed up the western coast of France and berth at France's most handsome of ports, La Rochefort, or later at the marina of Morgat on the Crozon Peninsular and dine on the delicious langoustines, as originally planned but make a direct transit of the Bay of Biscay from Cedeira to Camaret and then into the English Channel, a total run of 1,124 nautical miles from Gibraltar.

He was relieved to be clear of Gibraltar. Whilst berthed in Gibraltar he had been concerned to read in the daily

Gibraltar Chronicle a report of the murder, mafia-style, of two men in Rome. One middle-aged man, Alessio Bianchi, murdered in his comfortable apartment after being bound, gagged and tortured; the other, a slightly younger Marco Rossi, gunned down four days later in a dingy back alley as he took his dog for her regular late-night walk. The report had said that both of these men had worked in the Vatican Library. This fact made Delisle wonder. He was sure that some of the writing on the package he had been asked to smuggle, and was now concealed beneath one of the treads of the for'ard companionway steps, was in Latin. There was no going back now, he reasoned. Nor was there any sense in disposing of the package, even at sea. He had little choice but to go on.

Back in Gibraltar his most immediate concern had been that the Gibraltarian customs authorities, pressured by the Spanish seemly obsessed with detecting cigarette smuggling, might have decided to carry out a routine rummage of his boat. They hadn't. But whilst the Gibraltarians may not have been interested in the *Angeline* and her skipper, they were both of great interest to the United States of America and every change of course made by the *Angeline* was being tracked by one of NSA's spy satellites. Those details were relayed, via a secure link, to alert and anxious staffers at the United States Embassy in Grosvenor Square, London.

***

The morning had been taken up with the briefing in Red One. There were now five police officers and one civilian who comprised Operation Snowy: Detective Superintendent Mark Faraday, Detective Chief Inspector Kay Yin, Detective Sergeant Pippa Blanchard and Sergeant Peter Jean Purchell, assisted by Detective Constable John Butcher, a computer specialist, who would also act as Logistics and Supplies Officer, and Jane Flood, one of Special Branch's junior administrators who would act as Office Manager who, incidentally, had suggested the operation's name after her West Highland Terrier, Snowy, a lively, friendly and loyal dog but originally bred as a ratter and well known for their determined capacity to dig.

The team had been given a two-page briefing paper filled with bullet-points, some speculative, others directly relating and cross-referenced to information contained on the magnetic boards. Mark had allowed the team thirty minutes to familiarise themselves with the material which included the street map of Bristol with its blue and red markers; photographs of Adrian Harvey, the exterior and interior of Harvey's water-side apartment, his Volvo saloon, the scene of the road accident, and his clothing and personal possessions at the time of death; photographs of Miss Understanding, although not the exotic ones; photographs and floor plans of the Trans-European hotel; photographs of Mrs Annette Harvey and details of her private vehicle.

Once the team had settled into their seats, Mark, Kay and Pippa had taken it in choreographed turns to up-date this small group on the events so far, details of Harvey's life and work, including his treachery, the fingerprinting of Harvey's apartment on Monday where only his fingerprints were found. They referred to Miss Understanding and her clients, although omitting any reference to the Assistant Chief Officer (Administration and Finance). As they spoke, they walked from one computer screen to another, seven in all; from one magnetic dry-wipe board to a second; a large scale street map of the city of Bristol and one of the West Country, another of the south coast. They encouraged questions, welcomed suggestions, allocated tasks and actions.

Finally, Faraday stood before his seated team again with his back to the map wall. He reminded them of the main objective of the operation: to find Harvey's second home; the limited time frame, the sensitivity of their enquiries as well as the unknowns.

'We are a small team and so the various actions which will be undertaken will mean that some of you will work alone for a period, maybe a short one, then together. What will happen, without a doubt, is that on many occasions there will be overlap. Consequently, what we will be doing is listing all actions here,' he said pointing to one of the magnetic dry-wipe boards, now formed as a matrix detailing ACTIONS, DATE AND TIME ALLOCATED, OFFICER/S DEALING and RESULT, 'so that we all know what we are all doing and what progress we are making. I suspect that this will generate mini-briefings, but that's fine with me. So, in no particular order, I will start with you, Peter,' he said to the Anglo-French Sergeant Peter Jean Purchell, 'could you concentrate on Harvey's passports please. Kay has made some initial checks but I want you to do so again with your French hat on. Check airlines and all ferries, Immigration and Customs here and in France and Spain. Also anything to do with the French names he was using, maybe any historical or geographical significance of the name Melies; his family history both sides of the Channel, including St Lô and his French university diploma; in fact, any French connection that may or may not be pertinent. Can you also check, with Pippa, on Harvey's friends and associates. He was a loner but he must have had acquaintances at restaurants, cafés, clubs, societies, his barber, that sort of thing. Bring everything you can glean to the table and I don't mind how bizarre the information or connection may appear to be.' Then added, looking at them all in turn, 'I don't want anything overlooked.'

'I'm on it, Boss,' replied Purchell, eager to play his part.

Faraday then focused his attention towards DC Butcher. 'John, I would like you to concentrate on Harvey's phone records, both mobile and landline, frequencies of calls, patterns and similarities, friends and associates, remembering that at the moment Harvey is supposed to be on leave, and so, discreet enquiries everyone please. It goes without saying that we need to tread carefully on this one.' Butcher nodded in acknowledgement. 'And,' Faraday continued, 'his computer, if we can identify passwords at the earliest stage, that will be helpful, maybe linked to a favourite holiday destination, a wife's name, a pet's name, a film star, his grand-father's battleship, or simply Miss U or Miss Understanding, that may allow us access in other areas. You know the drill. I'm particularly interested to identify patterns of speech, the use of words that may be used in any communication he makes that might appear to be a casual remark but could contain a warning or an instruction to act. I think you have some software that can help us here?'

'Yes we do, sir,' he replied as he scribbled notes on his briefing sheet.

'Pippa,' Faraday said, 'the briefing sheet mentions Harvey's apartment.' DS Blanchard nodded. 'It could be that when he chose his apartment, the views from the lounge were simply a pleasant bonus.' Faraday tapped one of the screens containing a photograph of the view from Harvey's lounge. 'I'm not so sure. And so, please check with the estate agent who sold Harvey the property as well as how be paid for it. I'm thinking here that may be many apartments were on offer at the time but one of the reasons why Harvey chose his apartment was because of a very specific view. Team up with Peter and find out all you can about *True North*, the *Matthew* and the *SS Great Britain.* There may be no significance or connection, but let's just see if there are any. Finally, you will see on the notes that Helen Cave referred to the Spanish and Argentinians, the Antarctic and oil, yet, Harvey's empty drop-file tags refer to the Hudson Bay and Arctic. See if there's any connection, would you please.'

Pippa Blanchard ran her eyes over the briefing sheet. 'Yes, of course, and the painting hanging in his lounge over the fireplace, sir?'

'Oh, yes, you're quite right, Pippa. Thank you. Please find out all you can about the painting, who the artist was, where Harvey bought it, how did he pay for it and, particularly, were the scene depicted actually is.'

Whilst Mark Faraday concentrated on delivering his briefing and the questions and answers, Kay Yin was concentrating too – gauging the demeanour of and reactions to the tasks each had been set. As DS Blanchard made her notes, Kay glanced at DC Butcher who was looking at Pippa with, what appeared to be, a look of resentment or cold envy in his eyes as if her life had always be a leisurely walk in in the park. Pippa was a beautiful woman with a private school and university education, but, both Mark and Kay knew that her life had not always been so easy, particularly when her boyfriend, Captain Paul Hutchings, had been killed in Afghanistan four years ago.

Faraday finalised his briefing with some general comments. 'Clearly there will be overlap, thus the reason for the daily reviews. For my part, I will be visiting Harvey's bank and following up on some enquiry regarding Harvey's vehicle. I need to go back to Harvey's apartment and to speak with his neighbours. I will be going there later on with Kay who will continue to delve into the backgrounds of Annette Harvey and Miss Understanding.'

Faraday turned to check the various displays, screens, white boards, photographs and maps to ensure that he had not overlooked anything. DCI Kay Yin did not overlook anything either. She had been noting the expression on DC Butcher's face. As Faraday had spoken of his and Kay's return visit to Harvey's apartment, Butcher had raised an eyebrow and his lips became taught and hard. An indication of envy or irritation, of suspicion or resentment, she wondered. She wasn't certain. Whatever, DCI Yin scribbled two letters on her note pad: 'HR' and enclosed these letters within a double circle of red ink.

Chapter 9

Thursday, 5th May.

39°47'N 09°49'W and London and Bristol, England.

THE PASSAGE WAS PROVING TO BE EXCILIRATING. The *Angeline* had been romping along at an average speed of fourteen knots and Paul Delisile had not had late Spring gales to contend with, although winds remained strong. He was enjoying a quiet passage. Day-time visibility had been about ten nautical miles with the previous day having been overcast.

Today, the clouds had almost completely disappeared and the sun shone through. Night-time sailing had, of course, required Paul to be vigilant and cautious, planning his cat-naps according to the time, the predicted weather and the charts, particularly as his present course had taken the *Angeline* between the sheer, rugged cliffs of Cabo Carvoeiro, the western-most point of Portugal's Peniche Peninsula, and the Beriengas Archipelago to port.

Now, with the sun shining through, Paul Delisile was having a comfortable voyage and enjoying *Angeline's* escort provided by a pod of playful dolphins.

***

Life should have been real comfortable for Commander Walt Bergman too. He had a big office. Walt liked that.

Walt felt he deserved a big office. He also had the exclusive use of a very, very comfortable embassy-owned apartment near-by. Since arriving in London he had attended grand formal functions and informal parties. He had visited the top bars in Wardour Street and high-end restaurants in Charles Street. But Walt remained a lonely stranger in a city of more than eight million people. At night he would lay awake. He would imagine that he had single-handedly thwarted a Soviet plot and had been presented with the Distinguished Service Medal by the Secretary of the Navy or even the President herself for 'distinguished service in a position of great responsibility'. Walt liked the words. He reflected on them. 'Distinguished'. 'Great responsibility'. Or he would fantasise that he had left the Navy, set up his own company and devised an unbreakable encryption programme that had made him a multi-millionaire, bought a Lamborghini and had proudly driven past Lucy and waved.

There was a knock on his door and Lieutenant Lightfoot entered with a NSA signal in her hand. Walt's anxiety levels rose as he eyed the TOP SECRET blue-rimmed flimsy.

'Is there anything else I can do for you, Commander?' asked Lightfoot. Inappropriate thoughts swirled through Walt's mind. Walt's heart rate increased.

'No, thank you. I'm just fine, Janet,' he lied. He wasn't just fine at all.

Lightfoot left his office, his eyes following her to the door. Walt pulled open his right-hand top drawer and fumbled about for the little elongated box. He found the box. He opened the box. He pulled out a foil strip of tablets, pressed one Propranolol into the palm of his hand and popped it into his mouth. Within minutes Walt's heart rate and anxiety had lessened. He picked up the blue-rimmed signal and read its contents:

WB-674536/EHT-681 – MV Angeline
10:00 GMT
39˚53'N 09˚49'W
Maintaining course. Destination unknown.

Walt was a Navy man. He didn't need to consult an atlas. He pretty much knew where the *Angeline* was. Due west of Cabo Carvoeiro.

He leaned back into his comfortable chair. He was in real deep. And once you are in, you are never out. How had he gotten in so deep? Walt pondered. Maybe it was the lonely evenings and restless nights. Walt knew that his lonely evenings had provided a fertile breeding ground for resentment and bitterness to grow. And hadn't they grown. The posting to the UK had been good, but not that good. Back State-side, Lucy now had legal possession of their home and she had successfully brought a case to secure part of Walt's Navy pension when it was due. At long distance he had not been able to fight the case, and he blamed the Navy for that. Of course, there was always his daughter, Debbie-Anne, but she was three-thousand miles and nine hours flight-time away. And then there was that idle son-of-a-bitch, Lieutenant-Colonel Trumbell, who had gotten a posting to Berlin, only miles from Walt's grand-parents' family home in Fürstenwalde. And now Lucy was partying with Colonel Clarke Jackson.

Walt had never thought of becoming a traitor. But Walt was a traitor now. It had kinda crept up on him unawares. It had all started as a result of one of those red London buses. Walt blamed the Navy again. Walt had gone for a walk to get away from the unpleasantness of office politics. If there hadn't have been the pressure of office politics he wouldn't have needed to have a stress break. It had started to rain – it was always raining in London – and he just dove into a shop doorway. A red bus came by. It was the number 35. That was all. Number 35. And, standing in the shop door, the rain driving down hard, Walt started to consider the implications of Section 35 of the Constitution Act all over. And thinking it over led him on the road to treason.

He pulled the foil strip from its packet again and pressed another Propranolol out of its little plastic bubble and into the palm of his hand. He looked around his office furtively before he quickly put the tablet into his mouth. This furtive behaviour was a pointless thing to do. No one shared Walt's office. There were only two doors. One to his bathroom. The other to a general office and Lieutenant Janet Lightfoot. But, maybe, this act served to illustrate the extent of Walt's guilt and anxiety.

***

Detective Superintendent Faraday and Detective Chief Inspector Yin drove along Hotwells Road towards The Great Engineer's House.

'I called into HR earlier,' said Kay, 'to look at John Butcher's file.'

'Find anything interesting?' Faraday asked casually, but he knew Kay was shrewd and would not waste her time.

'Oh, yes. I think we can say that. He could be a problem for us.'

'Why do you say that?'

'I've been watching him. He's not a happy man. There's resentment there somewhere. Envy, maybe. I saw in his file that two years ago a complaint was received from his next door neighbour, a complaint of noise, constant loud arguing between Mr and Mrs Butcher.'

'I can't remember hearing anything about that,' he said with an interested frown.

'No, probably you wouldn't have. No formal disciplinary action was taken. Words of advice given and no recurrence.'

'And what was Butcher's explanation?'

'He said that the long hours and lack of sleep had taken their toll.'

'And Mrs Butcher?'

'A bit of a bitch, apparently.'

'Well, I can understand how Mr Butcher must feel,' said Faraday in mock sympathy. 'I can well understand how difficult it must be for him.' Kay ran her hand along his thigh. 'Kay,' he said taken by surprise. 'Stop. Stop or I will be having an accident.'

'Which kind?' she purred.

'Okay, okay, I give in.'

'Well,' she said, still purring, 'I might have to resume this line of intimate questioning later on as we are already here.'

Mark Faraday pulled into the parking bays as Kay removed the keys from the glove box. The pathway had been swept. 'Let's see if we can find the groundsman,' suggested Mark, but enquiries with Mr Etheridge proved fruitless and the officers walked down the steps to the garages. They opened the garage allocated to apartment number 16. The garage was completely empty. No shelving, no oil cans, no tool cabinet, no spare wheel. Just a dry emptiness. They both went up again and returned to Harvey's apartment.

In Harvey's apartment the mid-afternoon sun shone through. The apartment looked good. It was a restful place, not a home exactly, but tranquil. Mark concentrated his attention upon the anthology books as Kay made discreet enquiries with neighbours. Many of the books had been highlighted identifying particular species, their habitats, their migration patterns, food and nesting habits. When Kay returned she had been able to speak with seventeen of the other thirty-one residents. They all told the same story.

Mark Faraday's facial expression also told a story.

'You found something interesting, didn't you?' she asked.

'I think we know where his second home is, well, the town at least.'

Chapter 10

Friday, 6th May.

Bristol, England and 41°37'N 09°32' W.

THEY HAD ALL ASSEMBLED IN RED ONE. As Mark Faraday walked to the lectern, the team took their seats, Kay, as usual, seated on the extreme right with a bundle of files on the seats between her and the team.

'I want to follow the usual pattern and I will ask you all for your input in turn. It may be that some of your enquiries have drawn a blank. Don't worry about that. Because, that's good. It means that an avenue of enquiry has been explored and can now be closed down and we can turn our attention elsewhere. Okay, let's start with you, Peter, please.'

'Thank you, sir,' replied the Anglo-French sergeant. 'Nothing as startling, I think, as John's contribution later on, but I do have some interesting little pieces of the jig-saw. For what it's worth, my checks with airlines have proved negative. Enquiries with the ferry companies merely confirm the journeys that were taken, in the name of Harvey, during authorised annual leave and known to MI5. No journeys appear to have been made in the name of Melies. The Family Melies are well known in Alsace as a respectable family who have been committed to France and suffered for that loyalty to France. Harvey does have relatives, very distant relatives that is, living in St Lô, but the local police have not been able to help here, although,' he continued as he walked towards one of the photographs pinned to a display board, 'interestingly, I had assumed that the white porcelain head of the unicorn was connected to the rampant golden unicorns featured on the City of Bristol's coat-of-arms, but a white unicorn actually appears on the coat-of-arms of St Lô. It's only significance may be to show a close affinity to family or France. Of more significance is Harvey's French university's diploma. Firstly, the diploma is in the name of Harvey, not Melies, and the French shipping agent and Consul, a client of Miss Understanding, was a first-year student when Harvey was there as a second-year student. That said, neither was an active player in any protest or radical groups or student societies. However, both the French Consul and Harvey frequent the Café Rouge restaurant in Park Street. Pippa and I enjoyed a very pleasant supper there of Poulet Breton with extra French beans, of course,' he said with an exaggerated Gaelic shrug. 'I have discovered nothing else other than he has an excellent barber.' Sergeant Purchell ran his fingers through his thick, dark hair. 'I am, however, very disappointed, sir, that you haven't noticed the attention I have lavished upon my appearance. Meanwhile, I leave the rest to John, if I may.'

There was a great deal of well-meaning mock disbelief and shaking of heads at Paul's humour, a defence mechanism for what he knew he would have to explain later.

'Thank you, Peter. And I will make a note to inform the chief constable that you have had a superb haircut. I will pass on the barber's details to him,' said Faraday with a grin. 'Okay. How did you get on, John?'

'Nothing of significance so far from his mobile and landline, sir. No apparent friends or associates. I have accessed his computer. The code is "511MU", that is Miss Understanding's hotel suite number.'

'Excellent,' remarked Faraday.

'The only thing that seems to be of significance is a pattern of phrases used in e-mail and text communications via a French provider. There are two phrases that crop up just before some of Harvey's long weekends or week-long periods of leave. I've been greatly helped by Peter.' He paused and invited Peter Purchell to stand with him at the lectern.

'I'm not sure I have been a great help,' said Sergeant Purchell as he took his place alongside DC Butcher, 'this has all been down to eye-aching persistence by John, prompted by one of the books listed in the briefing sheets: *Between Silk and Cyanide*, a book by Leo Marks which dealt with the war-time Special Operations Executive and French Resistance. I was simply asked to help when all the hard work had been done.' DC Butcher was about to speak but Purchell silenced him with a gentle hand gesture as he stood by his side. 'During the last war,' continued Sergeant Purchell, 'between 1940 and 1944, obscure personal messages were sent from Radio Londres to Resistance fighters in France: *"Ici Londres! Les Français parlent aux Français"*,' he said in beautifully melodic French. 'I think most of us have heard of some of the rather more bizarre ones such as: "Jean has a long moustache" and "the dice are on the carpet". The most famous, I suppose … ,' he began to say but seemed to falter as if his use of the beautiful language of his mother brought back memories of history past, ' … was "wound my heart with monotonous languor" from … from a poem by the French poet Paul Verlaine: *"Blessent mon cœur d'une langueur monotone".'* For a moment Peter Jean Purchell remained silent. He started to bite his bottom lip and tears stung his eyes as the significance of these famous words reminded him of his French mother's family who had fought with the Resistance and had died for France. Kay Yin quietly rose from her seat and walked slowly towards the lectern apparently reading her notes. She stood behind both officers but, as she did so, she put her hand unobtrusively on Peter's waist. He cleared his throat. 'Yes, … ' he continued, ' … this, this message meant that the D-Day landings would commence within twenty-four hours.' He cleared his throat again and gathered himself. 'Often such messages were in two parts. One message would be sent to inform the recipients that action was imminent; the second was the trigger to take action immediately. For example: "It is hot in Suez" could mean to prepare for an agreed eventuality, followed later by: "There is a fire at the insurance agency". When John searched through Harvey's laptop and mobile phone he spotted a pattern: "I will reserve a table" and "I understand that the garage is excellent", phrases that had been used during the last two years, at times a little before Harvey appeared to have taken week-end or week-long breaks. The first: "I will reserve a table" was sent as recently as the 20th April which we believe means that Harvey should now be alert and on stand-by for the executive message. If we look at the timings and intervals of previous messages, then our best guess is that the executive message: "I understand that the garage is excellent" will be sent at any time between the 14th and 17th.'

There was utter silence in Red One. 'The only problem,' interrupted DC Butcher, 'is that I haven't been able to work out what act the executive message will trigger and where.'

'Okay. Good work, both of you,' said Faraday, 'I am prepared to run with the coded message scenario and all due to your excellent work, but ... '

'Sir,' offered Pippa, 'I don't know where it is likely to be either, but I believe I know where Harvey's second home could be.'

'Go on,' encouraged Faraday.

Pippa rose from her seat and approached the photograph of the painting which hung above the fireplace in Harvey's lounge. 'I thought this was a river with hills beyond, sir. Then I noticed this white paint smudge on the hill top with what looked like a flag pole protruding from it,' she said pointing to a small detail on the photograph. 'I thought it was just a house, but as Harvey seemed to be drawn to Dorset, I checked the eighty-eight miles of the Dorset coast line. This is not a house, sir. It's a Coastguard station with a communication tower. This is Hengistbury Head between Christchurch Harbour and the English Channel. I think that this painting could be a view from Harvey's other home. I think his second home is in Christchurch, sir. I'm certain of it.'

Pippa Blanchard remained silent. She had risked her reputation on this speculation. Red One was silent too until a smile creased the faces of Mark Faraday and Kay Yin. 'I'm equally certain you are correct, Pippa.'

The relief could be felt in the room. The team looked at each other, smiles creasing their faces too at the realisation that they had achieved a break-through.

'Marvellous work by all of you. Really, really good work,' said Faraday full of admiration for these good people. 'Take your seats again please.' Kay remained at Faraday's side. Once seated, Faraday spoke again. 'As you know, Kay and I went back to Harvey's apartment. We didn't find much. We listed the expensive wines that were in a rack. We checked his books more carefully. We spoke to neighbours who confirmed that Harvey was a loner. Harvey didn't get involved with the management committee which managed the communal areas of his apartment block; he didn't socialise at Christmas time or the New Year, and so on, although the observant neighbours did notice SOCO arrive on Monday dressed as electricians. Significantly, the ornithology books had been highlighted by Harvey. We crossed-referenced these and found that of the species highlighted many frequent Stanpit Marsh, a one-hundred and sixty acre nature reserve of Scientific Special Interest between Christchurch town and Christchurch Harbour itself . This was a *could be* location. But we then examined a small wooden display crate containing flower pots and an ingenious little irrigation system. We removed the pots and on the bottoms were price stickers for a nursey: Stewarts of Christchurch, a well-known local company. Well, they should be well-known having been established in the town way back in 1742. And so, I think that we can now reasonably assume that Harvey's second home will be in the Christchurch area. And Christchurch is within the estimated radius of 140 and 170 miles. Unless anyone has another suggestion, I think that it would be wise to conclude that Christchurch will now be the focus of our attention.'

'And St Lô is twinned with Christchurch,' confirmed Sergeant Purchell.

Faraday's own up-date was a slight anti-climax but, nevertheless, he did mention his enquiries with Harvey's bank; Harvey's membership of the breakdown organisation, the Automobile Association, and the garage where maintenance on Harvey's car was carried out. 'Nothing conclusive has been forthcoming from these enquiries or from forensics, although examination of Harvey's car tyres and underside did reveal,' he paused to pick up a report from the little table, 'here we are: "traces of acidic and lime soil with a pH of between 4 and 5.5 which is mainly found on free-draining, sand and gravel soil with few nutrients" which are apparently consistent with the salt and freshwater marshes of Stanpit Marsh. And so, I think we can say that we will be concentrating our enquiries in the right area.'

Pippa's enquires were certainly not an anti-climax. Her enquiries in respect of passengers and crew of the *SS Great Britain* and members of the restoration gangs and the trust also proved fruitless. Pippa was able to confirm that *True North* was a Canadian 12 metre America's Cup racing yacht, now available for charter out of St Maarten in the Caribbean, which fitted with one of Harvey's holidays. However, her enquiries regarding the *Matthew* were very significant. DS Blanchard said that whilst the *Matthew's* original crew and the teams responsible for building the replica had no connection with Harvey, the *Matthew* did have a direct connection with North America.

'Some of you may not be aware of the precise details of the *Matthew* which is a replica of a caravel,' she said, 'that sailed from Bristol with John Cabot, or Giovanni Caboto, an Italian born in Venice, and landed at Bonavista on the Newfoundland coast on the 24th June 1497. Your briefing sheets mentioned the empty drop files in Harvey's bureau with the little inside-out tags that contained the words: "Carbonaris", "Frobisher", "Nanvuti", "Inuits", "Newfoundland" , "Mi'kmaq" and "Oviedo".'

Pippa Blanchard walked to the display screens. 'Carbonaris was a priest from Milan and the Deputy Papal Tax Collector in England. He was close to Henry VII in whose service Cabot sailed, and Carbonaris arranged loans from a variety of Italian banks with whom his family was, and is still, connected. It was this man who established church missions in Newfoundland and Labrador.' She tapped the screen. 'Frobisher Bay,' she continued pointing to the screen again, 'was named after Sir Martin Frobisher who attempted to discover the North West Passage in 1576. Frobisher Bay is situated in Nunvut territory, an area which once formed part of the Northern Territories, including the Canadian Arctic Archipelago.' Pippa returned to the lectern. 'The Inuits, once referred to as Eskimos, had been formerly recognised as a distinctive group of Aboriginal Canadians by way of Sections 25 and 35 of Canada's Constitution Act of 1982. This group live in Alaska, the North West Territories and the northern third of Quebec.' Pippa checked her notes before she continued. 'Last Sunday, Helen Cave referred to Spain and Argentina, the Antarctic and oil, but not Canada or the Arctic, yet this area seemed to have been of interest to Harvey. Interestingly, Canadian oil reserves are only third to Saudi Arabia's, 28% of which are found off-shore of Newfoundland. Canada is the fourth largest producer of natural gas, most of which is to be found in Newfoundland and Nova Scotia. That's it, sir. Although I haven't found out anything of interest in respect of Oviedo.'

Faraday took four or five steps in silence. Turned and paced again. He stopped and faced his team, nodding. He had made up his mind. 'Well done, Pippa. In fact, all of you. Really excellent work.' He remained silent for a few long moments then addressed them again. 'I said to the ACC that we would need to poke about in the darkest of shadows. By your efforts we have discovered more dark shadows. I suspect that these shadows are very likely to become much darker, if not black, as our enquiries progress.'

***

Night had covered the *Angeline* like a black shroud. There were no stars in this moon-free sky. The only lights were the bright red and green navigation lights to port and starboard, the pale blues, greens and yellows of the illuminated instrument panels and the golden glare of the lamp over the chart table.

There was a Force Three sea running and Paul Delisile had donned his Helly Hansen Koster oilskins. These Scandinavian inspired Koster jacket and matching high-fit trousers were perfect for this part of the passage. Usually worn on sail boats, Paul liked the ease of movement the design provided, together with the warmth and dryness. The sea state was good and pushed against the *Angeline* counter and drove her along nicely, but any skipper would be fool-hardy to be complacent in these treacherous waters.

Paul was now approaching part of the Spanish Galician coast. It was pitch black but he knew this coast, a rock-bound coast known as the Costa da Morte – the Coast of Death – between Muro and Malpica. In particular, he knew of the rocky peninsular of Capo Vilán – Cape Villian. It was here in 1890 that *HMS Serpent*, an Archer Class cruiser, foundered in a storm. Of the one-hundred and seventy-six crew, only three were rescued. The dead were buried in the tranquil Cemiterio dos Ingleses, a sad place overlooking a rocky shore and ever dangerous sea. The enquiry that followed this tragedy determined that there was a design fault in this class of warship. *HMS Serpent* was too heavy in the bow and with a heavy sea running she would pitch badly. Added to this fault, the enquiry determined that there had been navigational errors by the watch-keeping officers. By contrast, Paul knew that the *Angeline* was a sturdy and honest boat with excellent sea-keeping qualities. He was also determined not to make the navigational errors that had been made on the bridge of the British cruiser on that fateful November night. Accordingly, Paul had thoroughly checked the expected weather by way of the synoptic charts; calculated his course carefully and entered the way-points into the Garmin plotter, working his rest and refreshment times around these calculations. But there was a not insignificant low developing in the mid-Atlantic and Paul knew that rest would be a rare luxury as he maintained his course to round Cabo Tourinan on the 7th and 8th , eventually to enter the calm shelter of the Ria de Cedeira on the 9th. That was the plan.

Chapter 11

Monday, 9th May.

Bristol and Christchurch, England.

FARADAY HAD GIVEN THEM THE WEEKEND OFF. But there had been no rest for Detective Superintendent Faraday. He had spent most of Saturday with Assistant Chief Constable Perrin who was in, what seemed to be, endless but necessary discussion with his opposite number in the Dorset Police.

Operational protocols were discussed then drafted, to be re-drafted again and again. This was particularly so in connection with the need for Faraday's team to be issued with firearms. Understandably, Dorset's ACC did not wish to be excluded from events happening in her police area which, with Faraday's very limited knowledge of the county of Dorset, might spiral out of control and result in adverse publicity for her force. Nevertheless, channels of communication were agreed as well as access to magistrates should warrants be required. Liaison officers were appointed and local tactical teams were identified and briefed. The ACCs considered how detailed these briefings needed to be and at what level. Compromises were reached, decisions made and protocols eventually signed off.

Now it was Monday morning and the teams were set. There were two RV points, three pairs and three routes to Christchurch, Dorset.

Christchurch is a borough on the eastern margins of the county of Dorset, abutting onto the New Forest and the county of Hampshire. But Christchurch is also a town of 54,000 residents within the borough. More than thirty per cent of the population is aged over sixty-five years, double the national average, and life expectancy is much higher too. The town was established in the seventh century between the rivers Stour and Avon. It boasts its own eleventh century church which is larger than some English cathedrals, a twelfth century castle and a beautiful lake-like harbour protected by a headland which was once an Iron Age settlement. The pace of life in Christchurch is sedate, if not slow, with the town's slogan being: *'where time is pleasant'*. It was to this pleasant town that the three pairs of officers would be heading.

One pair, comprising of Sergeants Purchell and Blanchard, drove to The Mall, the large, sprawling shopping centre on the northern outskirts of the city of Bristol. They both arrived separately at 7.50 and 7.55am. Paul Purchell parked his private car in the underground carpark adjacent to the John Lewis department store, Pippa Blanchard being driven there by her husband, Charles - but not in the Bentley. In the semi-seclusion of the carpark Charles helped them load their kit into a dark-grey Land Rover Discovery rental. Their go-bags contained enough clothing and personal toiletries for ten days. All would bring plastic suit-carriers but, for the most, their clothing was that of young people taking a Spring-time seaside holiday, but also smart-casual and foul-weather, including Hunter boots, together with plastic crates containing Red One's display material, manuals, stationary and computers.

Once loaded, Peter and Pippa drove from under the carpark to the M32 motorway and then onto the M4 towards London, leaving this motorway at Junction 13 and on to the A34 and A31, through the New Forest to their final destination in Christchurch. It was unlikely that any of this team would have been under surveillance, but Faraday was cautious as to the interest of MI5, MI6 or the US intelligence services. He considered that there was the ever-present possibility of satellite or drone surveillance, and so, anyone who would have been tracking the two officers, unless they had actually been followed into the underground carpark, would assume that they had become lost amongst the thousands of daily shoppers to this, the largest shopping complex in the West Country.

The second pair, consisting of Jane Flood and DC Butcher, had arrived at Brunel's Old Engine Shed carpark, a large covered carpark directly linked to Bristol Temple Meads rail station. DC Butcher and his wife, Sandra, had arrived fifteen minutes early at 7.45am and were now arguing alongside her orange-coloured Ford Escort SR – so much for a discreet arrival asked for by Faraday! Mrs Butcher was early because she wanted to get to her gym appointment by 8.15 and had no intention of wasting her time by meeting the other team members. Jane had arrived shortly afterwards and, embarrassed, had sat in her Renault car some distance away viewing the argument. Mark Faraday and Kay Yin arrived in Kay's GTi at 7.55. Kay parked her

Volkswagen near a green Land Rover Defender rental and started to unload their kit and transfer it to the Land Rover. In addition to personal clothing, this kit consisted of additional Red One computers, Ordinance Survey county and street maps, visitor guide books, Samaritan leaflets, six folding camp beds and bedding, food and emergency rations and lighting supplied by Ops Planning, surveillance equipment and, a hardened secure case containing firearms and ammunition.

Faraday approached Mrs Butcher and introduced himself. 'I'm Mark Faraday, Mrs Butcher. I'm sorry that I am taking John away from you for a few days and that he won't be able to contact you, but it shouldn't be for any longer than the 16th, maybe the 17th. Should you need to speak with John you will be able to make contact via the ACC. I do hope John's absence won't be too much of an inconvenience for you.' Sandra Butcher expressed her thanks but her attempt at a smile was more like that of someone who was suffering from constipation. By any measure, a physically attractive and well-groomed woman, Sandra was as cold as ice and the short-lived conversation became a struggle.

Whilst Mark was attempting to make conversation with Mrs Butcher, Kay was joined by Jane and they both began to load the Land Rover and the dark blue Ford Mondeo estate rental, allocated to Jane Flood and John Butcher, with, amongst other items, electric extension cables and torches; two kettles, cutlery, plates and mugs; fresh milk and bread; soap, towels and toilet rolls; dish washing liquid, kitchen and bathroom cleaning sprays and materials.

Once Mrs Butcher had driven away, the small group discussed their respective routes. The Ford would drive towards Bath on the A36, onwards to Salisbury and finally Christchurch, whilst the Defender would take a southerly route on the M5 towards Taunton, east along the A356 to Dorchester and then the A35, skirting Poole and further on to their rendezvous at Christchurch.

As with The Mall, any casual observation of the drive-in by Superintendent Faraday, Chief Inspector Yin, Constable Butcher and Miss Flood should appear to be not unlike the nine and a half million annual commuters entering the rail station hub with its fifteen platforms and direct links to Cardiff and Wales; Birmingham, The Midlands and Scotland; Exeter and the South West and east to the metropolis that was London.

***

The Maritime and Coastguard Agency is the body that, amongst other responsibilities, co-ordinates search and rescue operations and is responsible for Her Majesty's Coastguard. At Steamer Point, on the outskirts of Christchurch, is HM Coastguard Training Centre, now lying vacant whilst a new complex was being built at Southampton. The Steamer Point Centre, amongst salt-tolerant trees, the Home Oaks, Scots Pines and Monterey Pines, consists of nine large buildings, two smaller ones, together with a secure store and ample car parking. Originally opened in 1943 as the Ministry of War's Signals Research and Development Centre, it is enclosed by tall wire fencing topped by barbed wire. Entry can only be gained through one set of large double gates.

Sergeant Purchell and Detective Sergeant Blanchard were the first to arrive at the double gates at 10.21am. Although the mileage from Bristol to Christchurch was much more than the A and B routes taken by the others, the route via the motorways was quicker. Second to arrive were Detective Superintendent Faraday and Detective Chief Inspector Yin at 10.34, with Detective Constable Butcher and Miss Jane Flood arriving eight minutes later. There, standing at the double gates, was District Officer Greaves, resplendent in his uniform identical to that worn by a Royal Navy Commander.

Dennis Greaves ushered the vehicles through the gates and welcomed the police teams with coffees and biscuits in the kitchen, followed by a conducted tour of the centre. Two of the larger buildings were chosen as ideal for the team's needs. Although dust hung in the air and some of the rooms were a little musty, the accommodation was spotlessly clean. All rooms had blinds or curtains. There were two bathrooms. The kitchen-cum-mess room had three good sized table and twenty-six chairs, a stack of trestle tables in one corner, a working six-hob cooker, a large micro-wave oven and fridge, but no freezer. Dennis had thoughtfully provided plates, bowls, mugs and cutlery, together with tea towels and kitchen rolls, both of which had been overlooked. Faraday quickly suggested an allocation of rooms: two rooms to serve as bedrooms; a large classroom as the ops and briefing centre; two smaller rooms for stores; another small room for use as his office, the mess to remain as the dining room and what had been the teaching staff's common room, equipped with an odd collection of comfortable easy chairs, to act as their lounge.

Whilst the team shifted tables and chairs from the store room, Faraday and Greaves checked the perimeter, security lighting and alarms. As they approached the entrance gates, Mark thanked the Custom's officer. 'Thank you so much, Dennis, for all your help and preparations. If you make us any more comfortable here by the sea, we won't want to leave.'

'I'm pleased to help. There are only two phone lines left operating, but the heating is on, although the boiler is old and temperamental like me,' he said with a great chuckle in-keeping with his ruddy complexion. 'I don't know what you people are up to and there's no need for me to know, but, I expect you will be needing privacy and this sign should do the trick.' He produced from his battered briefcase a laminated notice, mounted neatly on hardboard, which he fixed to the outer gate with plastic ties:

HM Coastguard Training Centre

'Exercise Fortitude'
9th May – 27th May

All enquiries to:
District Officer D Greaves
Phone: 01202 488 116

Faraday returned to the main building and large classroom in which Red One was being replicated, but with the addition of Ordinance Survey Maps of the counties of Dorset and Hampshire and of the borough of Christchurch, as well as detailed street plans of the town itself. Photographs were cut from visitor guide books and pinned alongside key features on the various maps. By mid-day the Centre was well on the way towards completion with doors neatly labelled: 'lounge', 'ladies bathroom', 'gents bathroom', 'The Boss', 'store', 'Red One' and bedrooms suitably designated, although this would change. It was time for lunch and Faraday drove out to collect locally caught fish and chips. Faraday noted the buoyant team spirit although, maybe not so with DC Butcher. Nevertheless, all became involved in washing and drying dishes, wiping down tables and generally tidying the dining room before the briefing.

After lunch, whilst the team continued to set up the accommodation, Faraday drove off-centre and reconnoitred the Christchurch area and surrounds, returning in time to commence the first briefing at 3.45pm.

Faraday entered what had been designated as the Ops and Briefing Centre and now called: Red One/Two, and looked around. Everything was in place: the magnetic dry-wipe boards, computer screens and display boards; a central table with six matching chairs and a small table that acted as a lectern, together with a rather incongruous bed-side lamp with a pink-coloured shade, with two chairs either side; a large clock mounted on the wall, trash bins, a shredder and an HP Officejet copier; and the ACTION, DATE

AND TIME ALLOCATED, OFFICER/S DEALING and RESULT board. Faraday was also pleased to see that all eight windows had been sealed with black-out sheets. Faraday spent a short time discussing his reconnaissance and notes with Kay Yin, then turned to address the group.

'Very impressive and business-like, everyone. Perfect. And I like the pink shade,' he said as he commenced the briefing by asking if there were any significant problems with the facilities and was there any essentials that had been overlooked. Suggestions were made and notes taken. It was agreed that all unused rooms could be taken into use as bedrooms to cater for restless or noisy sleepers. Pippa, Jane and Kay wanted to share one large room, with the men preferring to take separate rooms. The bedroom signs would be changed accordingly. None of this presented a problem and there was a unanimous decision that each day should commence with an English breakfast of eggs, bacon, sausages, beans and tomatoes. It was agreed that a roster would be made for two members of the team to prepare breakfast, another pair to clear away. It was light-heartedly agreed that there would be no exceptions – even for those who hitherto had never successfully boiled an egg, or those who might be vegetarians or those more used to French or Chinese cuisine.

'This evening,' continued Faraday, 'we can use the vehicles we came in and familiarise ourselves with the town. You will see that I have acquired a selection of brochures from a variety of estate agents that you should leave in your vehicles in prominent positions. These should serve to account for your presence in the town. I suggest we spend no more than two hours, but not in convoy. Independently please. Our focus must now be directed towards identifying Harvey's home, whether a house, bungalow, apartment or caravan; rental, short-term let or permanent second home. Tomorrow, I would want Kay and John to post generic Samaritan leaflets through every door along these roads here at Stanpit, the purpose will be to survey every home for the slightest indication of where Harvey may live.'

Faraday ran his index finger over the street map of Christchurch, particularly the Stanpit and Mudeford areas, and the roads which overlooked Christchurch harbour and Hengistbury Head beyond. 'I'm guessing here, but there must be at least ninety homes along here at Stanpit. There are a number of large and impressive properties, like Mudeford House here, with coach houses and other buildings in their grounds which appear to be occupied. Maybe independently occupied and now privately owned. I don't know. There are small apartment blocks here in Inveravon and Rushford Warren, some of which would give views over the water, and others standing way back, such as Mudehaven Court and Donny Brook with line-of-sight views probably from the top floors towards Hengistbury Head.' Faraday examined the street plan more closely then pointed. 'And here is Masthead, the luxury water-side apartments near the Christchurch Harbour Hotel. These all have to be leafletted. There are quite a few smaller roads, such as Argyle Road and Chichester Way; Coastguard Way and Smugglers Reach. Some of the small roads and tracks have at their entrance: "Private. No Thoroughfare" notices. This will not apply to us. We have to find Harvey's property.' There were smiles of approval at this remark. They all seemed to be on-side. Faraday nodded towards Kay.

Kay stepped forward and turned her attention to Jane Flood. 'Jane, I would like you to check the local council offices, residential and holiday caravan sites, the Planning Inspectorate, HM Land Registry, in fact, any department that might give us a clue as to Harvey's property.'

'Yes, ma'am.'

'Peter and Pippa,' said Kay, 'I need you both to concentrate on French restaurants, wine outlets, the three sailing clubs and the Harbour Master. Also check out Highcliffe Castle. Apparently Kaiser Wilhelm visited the castle in 1907. Paul, if you see him wandering about you could ask him if he approves of your haircut.' The group erupted into laughter. Once they had settled, Kay Yin continued: 'A lot of exhibitions and musical shows are held there. There may be something connected with France. And, likewise, check out The Red House Museum, the Regent Centre and the Priory Church.' She paused to collect a blue plastic crate which she left on the small table. 'As far as communications are concerned,' Kay said, 'all of you will have left your personal mobiles at home. You can collect from this blue crate your police-issue pay-as-you-go phone. These will only be used during surveillance or in an emergency. Chargers are also in the crate.'

Faraday interrupted. 'I think I better take the next bit, because I would prefer it if you thought that I had gone mad, and not Kay.' He had their attention now as he had wanted. 'We know that communications are constantly monitored by our own intelligence services and foreign agencies too. We also know that the United States use a "trap and trace" system and that intelligence is shared through the "Stone-ghost" and "Stateroom" programmes. We know that criminals and private security contractors monitor police communications. We must, therefore, assume that anyone could be monitoring us and that they would very likely be familiar with police procedures and jargon. We know that key words and phrases can be targeted. And so, we are going into the restaurant business.' The team looked both bemused and intrigued at the same time. 'There is a possibility that our calls will be actively monitored,' he emphasised, 'but, we have to speak with one another from time to time. Some of our names are certainly known to MI5. They could be known to other agencies. And so, from now on, we will be using our second names.' There were some uncomfortable looks from some of the team. 'Okay, Peter, your middle name is Jean. That is the name you will use from now on.' Kay stepped forward and stuck a label on his chest with his second name written upon it.

Faraday spoke of every member of the team. Kay would now be Moon, John would be Frederick, Pippa would be Francesca and Jane would be Emily.

'We need to be imaginative here. It may seem to be imprecise and in an emergency we would revert to our usual call signs and ordinary operation speech. But, for the moment, humour me,' he asked. 'Let us assume that we are maintaining observation on a suspect outside The Priory church. If we see him enter, we would merely say something like: "customer entering restaurant". If we saw this suspect talking to someone in the church, we might say: "customer discussing menu with another customer" or "customer has joined our only other customer" or "I don't know what happened but the first customer has just walked out". We will have to add-lib, but this, I know, can work. At the outset, the scenario should be straight-forward. We are assuming that Harvey's intention was to have met someone here, or here abouts, otherwise, I can't see why his visits have been so clandestine. This meeting could be anywhere. It might be in a café, a restaurant, a shop, in a park. It could be a dead-drop. We don't know. And so we might say: "the customer has left his bag in the restaurant" or "on his seat" or "I am following a customer who hasn't paid his bill". If a suspect gets into a vehicle, we might say: "The customer is having a drive-thru take-away" or if he gets off a sail boat we might say: "the customer has left the Ship Inn". If something significant happens and we need to have an urgent meeting, we should say: "all staff come to the kitchen". What I am asking is for you all to think this through, imagine an operational scenario and think how you could apply this. Oh, I will be "patron".'

'Sir,' said Peter Purchell, running his fingers through his recently cut hair, 'as I am very likely to become a personal friend of the Kaiser, I am emboldened to say that your title of "patron" is entirely befitting your role,' a remark that was greeted with good humoured banter, Pippa and Jane screwing up pieces of paper and throwing them towards

Peter. It was a good way to end the briefing on this harmonious note. But the harmony would be short-lived.

Chapter 12

Tuesday, 10th May.

41° 30’ N 04° 11’ W and London, England.

HE HAD LEFT RIA DE CEDEIRA FAR BEHIND, avoiding the rocky reef a mile from its entrance and the shoals in the bay. It had been a sensible precaution to rest before the transit of the Bay of Biscay. And de Cedeira had provided that prudent opportunity, twenty miles north-east from La Coruna where the local police and the Guardia Civil would certainly have been more vigilant. At de Cedeira these agencies were nowhere to be seen.

Yes, de Cedeira had suited Paul Delisile’s needs perfectly. True, there were no bunkering facilities, no fuel and no water, other than bottled water in the town’s supermarket, but it was well recognised as a good sheltered bay in virtually any weather conditions. There was no harbour, just a long breakwater and good holding in the sand for the *Angeline’s* 110kg anchor.

Popular with Spanish tourists, no one seemed to take the slightest notice of Paul as he walked the pleasant little shaded streets and sat in the cool bars, all of which had televisions where he had been able to see the local and national news. And it had been good news. Good news regarding the weather. Good news also because there had been no follow-up broadcasts regarding the murders of Alessio Bianchi and Marco Rossi in Rome.

Maybe the Spanish tourists were in care-free mode, and the local businesses more concerned to capitalise upon the pleasant weather, than to have bothered to notice Paul as he walked along the unhurried little streets or lounged in the lazy bars. But NSA had noticed him. They always did. Every leg of his journey.

***

Lieutenant Janet Lightfoot tapped on his door. 'Come', called Commander Walt Bergman. She walked in and stood before him at the front of his large desk. He saw the Top Secret blue-rimmed NSA signal in her hand. He fidgeted in his chair.

'Two signals, sir,' she said standing perfectly central to his desk, as if on parade. He liked that. It showed respect, at least, that's what Walt assumed. 'One directly from NSA, the other from Menwith, sir.'

Her comments took him by surprise. Walt's mind wandered. She sure did look good in her blouse, he thought, crisp and white, and the perfect twin creases at the front. His mind wandered some more until his lustful eyes moved towards her shoulders and the insignia of her rank, one thick and one thin gold tape on her neat, sloping, black epaulettes. They kinda set her off, he continued to think, somehow directing his attention upwards towards her handsome face. Walt was now beginning to re-appraise Lieutenant Lightfoot. Walt had concluded that his original opinion had been premature and misjudged. The description of handsome had been far too hasty. He was more certain now. Janet Lightfoot was beautiful. Whilst Commander Bergman was arriving at this conclusion, the lieutenant remained patiently silent, patiently still. His mind continued to wander. He glanced down at the NSA signal she had handed to him:

WB-674536/EHT-681 MV Angeline
10:00 GMT
43°56'N 05°53'W
NW Ria de Cedeira. Destination Unknown.

'The NSA signal is simply an up-date, Lieutenant,' he said dismissively, extending his hand so as to take the second piece of paper from her. 'What's the other?' he asked as if these signals were something of a nuisance for such an important official.

'It's an "Echelon", sir,' she said, referring to the NSA's satellite global surveillance system that is able to capture every telephone call throughout the United Kingdom which is then fed into the United States CRC at RAF Menwith Hill in North Yorkshire. 'If you recall, sir, you asked me to task "Echelon" with the key word "Faraday". They have just had a hit.'

'Oh yes. So I did,' he said, recalling perfectly but adopting a casual and superior demeanour.

'Is there anything else, sir?'

‘No. No, thank you, Lieutenant,’ he replied impatiently.

Janet Lightfoot walked from the office, his eyes following her. It was becoming a habit now, following her with lecherous eyes. Walt seemed to be thinking of the young lieutenant all the while. She closed the door. He looked furtively around his office, foraged in his drawer, removed the little box and took a Propranolol. He spread the second signal on his desk with both hands and read its contents intently. It took some few minutes. The signal was a transcript of a conversation between unknowns. Faraday’s name was mentioned three times. The Dorset town of Christchurch was mentioned once.

The door suddenly opened. Walt stood up. Captain Martin Turner sat down.

‘You have the latest signal, Walt?’

‘Yes, I sure do, sir,’ replied Walt enthusiastically, although Walt wasn’t sure which signal the captain was referring.

‘Well, my judgement is that the *Angeline* is heading for Cornwall or Devon,’ said the captain. ‘Why sail way up the God-damn Channel?’ It was a rhetorical question. ‘I think it will be Cornwall. There are some good ports along the coast down there, just right for a cabin cruiser. You had better go plan to go mobile, Walt, and you’ll be taking Lightfoot with you. Good training for sure.’ He stood up and walked towards the door. ‘Keep me appraised, Walt.’ Then he was gone.

Walt was thoughtful. Walt was troubled. Menwith Hill was notionally a British base commanded by a Group Captain, senior Royal Air Force officer. In reality, Menwith Hill was a Little America with thousands of US personnel. In reality, it was a sophisticated monitoring station. Walt reasoned, correctly, that the intel from RAF Menwith Hill could not be misinformation. But, for appearance sake, he couldn't drive straight to Christchurch, he would have to travel down to Cornwall. And what was Cornwall but a dreary, rain-swept and craggy place shaped like a piece of God-damn cheese with no Interstates, just a bunch of narrow, twisting little roads. His plan had been to be near-by when the hand-over took place. Now he would have to be chasing his ass around Cornwall for appearance sake when he was now certain that *Angeline's* landfall would be on the Dorset coast. That was a complication he didn't want. What Walt did want was another Propranolol. Walt took two.

Chapter 13

Wednesday, 11th May.

Christchurch and London, England.

THERE HAD BEEN RAIN ALL MORNING. A lot of rain. But rain was good. Rain allowed the officers to shelter in doorways. The rain allowed them to observe their environment, spend extra time in porch ways, more time under shop awnings - observing.

DCI Yin and DC Butcher reported to the daily review that they had slogged along puddled streets, through water-logged lanes full of wet, overhanging bushes and branches and along muddy tracks. They had posted the Samaritan's leaflets through one-hundred and thirty-two letter boxes. They had not been able to gain access to one small apartment block and sixteen homes did not open their doors to their knocking; eleven homes appeared to be vacant and seven were being renovated by local builders. They spoke to a carpenter sheltering from the rain at Tutton's Well and two French waitresses employed by the prestigious Christchurch Harbour Hotel. But no useful information had been forthcoming.

Jane Flood said that she had contacted by phone the local council and county authorities; the Land Registry and planning offices; the highways authorities and utility companies. Those who were co-operative were unable to provide any useful information. Those who were not co-operative provided nothing at all.

Sergeants Purchell and Blanchard had had no success at any restaurants visited by them, although an up-market wine store had recognised Edouard Melies' photograph as someone who visited the store from time to time and purchased the higher priced wines, names which appeared on the briefing sheet as having been found in Harvey's Bristol apartment. The Harbour Master was willing to be of help, but his record-keeping arrangements were so poor that he promised to speak with both officers in two days' time when they agreed to meet with him again.

As the team continued the review, Faraday's pager bleeped on his belt. He pulled the pager from its holder and looked at numbers on the little screen. Just six numbers. 250960. But important numbers. Numbers not to be ignored.

'Kay,' he said looking at his watch. It was 9.40am. 'I have to go. More foot-slogging I'm afraid. I will leave you to wrap-up here.'

'Right, sir. Shall I wait here for you to return?' she queried instinctively.

'Good idea,' he said and, without turning around, he walked straight for the door.

Faraday used the Land Rover Defender and drove along Stanpit and parked outside the newsagents a little way past the hotel. At the junction of Stanpit and Mudeford is a quaint Victorian post box, painted Royal Mail red, with an unusual vertical, hinged letter opening. But it was not this post box that he was eager to use but the public phone box next to it. He pulled the heavy door towards him and entered the box with its aroma of stale cigarettes. Faraday waited. He knew he had to wait. Wait until the top of the hour. He thought of the number '250960' which was the date of birth of Assistant Chief Constable Perrin's wife, Barbara. He knew the call would be important. At ten o'clock precisely he rang the ACC's mobile. The ACC, standing alongside the carrots, potatoes, onions and runner beans in the large, crowded Sainsbury's supermarket at Portishead, answered his phone. The exchange was brief.

'Hullo Uncle, you left a message?' queried Faraday.

'Yes. Sorry to trouble you, but you should know that your ex-girlfriend has told me that one of your most junior colleagues is speaking to his wife about you,' said Perrin.

'I thought he might. Thank you. Give my love to Joan,' knowing full well that Perrin's wife's name was Barbara and he wasn't his uncle. Then Faraday rang off.

Faraday returned to the Land Rover and drove the short distance onto Mudeford Quay and parked. Mudeford Quay, the site of the infamous 1784 Battle of Mudeford Quay, is at the mouth of Christchurch Harbour. The harbour is like a great lake of some 900 acres. Because of the tidal harmonics created by the Isle of Wight and the proximity of the French coast, the harbour and its approach experienced double high tides. The water moved at significant speeds, with the low tide water flow being as much as eight knots, slightly less on the flood. Faraday stood on the bank of Mudeford Quay looking across to Mudeford Spit, with the sea ebbing furiously through the navigable gap between these two points. Known as 'The Run', these waters were a treacherous hazard for the unwary sailor, particularly as the dimensions of this sand spit, its length and width, could change by the week. Faraday returned to his Land Rover, opened the driver's door and leaned on to the open door as he looked over towards the Isle of Wight and The Needles directly in front of him – thinking. His thoughts skipped between the battle of 1784, Adrian Harvey aka Edouard Melies and the phone message from his ACC. He considered what would be the most useful action for him to take. He thought for a long moment He made his decision. It would be to confront and turn it around. Resolved, Faraday climbed into the Land Rover and drove towards the Coastguard Training Centre. He had driven less than a half-mile when he received another message on his 'as-you-go' mobile. It was from Detective Sergeant Pippa Blanchard, a message delivered in a calm, unhurried voice.

'Francesca here. Everyone back to the kitchen, please.'

Within eleven minutes, all had assembled expectantly in the briefing room.

'Okay, Pippa, Peter,' said Faraday, 'the floor is yours.'

'Thank you, sir,' replied Peter 'Probably simpler if I start. The briefing sheet mentioned that Harvey had been prescribed Piroxicam. Whilst in Christchurch, his local doctor's surgery would more than likely be at the Purewell Crossroads. On Monday, Pippa and I wandered along there. I went in and, in the foyer, was a little desk with a pile of Repeat Prescription Request forms, some pencils and a little post box. The forms simply required the patient to fill in their first name and surname, date of birth, a contact number and the medication required. So I took a chance and filled in Edouard Melies' details and put in a local phone number, namely this training centre. I went in today, waited for a long queue to gather and then asked the harassed receptionist for the prescription, deliberately confusing her with a mixture of garbled French and English. It was so garbled I nearly confused myself,' he added lightly with a smile. 'The flustered receptionist gave me the prescription. Edouard Melies' address is listed as: 'Sea Fern' which is one of the cottages along Stanpit, near Tutton's Well, where the occupants appeared not to be in,' said Peter, adding modestly: 'I think we are nearly there, sir.'

'Well done, Peter,' said Faraday. The team smiled and clapped, delighted that the enquiry was moving forwards.

'Do you think I should mention this development to the Kaiser when I see him, sir?' suggested Peter.

This jocular remark was greeted by more spontaneous laughter. But Kay had noticed her lover. She could see that he was pleased and relieved at the progress. But his smile had soon faded.

'Okay,' Faraday said. 'Pippa and Peter, in your best French accents, check out 'Sea Fern', but do not enter the premises. If someone answers the door, exercise your Gaelic charm. Gabble or garble – you seem to be very proficient at both, and back away. Report back in person, here, within thirty minutes. And well done the pair of you.'

As Jane Flood and John Butcher made coffee, Faraday retired to his little office. Kay Yin instinctively followed. She closed his door. 'There's a problem, darling, isn't there?' she asked softly.

Faraday explained the problem. He suggested a solution. They both agreed. She called DC Butcher to Faraday's office.

DC Butcher entered the office. He was dressed in casual jeans and opened-neck shirt, as was Kay Yin. Kay closed the door and stood behind him. Faraday was seated at his desk in front of him. Faraday's equally casual clothing did not, however, diminish his natural authority. Faraday extended his right hand.

'Kindly give me your personal mobile phone, officer,' he asked formally.

For a moment DC John Butcher was speechless. Blood drained from his shocked face. His heart raced. His throat became dry. Faraday's hand remained outstretched, his left eyebrow raised accusingly. Butcher foraged in his jacket pocket. He handed it to Faraday who in one swift movement tossed it towards Kay. Her right hand shot upwards. She caught the phone in her hand and held it alongside her face. Butcher turned but he didn't look at the phone. What fixed his attention were her angry and menacing eyes. He may not have known for sure the relationship between Mark Faraday and Kay Yin but he knew for sure that she was angry and, maybe, unforgiving.

'You have been calling your wife, haven't you?'

'Yes, sir,' he replied after a long awkward pause.'

'You have disobeyed a very precise and clear order,' said Faraday quietly and calmly. 'Additionally, you have committed a criminal offence by obstructing this enquiry,' he continued. 'Is there some pressing reason why you should wish to contact your wife, a health issue, maybe?'

'No, sir.'

'You are a capable officer, but, you have let down your colleagues. In fact, you may well have put them in harm's way.'

'I've let you down, sir. I know that. I'm really sorry.'

Faraday clenched his fists. His voice was less calm now. 'It's nothing about *me*.' He looked up and stared into Butcher's face with his penetrating, fierce, brown eyes. 'Don't … you … understand?' he said slowly. 'You have let down *your* colleagues.'

Butcher didn't answer. There was no answer. Faraday became calmer. 'When is your wife expecting you to call her again?'

'Tonight, sir.'

'Good. Then you will ring her. You will be on speaker and Miss Yin and I will be present. I don't care what you talk about but in your conversation you will include comments and remarks that we will require you to make. We will provide you with a piece of paper with what we want you to drop into your conversation. Tonight we may not require you to say anything. Tomorrow we may. Do you understand me?'

'Yes, sir.'

'Miss Yin will co-ordinate. Meanwhile, only make contact with your wife when we are present.'

'Yes, sir.'

'Your private life is a bit of a shambles at the moment?'

'Yes, sir, it is really,' he replied sorrowfully assuming that Faraday was about to offer some sympathetic advice.

But he was wrong. Faraday was always quick to help those in difficulties, but self-indulgent self-pity cut no ice with him. 'Life can sometimes be a shambles. In fact, it very often is. It is also easy to think that the world has been unfair and for individuals to become resentful of others,' observed Faraday. '*We* have noticed *you*, officer. You seem to be quietly resentful towards Peter's charming and easy manner, his popularity. Yet he is the one who ensured that *you* received full credit for discovering the … .' Faraday looked towards Kay.

'"I will reserve a table" quote', she said.

'Yes, that was it - what appears to be the coded messages. Yet I sense resentment. But you know nothing of his life or that of his family.' Then added harshly: '*Nothing.*' He paused to allow his anger to subside. 'Likewise, you think that Pippa by marrying Lord Chelwood, has landed on her feet and that her life has been one great big bed of roses.'

'I know she lost her boyfriend, sir.'

'Have you *any* idea of her pain?' his anger rising again. 'Her boyfriend's convoy was attached. He raced across open ground to attend to his injured men, then a second road-side bomb caught him. It blew off his right forearm and right leg. He was evacuated by chopper to one of those big military aircraft fitted-out as an operating theatre. Seventeen doctors and medics worked on him but they lost him just before they landed back home. He should have received a gong but, unfortunately, the dead don't provide very good references.' He paused, his fist at his lips. 'And Lord Chelwood tragically lost both of his parents in a gas explosion.' He paused again, wondering whether he should speak of his lover, to explain that, as a result of a savage beating in the back streets of the Kwai Tsing Police District of Hong Kong, she would never, never be able to have their children. 'And you certainly know *nothing* of Miss Yin.' Faraday nodded towards Kay.

'Go for a walk outside, officer, away from this centre but in sight of it,' she said coldly. 'Return only when Peter and Pippa arrive back. Then join them for the review as if nothing has happened at all.'

'Yes, ma'am.'

***

There had been a public house in Thayer Street since 1852. Now called the 'Angel in the Field', it was where they had agreed to meet. Commander Walt Bergman walked along George Street in the rain and arrived first. He entered this very traditional English public house through the stained-glass doors. There was a sign in the entrance way: 'Dining Upstairs' and 'Beer Downstairs'. Walt did beer downstairs. Walt walked into the bar, a bar with green stained- glass windows and a roaring log fire in an ornate stone fireplace. He removed his raincoat and sat in the left-hand corner with a beer and a copy of The Times. Walt had done the numbers. He had calculated the earliest landfall in Christchurch. And he calculated that the earliest date would be the 16th May.

Two beers and fifteen minutes later, Jim Hogan entered and walked straight up to the bar counter. He removed his jacket, ordered a beer and a packet of peanuts. The beer was pulled. Hogan paid the barman, took the pint glass and peanuts, and looked about the bar as if to find a vacant seat. He saw a vacant seat. It was occupied by Bergman's raincoat. Hogan crossed the bar and occupied the seat.

Bergman drank his beer and continued to read his paper. Neither man acknowledged or spoke to the other.

Bergman finished his drink, picked up his raincoat and, leaving his edition of The Times on his seat, placed the empty glass on the bar and walked out without a glance towards Hogan. Hogan picked up The Times. He noted that on the top of the first page, written in blue biro ink, were the figures '1' and '4', figures that would appear to a casual observer to be those of a house number, maybe. Hogan read the paper slowly, page by page. At page fourteen Hogan noted the message: 'Christchurch - 16 ', again written in blue biro half way down the page. Hogan thought about the 16th May. Hogan liked to be prepared. Hogan concluded that he would be in Christchurch on the 14th. But the 14th would be a mistake for him. Oblivious to the danger, he continued to read The Times and munch his peanuts.

***

Twenty minutes later the team reassembled for review. Pippa spoke first.

'No one answered our knocking at Sea Fern, sir,' said Pippa. 'The property is a very pleasant, neat, mid-terraced, red brick cottage. The front area is small without a garden, but has a well-swept flag-stone path and gravel. Conveniently for us, the cottage has a deep recessed porch. There is some mail and circulars in the little vestibule which seems to lead straight onto the staircase and into a small front room. There are French doors which lead from this front room into an open-plan dining-cum-kitchen area. We were able to walk around to the back via a public grass area which leads onto a public footway.'

Pippa remained silent as Faraday peered at the street map. 'This would be Fisherman's Bank?'

'Yes, sir,' she continued. 'And, as you can see, the pathway at the rear of these cottages goes along the water's edge for about five-hundred yards. Each of these properties, and the next groups of terraced houses, seem to have their own private jetty, or at least some have notices saying "private jetty". At the rear of Sea Fern is a long, narrow garden laid to lawn, neatly trimmed, with a path. Each of the three properties in this short terrace has high walls, about eight feet high, immediately at the rear between each property and extending for about fifteen feet. This allows each dwelling some privacy, although, we could easily be seen from the rear upstairs windows of the adjacent houses. Both adjacent properties appear to be occupied. There is a little shed at the rear of Sea Fern but no garage. There is no boat or kid's swings, but there is a nice conservatory giving a perfect view towards Hengistbury Head, in fact, that view,' she concluded, pointing to the photograph of the painting that hangs in Harvey's apartment.

Faraday nodded. Pippa had covered everything clearly and precisely. 'Okay. Jane. The man at the council who wasn't very forthcoming. Your assessment of him, his age, his attitude, his manner?'

'Young, sir. A wee bit pompous. Told me twice that he was the manager and kept asking me if I was a police officer or *just* a civilian.'

'Oh, good,' said Faraday with a grin. He checked his watch. 'Kay and Pippa, you both like dealing with pompous managers. It's five twenty-five. Too late now, but I want you at his office tomorrow at nine. I want to know who owns the property and the properties on each side for good measure.'

'On it, sir,' replied Pippa.

'We could apply to the magistrates for a warrant this evening, but that will take time and might create a fuss, with magistrates scratching their heads, getting their clerks back to ask for guidance and, maybe, calling the local chief constable. We can do without that. I want this operation to be as low key as possible. We can use Section 17 of the Police and Criminal Evidence Act, I know, but we had better not go blundering into Sea Fern tonight. Peter, is there any vantage points were we could keep obs on Sea Fern tonight?'

'Our vehicles would be too conspicuous on the narrow road at the front, but, because of the open-plan nature of the house and the conservatory at the back, we should be able to detect any activity from hides on Stanpit Marsh.'

'Let's do that. Let's eat first and we have thermos flasks. Sort out a roster and include me please. If Harvey was going to meet up with anyone, I don't want to miss him.'

Chapter 14

Thursday, 12th May.

Christchurch, England and 47°33'N 04°31'W

THE OFFICE OF JOHN HARRINGTON was situated in the corner of the council building. It was small, but it was *his* office. It overlooked the staff carpark, not the park or the river, nor the visitors' car park. And so, Mr Harrington didn't see the two officers arrive, but Miss Catherine Boyle did. Miss Boyle, a grumpy looking spinster with a face like a sea turtle, took an instant dislike to the two attractive young ladies with their confident walk who had just parked their Land Rover Discovery. She liked them even less as they approached her counter.

'Good morning, Miss Boyle,' said Kay reading her name badge. The middle-aged Miss Boyle considered that addressing her by her name was far too familiar, indeed patronising. 'Could we please speak privately with Mr John Harrington?'

'And what is the nature of your business, miss?' she asked condescendingly as she looked through her glasses perched on an unsmiling and sour face at the two casually dressed young women in jeans and expensively cut jackets.

'It's rather confidential, Miss Boyle. I am Detective Chief Inspector Yin and this is my colleague, Detective Sergeant Blanchard.' The officer said no more but slipped her gilt police badge surreptitiously across the counter. Miss Boyle glanced down. There was a pause. Miss Boyle then made an irritated pantomime of shuffling some papers together in front of her, replacing the cap on her plastic pen pedantically and placing a 'Partition Closed' notice in front of her before stomping off into a corridor and lost to view.

Mr John Harrington, office manager, thirty-four years of age with prematurely thinning hair, had adjusted his tie in anticipation of their arrival. He sat smugly behind his little desk, papers and pens neatly aligned. At first glance a visitor would have assumed that the seated Mr Harrington was about five-nine. He didn't stand as the officers entered. Then he did, but clumsily. He was five-three. Miss Boyle introduced Kay and Pippa: 'The *police*, Mr Harrington,' she announced disparagingly.

'Thank you, Miss Boyle. I can take this now.' Miss Boyle stomped out. She clearly thought that stomping was a good thing to do in her role. 'How can I help you, chief inspector?'

'I'm Detective Chief Inspector Kay Yin and this is my colleague, Detective Sergeant Pippa Blanchard.' He scrutinised both officers as he resumed his seat. He was becoming impressed or was it overawed. 'Can we both thank you for seeing us at such short notice, sir,' said Kay. 'This matter is rather urgent and we understand that you would be able to help us.' Kay didn't wait for him to agree or disagree. 'Do you recognise this man, Mr Harrington?' she asked as she placed a photograph of Adrian Harvey in front of him.

He seemed surprised. He was supposed to be surprised. He had not expected such a question. He studied the photograph. 'No. No, I've never seen this man.'

'Oh dear. We have been misinformed,' said Kay looking disappointedly at Pippa. 'This is a Special Branch matter and we were led to believe that you were the go-to manager who would be able to assist us. You see, Mr Harrington, we are keen to establish this man's movements and know that he has visited a property called Sea Fern on Stanpit. We need to know who owns that property. You can, I'm sure, help me here, Mr Harrington.'

Harrington's pompous ego was such that he would like to believe that he was the sort of go-to man who would be called upon to assist these extremely attractive Special Branch officers. But, he was now deflated. He had not recognised Harvey. Of course, the officers knew that it would have been very unlikely that he would have been able to recognise Harvey at all, but their approach had the desired effect. Mr Harrington now felt that, at this critical moment in an otherwise humdrum week, he had disappointed these police officers. Clearly, his ego needed restoration and so he made the pretence of giving his decision the serious consideration that it demanded before consulting his computer screen. After a suitable pause he spoke.

'In these *particular* and *urgent* circumstances, I can tell you that the property is owned by Josephine Savary Bennett. Currently, Miss Bennett, who is seventy-eight years of age, lives at The Saltings, a residential home here in Christchurch.'

'Mr Harrington, that piece of information has been quite critical. Thank you so, so much,' said Kay effusively. 'And we would be very grateful for the details of the occupants of the two cottages each side of Miss Bennett, if you would.'

***

There could be a legal argument that a warrant to search Sea Fern was unnecessary, namely that the cottage was in the occupation of Adrian Harvey who was now deceased and that Section 17 of the Police and Criminal Evidence Act allows the police to enter and search premises in order to protect the public from injury or harm, but there had been no activity at Sea Fern during the previous night, observations were still being maintained, and Faraday sought the flexibility provided by applying for a warrant. Consequently, Faraday appeared before the local magistrates in camera and obtained a search warrant on the grounds that he suspected that an indictable offence had been committed, contrary to The Official Secrets Act, and that the premises in question, namely Sea Fern, may contain evidence of that indictable offence or 'material that would be of importance to a trial'.

The three magistrates, correctly, questioned Faraday and considered the application before signing the warrant. Thirty-four minutes after his arrival, Faraday left the court with the warrant that would be valid for three months.

Faraday determined that a discrete approach was called for. Street plans were studied and deployments made a suitable distance away. Once the deployments were in place, Sergeant Peter Purchell approached Sea Fern on foot. He inserted the Chubb key into the door just below the door knob and turned it to the right. He then inserted the Yale key into the cylinder lock just above the knob, turned it to the right and gently pushed. The door opened. He stepped inside Sea Fern and closed the door, then opened the inner door of the vestibule. It had been cold outside. It was warm inside, the conservatory capturing the heat of the sun. Purchell quickly check the ground floor. It was open-plan, the partition wall between the front and rear rooms having been removed. Not a great deal to check, other than the under-stairs cupboard. He mounted the steep stairs to the first floor and its two bedrooms and neat bathroom.

'Patron, this is Jean. All the tables on both floors are clear,' he said as he drew closed the front, ground floor curtains.

Fifteen minutes later, Mark and Kay arrived, also on foot, and entered through the front door. Harvey's second home was spotlessly clean. There was no wallpaper to the ground floor but the rendered walls were painted a restful soft, pale green. The two old fireplaces had been retained and made attractive features. The kitchen-diner was expensively equipped and the French doors led to a delightful conservatory furnished with Indonesian cane, upholstered chairs and equipped with a Canadian manufactured Olivon T800 angled spotting scope mounted on a tripod. It was clear that this cottage was a restful place. On the first floor was a comfortable bedroom to the front, a small but cleverly designed bathroom, shower and toilet and, to the rear, a second bedroom now equipped as a comfortable study with an excellent view over the harbour and Hengistbury Head beyond.

The front bedroom had an expensive Serta double bed. But otherwise, it was in single occupancy, that is, other than a framed, bed-side photograph of Miss Understanding. The wardrobe had two pairs of trousers and a pair of shoes neatly arranged as were a small number of shirts, pants, vests and socks and one heavy-knit jumper in the drawers – all brands and sizes as Harvey's Bristol water-side apartment. In the bathroom were men's toiletries and one remaining bar of Marseille soap. In the study were more ornithology and sea-faring books, a collection of French novels by Balzac, Hugo, Dumas, Verne, de Beauvoir and Loti, but no computer. A place for Adrian Harvey to relax.

The officers returned to the ground floor. Under the stairs were a hardy walking-stick, a large RNLI umbrella and a Tayberry coat, plus a pair of Wellington boots. The contents of the kitchen replicated that of Harvey's apartment. The fridge was empty except for some bottles of Gaillac Perlé and the freezer contained frozen vegetables and lamb shanks. The wine rack contained five bottles of Gewurztraminer and three of Châteaunef-du-Pape, together with two square tea towels. But they weren't tea towels.

Kay pulled the coloured cotton squares out. The first appeared to be the tricolour with toggles. 'Here's a French flag, for the flag pole at the bottom of the garden, I suppose.'

Peter stepped forward. 'No, ma'am, that's not the tricolour. The French flag consists of equal vertical segments of blue, white and red, with the blue closest to the flag pole.' He said as he fiddled with the toggles. 'This pattern is wrong, the red, followed by white and then blue.'

'Then what is this one?' asked Faraday, holding up an identically sized flag but consisting of two vertical colours, one yellow, one blue.

'Give me a moment, sir,' said Kay as she mounted the stairs to the first floor. Within minutes she walked down the stairs reading a little blue book and clutching another much smaller, soft-backed edition.

'This little book,' she said, holding up a copy of Christchurch Harbour Tidal Predictions, 'contains the tide tables for this harbour and this one is all about navigation and contains the International Maritime Signal Flags.' Mark and Peter gathered around, Kay between them, as she pointed to a picture of the yellow and blue flag. 'This flag is K for Kilo, which also means: "I wish to communicate with you". The other, red, white and blue, is T for Tango, which also means: "Keep clear of me".'

'Very neat,' remarked Faraday with an admiring smile. 'Rather like the British rarely notice if our Union Jack is flying up-side-down, I doubt whether anyone around here would notice that the T for Tango flag wasn't the French tricolour. They would assume that Harvey was French and that the flag was French, and not a warning signal. Simple, but absolutely brilliant.'

'And the K for Kilo would be signalling the all-clear,' observed Kay.

'Exactly,' agreed Faraday only to be absorbed in thought. 'I think we can reasonably assume that Harvey's contact *may* come by sea.'

'It's certainly a possibility,' agreed Kay, 'I found nothing in the study to indicate ownership of a boat; receipts for the purchase of equipment, refits, fuelling or moorings, and so, why would Harvey need to know about tide times?'

'True,' Faraday replied, his mind juggling with possibilities and questions. 'We need to get John to go back to the Harbour Master and see if any boats came in during the times we know Harvey was away from Bristol. But there is another question. This house has been decorated, I suspect, exactly as Harvey would have wanted it. Certainly, it is not the colour schemes of a lounge or a study, or the dining room furnishings, which I would associate with an elderly person. And an elderly lady, living in a care home, is unlikely to spend a fortune on the kitchen and bathroom in a house where the stairs are so steep. So why is Miss Bennett allowing Harvey the use of this house? The yearly rent for a water-front cottage with a view like this must be significant for him. How does he afford that, I wonder?'

‘It could be that his treachery is much greater than we thought, but, there might be another explanation, sir,’ suggested Peter. ‘Harvey could have used a French connection to persuade Miss Bennett to allow him to use her cottage for a reduced rent or for no rent at all.’

‘I’m not sure I follow,’ questioned Faraday with an intense frown. ‘You say a French connection?’

‘Yes, sir. I might be completely wrong,’ suggested Sergeant Purchell, ‘but the owner’s name is Josephine Savary Bennett?’

‘That’s right,’ agreed Kay.

‘Well, Savary was a French Socialist politician who was, I know, a member of the French Resistance during the war. I will have to check, but I am sure that he became governor of St Pierre and Miquelon.’

‘And that could be significant?’ queried Faraday.

‘It could be a coincidence, of course, but St Pierre and Miquelon are islands situated in the Cabot Strait, just off the south coast of Newfoundland. They are French and the last remnants of “New France”, that is, the former French colony of Canada.’

***

Low barometric pressure and the Spring westerlies had meant that the *Angeline* had romped northwards across the

Bay of Biscay. The crossing had been demanding. Even with all the modern high-tech equipment, sailing at night demanded constant vigilance, particularly in the turbulent conditions. It was a tiring business. The days had the colour of lead, the nights the colour of pitch. Delisile's sleep had been fretful for days and he recognised that he needed a short rest. As he approached Ushant, Paul considered whether he would make landfall at Audierne or Camaret.

Audierne, at the mouth of the Goyen, had been a major fishing port but now a large and popular yacht haven. But, from previous visits, Paul knew that the marina was the habitat of nosy officials. He didn't give the matter much further thought but sailed northward past the rugged granite cliffs of the Pointe de Raz and the safer haven of Camaret on the Crozon peninsula.

Camaret had a smaller population of just over two thousand. Once bustling with tuna and lobster fishermen, it was now a small but charming village, very Cornish-like and twinned with St Ives in Cornwall. Camaret had three small marinas and a curved, natural jetty with its fabled seventeen-century Golden Tower, an impressive brick fortification guarding the harbour. Paul moored the *Angeline* and strolled along the quay. The quay had changed little over the years, although the former sailors' homes had now been sympathetically converted into cafés, restaurants and gift shops. He knew this place well and visited his favourite restaurant and ate a seafood platter of mussels, cockles, oysters, prawns and crab with a dry white Muscadet.

The sun was warm and the streets dry after the rain. As the restful afternoon drew to a close, the sea began to lose its perfect azure-blue colour, this perfection being replaced by a beautiful golden and crimson sunset towards the Tas de Pois, the group of five pyramid-shaped granite rocks that stood out to sea. Paul would pass these rocks early the next day as he made his way across the English Channel – the most dangerous waterway in the world.

Chapter 15

Friday, 13th May.

London and Christchurch, England.

THE ACCUMILATED STRESS OF HIS POSITION was now beginning to tell. Lieutenant Janet Lightfoot had brought two further signals to Commander Walt Bergen's desk. The first notified him that the *Angeline* had departed the Breton coastal town of Camaret. He bit his lower lip. This didn't really help Walt too much. The second contained the latest 'Faraday' transcripts from Menwith Hill. He kept biting his lower lip. These didn't help Walt too much either.

Walt read through the transcript's seventeen pages. It was depressing reading. They reminded him of his own domestic situation. They were the transcripts of unpleasant exchanges between John, whom he assumed was one of Faraday's men, and John's wife, Sandra. Sandra was demanding that John return home. John had tried to explain that the operation was on-going, but slowly. John had tried to explain that they had not yet located Adrian Harvey but believed that they were very close to identifying Harvey's home in Christchurch.

Walt was beginning to have a lot of sympathy with John. Sandra's attitude to the demands of service life and the words she used seemed to mirror those of his ex-wife, Lucy. The transcripts reminded him of her unreasonable behaviour and treachery. Reading the transcripts had made

Walt feel even more frustrated. Walt considered that he had been betrayed by Lucy – which was probably true, and betrayed by the Navy – which was certainly untrue, conveniently suppressing the fact that he was betraying the United States of America – what the psychologists would call 'projection'. He was also frustrated that his plan was moving far too slowly, too uncertainly. Walt wasn't good with uncertainties. Walt needed to know the course that the *Angeline* would be taking once in the English Channel. Would the course be along the English south coast or direct to Christchurch? He needed to know this. He needed to know timings.

Like most rational human beings, Walt needed security and structure. The Navy provided for most of that, but it was something that he was irrationally rejecting. Subconsciously, an alternative would need to be found. Walt also needed to interact with other human beings. Of course, he did that at the embassy, but on a superficial level. He had no loving wife or daughter with him and so still felt like a real lonely stranger in this city of more than eight-million people. And like most normal human beings he needed companionship and affection. But he had lost that too. His wife had gone. His daughter distant. Now another beautiful human being began to figure in his mind and Walt was sure frustrated with her. Walt felt that Lieutenant Janet Lightfoot was warming to him, that they had gotten closer. As the days rolled by, she would no longer stand before him in front of his large desk, but had taken to standing at his left-hand side. Walt liked that. Janet Lightfoot would sometimes lean over his desk as she helped him with his papers. Walt thought this a very promising sign. He started to imagine. And Walt had a very vivid imagination. The proximity of Janet Lightfoot was becoming too much for a decent, honourable and reasonable man to bear, he concluded. He pressed the button on his intercom.

'Janet,' he said in a most congenial tone, 'I would sure like another coffee, please.'

'Of course, Commander,' she replied.

Walt smiled. 'Of course, *Commander*,' sounded real sweet and when Lightfoot brought in the coffee she looked real sweet too.

***

Detective Constable John Butcher returned to the Coastguard Training Centre with a memory stick in his pocket.

The harbour master's records went back twelve years but only the last three years had been computerised. John had the last two years. He down-loaded the contents and began a search programme. First he entered the dates when it was known from Harvey's annual leave requests, or surmised from his vehicle log book, that he had been absent from his Bristol address. He then entered details of all vessels that had entered the harbour beginning one week before these dates, then all vessels that had sailed from the harbour during that time or one week thereafter. This data was then crossed-checked with vessels owners' names and addresses. Finally, John narrowed down his search to any vessel that had entered before or during the times that Harvey was believed to be in Christchurch and the ones that had arrived well in advance of Harvey's scheduled breaks or who had sailed as soon as possible after these visits.

'I worked on the assumption, ma'am,' he reported, 'that any skipper coming to Christchurch could not guarantee when he would arrive – he may have had a problem with an engine, steering, navigation equipment or a sail; the weather could have been favourable, it could have been foul. But, once arrived, a crooked skipper wouldn't want to hang about too long and would want to be on his way as soon as possible. And so, tides and weather permitting, this skipper would be on the move quickly.'

'And?'

'I've got four likely suspects, ma'am. There's the *Gallant 11*, a Bermuda-rigged yacht, registered in Jersey and the *Bobbing Along*, a converted coastal fishing boat, registered in the Irish Republic; the *Angeline*, a cabin cruiser, registered in Malta and the *Almirante Farragut*, a Moody 64 sail boat, registered in Minorca.'

'And your best guess?'

'The largest number of hits is the *Angeline*, followed by the *Gallant 11*. If I can suggest, it might be good if Paul calls on Harvey's neighbours.'

'Good suggestion. Thank you, John.'

'Ma'am,' DC Butcher said, then hesitated a short moment before going on. 'I am really sorry to have let you all down. I think I'm losing my marriage, ma'am, and I need the police family more now than ever,' he said genuinely.

'Look, John. I know the superintendent. He would never, ever, let you down and so he's disappointed with you. And so am I. I also know that he will keep to what he said to you, that is, the matter is now forgotten unless, by your future conduct, you remind him of it. So don't remind him. Move on, John. Absorb yourself in your work and do what you are so capable of doing.'

***

Lying is not normally a sound strategy. Lying usually gets the liar into trouble. Liars have to have very good memories. Liars are very often caught out. The consequences of lying by police officers can take many forms. At the lowest level: embarrassment and appearing really dumb, the loss of credibility and mistrust. At the highest level: perjury and imprisonment.

And so, like most police officers, Sergeant Peter Jean Purchell avoided telling lies. He knocked on the door of the cottage next to Sea Fern, in the occupation of Miss Vera Winifred Kane. There was a creak as the slightly warped pale blue door was pulled open by the seventy-two year old owner, a striking lady with thick grey hair arranged in a bun, secured at the top with a Derwent 4B graphite pencil.

'Hullo, Miss Kane. I'm Jean,' he said in his very best French accent, 'and know your neighbour, Edouard.'

Miss Kane beamed and invited him in without hesitation. Which was good because he was one of the good guys. The pungent aroma of oil paints, turpentine and white spirit permeated the little vestibule and the front dining room but, particularly, the rear room with its clarity of light, which was her studio. The front and rear rooms were organised clutter. Framed and unframed canvases, mostly seascapes, finished and incomplete, were on display or stacked. 5ml, 56ml and 200ml tubes of paint were scattered about, in some semblance of order on little high table tops, together with a palette and its dipper. There were round and flat brushes, brights and riggers poking out of the top of jam jars and tall mugs, as were painting and palette knives. Miss Kane fussed as she arranged two easy chairs near the French windows, a coffee table and empty easel, and made them both a cup of tea.

'A beautiful view, Miss Kane,' he said as he looked down her garden towards Hengistbury Head. 'You must have painted the picture which hangs in Edouard's Bristol home?'

'Yes, I did,' she replied modestly. 'He asked me to paint it last year. He tells me that it has pride of place.'

'That is very true. It hangs over his fireplace in his lounge which overlooks the old Bristol city docks.'

Miss Kane smiled and nodded with pleasure. 'And you are visiting?' she enquired.

'Passing through really with Pippa, a friend of mine.'

'But he's not here at the moment, don't you know.' A statement, not in any way a question.

'He's still in Bristol, Miss Kane.'

'Well, I'm so pleased for Edouard that you are here. He seems to have so very few friends.'

'I'm surprised. This is such a glorious place. I would have thought he would have had quite a few visitors.'

'He's a very private person, don't you know,' she said affectionately, maybe thinking of the son she never had. 'He keeps himself to himself. He's a bird watcher,' adding a little defensively, 'a solitary hobby. More than 300 species live or visit here on the marsh. You see it's one of the largest salt marshes in England.'

Miss Kane appeared to Peter to have some affection for Adrian Harvey aka Edouard Melies. She had painted a beautiful painting for him. She was pleased that it hung in such a prominent position in his home and was defensive or, maybe, protective towards him. The policeman persisted gently. 'That seems so strange. I'm surprised but, maybe, you wouldn't see Edouard's friends coming and going, Miss Kane, you working here in your studio?'

'That's true, I suppose,' she conceded. 'Of course, I don't see who comes to his front door because I'm always, well nearly always, working here where the light is so good. Although I do see one of his regular visitors from here.'

'A regular visitor coming through the rear garden?' asked Peter casually as he sipped his tea.

'Well, he comes by in a lovely boat. I know when he comes because Edouard always flies his flags.'

'It must be lovely sight to see, his friend coming in by sail boat?'

'Oh, no. He has a lovely *motor* boat,' she emphasised.'

'Does he?'

'Yes. It is so beautiful that I painted it,' she said with such an engaging smile. 'Come through,' she said as she stood up, put her cup and saucer on the little table between the chairs, and beckoned him into the front room.

Sergeant Purchell followed Miss Kane into her front room where she pointed towards the painting. It was a beautifully executed painting of an Ormidale fifty-eight foot classic motor yacht, its pure white, graceful hull reflected in the calm sea. The painting showed her riding at anchor with Hengistbury Head in the distance, her hull punctuated by ten port holes, a companion ladder lowered in position at a 45° angle against her port side, with an aft deck sun-awning rigged over deck chairs and a wooden dingy. The deck was of teak, the deckhouse of mahogany. A mast with a radar dome was stepped before the deckhouse. But what attracted Peter's attention were the two flags at the mast head: the British courtesy ensign and the blue, white, red, white and blue horizontally stripped 'C' for Charlie flag. At the stern fluttered the red and white flag of Malta.

'This is another beautiful painting, Miss Kane. May I take a photograph?'

'Of course you may,' she said, standing back, pleased that someone was admiring her work.

Peter continued to admire the painting, then asked: 'This must be the scene just outside isn't it?' he said as he walked back into her studio and looked out through the French windows and over the water.

'Well,' replied Miss Kane as if to confide a secret. 'I've used a little artist's licence, don't you know. You see, the motor boat would be anchored further out towards Blackberry Point, the little island there. It's far too shallow here and so his visitor uses a little boat. I call it "the jolly boat". It has a tiny little motor and everything.'

'And the jolly boat can tie up to Edouard's jetty I suppose?'

'Exactly. She's called *Angeline* – not the jolly boat,' she said with a giggle, 'the motor boat. Such a lovely name for such a lovely boat, don't you think?'

'It really is. Do you sell your paintings, Miss Kane?

'Well, I have to,' she replied.

'And where do you sell them, may I ask? Locally?'

'Yes. At The Regent Centre or on The Quomps.'

'The Quomps?'

'Yes, The Quomps is a local grass area at Mayor's Mead near the Boat House. A nice restaurant for you to take Pippa,' she said mischievously, adding, 'I know Edouard would sometimes go there too.'

Miss Kane and Sergeant Purchell continued to talk about her career as an art teacher at Goldophin School in Salisbury, her success as a seascape artist and the sales of her paintings for between £350 and £1,200.

They talked for more than an hour before he left. Miss Kane was a delightful and gifted lady and Peter was conscious of the secret he knew but could not share. But he hadn't lied to her. That was important to him. He was glad he didn't lie.

***

Faraday had the team assembled for their latest review. There was good news. There was some disturbing news. But disturbing news would have to be turned around, turned around without leaving anger at worst, annoyance at best.

He reminded the team of the visit by DCI Yin, PS Purchell and himself the previous day and the discoveries they had made, in particular the signal flags and tide tables, before handing over to Peter Purchell who told of his visit to Sea Fern and his meeting with Miss Kane earlier. He described her home, the home of an accomplished artist who confirmed that she had painted the picture of Hengistbury Head found in Harvey's Bristol apartment. Peter detailed Miss Kane's opinion of Harvey, or of Edouard Melies as she knew him to be, saying that Edouard 'keeps himself to himself' and that he was a bird watcher, 'a solitary hobby' as she put it. Peter spoke of a visitor or visitors that Miss Kane had seen coming to Harvey's house, but via a boat and his back door. Whilst these visits had been infrequent, maybe two, three or four times a year, the sailor had been the same man on all occasions, a tall, tanned young man with long, wavy, fair hair. The sergeant described the apparent significance of the flags that would fly from Harvey's flag pole a little before these visits. Peter pressed a number of keys on the computer and almost instantly the photograph of Miss Kane's painting of the *Angeline* appeared on the screen.

'Miss Kane was so taken with the beautiful lines of the boat that would be involved in these visits, that she painted this picture of her. This is the boat, the *Angeline*.' Everyone craned forward to look at an enlarged photograph of the beautiful vessel as the sergeant continued. 'Miss Kane is clearly a gifted artist with great attention to detail. I think that we can assume that this painting is a faithful representation as is her description of its skipper, although Miss Kane says that she used artist licence and painted the vessel closer to the shore than the depth of the water would allow, even at high tide. Jane has checked this vessel out and can confirm that the *Angeline* is a fully seaworthy family boat, a go-anywhere vessel quite capable of circumnavigating the British Isles, sailing to the Canaries and around the Mediterranean.'

Sergeant Purchell moved towards the computer and pointed to the screen. 'The flag at the stern here confirms the *Angeline's* port of registration as Valletta, Malta. More significantly are the flags shown at her masthead. One is the British Red Ensign, a courtesy flag flown by foreign registered vessels as they enter British waters. This, however, is the key,' he said pointing his pen at the screen and leaving it pointed at the multi-coloured flag. 'This blue, white, red, white and blue horizontal striped flag is the signal flag C for Charlie that also means: "Affirmative". By the simple use of this flag, together with the others we have previously discussed, Harvey and the *Angeline's* skipper can signal and acknowledge.'

'Thank you, Peter,' Faraday said. 'I think we can assume that at least one of Harvey's contacts could come by sea. We know as a result of John's work that we can estimate that the executive signal "I understand that the garage is excellent" could be received any time from tomorrow onwards. From information the ACC has received from Helen Cave of MI5, it can be assumed that the Americans are monitoring our communications. Not our mobiles or my calls to the ACC. This fact will be used to our advantage.' The team looked quizzically at this comment, but Faraday continued. He wanted to set the scene, he wanted to present DC Butcher's behaviour, irresponsible as it was, as an advantage to be exploited. 'At the moment we are still poking about in the darkest of shadows in the hope that we will bump into a solution. A solution is now at hand. John.'

John Butcher stood up and faced the team, but Faraday stayed at his side. A sign of support, a sign that this was not the time for recrimination.

'Mr Faraday,' said Butcher in a strained voice, 'has been very understanding. But the bottom line is that I'm having a bit of trouble at home and, ah, contrary to the very clear instructions we had all received,' he said then looked towards Kay Yin, 'from you, ma'am, I brought with me my personal mobile.' He hesitated for a long moment as the team moved about in their chairs and exchanged glances. 'Mr Faraday and Miss Yin have made it very clear to me how stupid I have been and how I have potentially put you all in harm's way … ,' he cleared his throat before continuing. 'Mr Faraday now knows that my calls have been picked up by the Americans. In my conversations with Sandra I mentioned the boss's name a few times and I also mentioned Christchurch.'

Everyone seemed to exhale breath simultaneously. Their facial expressions showed clearly their annoyance. Faraday raised his hand. He expected their attention. He got it.

'John was irresponsible, totally irresponsible. In so doing, he has let you all down. To say that Miss Yin and I are unhappy about it is an understatement. However, this is a bump in the road and we will now turn this to our advantage. We now know for certain that the Americans are in the mix. Why? I don't know. Was Harvey intending to pass something on to the *Angeline*? I don't know. MI5 have been monitoring Harvey's activities. They know what files he had been accessing and they don't think that is likely. Was Harvey intending to collect something from the *Angeline* or someone else? I don't know. What we *do* know is that the Americans are interested in what Harvey would have been up to. And that means that he must be meeting with someone or collecting something.'

Peter Purchell asked: 'You say that the Americans are in the mix, sir. Are you saying that they are here in Christchurch?'

'If they aren't here now, I believe that they will be very soon.'

'May I ask a question, sir?' asked Jane Flood.

'Of course you can, Jane.'

'I'm not sure why the Americans would be interested in Harvey as we have apparently already told them that he had been passing intelligence to the Spanish and Argentinians?'

'I think the answer is in your use of the word "apparently". They probably don't trust us to tell them everything. And I very much doubt that we *do* tell them everything. There *could* be a lot of other things going on -no, there *will* be lots of other things going on - that could or could not be linked which has excited their interest. I don't know. What we do know is that MI5 want to have a clearer picture of Harvey's activities. MI5 know that the Americans are interested in Harvey, but the Americans don't know that Harvey is dead. And so, I intend to turn John's imprudence to our advantage. I said that we believe that the Americans will soon be here, if they are not already. I think that we should introduce ourselves to the American. It would be discourteous not to do so. And we should make our acquaintance with *Angeline's* skipper. We don't want to leave him out of it, do we?'

'Certainly not, sir,' responded Pippa, 'that would be very unfair,' she said with a huge grin, her blue eyes sparkling.

'How are we going to achieve this?' he said to the bewildered team. 'Kay, John and I have discussed this. I don't think that Mrs Butcher will be very pleased, however, but I am prepared to risk her displeasure. Mrs Butcher expects John to call her every other night. She keeps asking John, well, demanding, to know when this operation will be concluded. These conversations provide us with an opportunity to feed into the conversation information that will be to our advantage. Kay has prepared a list of words, statements if you like, that John should be able to drop into their conversation. If the Americans are interested in our conversations, we will give them something interesting to listen to.'

***

Mark Faraday and Jane Flood drove along Barrack Road to Pizza Hut in Bailey Drive and ordered the evening meal for the team. This Pizza Hut was in the best location, the restaurant's building itself obscured the carpark from the main road and, maybe, any observant unwelcomed motorists. They parked the Ford rental and Faraday and Jane entered the restaurant. They placed the order and he paid on his credit card, returning to the Ford so that he could observe the comings and goings in the carpark as Jane waited inside.

When Mark and Jane returned to the training centre, coffee was already brewing and Kay and the team had finalised their plan. There were still many unknowns. The plan had to deal with probabilities, not certainties. The plan had to be flexible and take account of these unknowns, their limited manpower and the peculiarities of Christchurch Harbour which, whilst a sheltered anchorage can, nevertheless, be very inhospitable, particularly when stormy weather combines with flood waters flowing rapidly towards the sea from the Stour and Avon rivers, only to encounter high in-coming tides creating significant turbulence in The Run. The plan assumed that the *Angeline's* visit would be in accordance with weather and tide predictions and that entry through The Run into the harbour would be undertaken during day-light hours in order that the green and red marker buoys at the approach to The Run could be clearly seen and Harvey's signal flags could be read.

Advanced warning of the *Angeline's* approach to the harbour would be gained from occupying the Coastguard look-out station on the top of Hengistbury Head. Anyone standing on a beach would be able to view the horizon at about three miles distant. From the top of Hengistbury

Head, and due to the curvature of the Earth, the horizon would be a little over twelve miles away. This vantage point provided excellent line-of-sight observations for the police in a sweep from Hurst Castle at the approach to Southampton in the east, through the Isle of Wight and The Needles, the three distinctive chalk islands at the western edge of the Isle of White, and across Poole Bay towards Old Harry Rocks in the west. This vantage point also provided for a panoramic view of The Run, the anchorages in Christchurch Harbour and all the cottages and homes backing onto Fisherman's Bank.

After supper, DC Butcher phoned his wife. Kay had prepared the dis-information statements, but she and Mark left John to make his call alone, assuming that it would be a more natural and convincing exchange if they were not present. And so it was.

Before the team went to bed, they checked the vehicles and parked them facing the exit gates. They also checked their clothing and kit for the next day. They would be ready to move at a moment's notice.

Chapter 16

Saturday, 14th May.

London and Christchurch, England.

COMMANDER WALT BERGMAN KNEW HE WOULD HAVE TO GO. He knew he was expected to respond to the NSA signal that Lieutenant Janet Lightfoot had brought to him:

WB-674536/EHT-681 MV Angeline
10:00 GMT
49˚52'N 05˚04'W
NE Lizard Point. On direct course for Falmouth.

He knew that the *Angeline's* destination was Christchurch but he could not ignore this signal that was indicating the Cornish coastal town of Falmouth. To do so would reveal his hand. He re-read the other signal from RAF Menwith Hill with Lightfoot still at his side. She waited patiently.

'I can't understand these Brits, Janet. These messages seem to conflict,' he lied. But, of course, they made complete sense to him. 'Well, like the good soldiers we are we will run with the NSA signal, they will know best,' he reassured, then asked: 'And you have your civilian clothes with you?'

'Yes, sir. And a go-bag. I'm good for five days,' she replied.

The thought of five days with Lieutenant Janet Lightfoot lingered in his mind, clouding his thoughts and delaying any coherent response. She waited patiently before speaking again.

'Shall I have the car standing by in thirty, sir?'

'Yes, do that,' he replied adding, 'it's a rental?'

'Yes, sir. One of our *special* rentals,' which meant that the rental company was a small, legitimate but stooge company owned by the CIA. 'A Skoda Superb. I think you will like it, sir.'

'Okay, but I don't want one of those stick shifts. It must be automatic.'

'It is, sir.'

'And I don't want one of those Micky Mouse engines. You know, 1.4 or 1.6. That's too damn small for me.'

'I've reserved the 3.6 V6 model for you, sir.'

He nodded appreciatively and watched her walk out of his office as her perfume lingered over his desk. God, she was so accommodating, so mindful of his needs, he thought. This was sure going to be an interesting five days, he concluded. He relaxed back into his chair with a satisfied smile. He absent-mindedly fingered the Menwith Hill signal. He re-read the signal. His satisfied smile faded.

He read the five pages of conversation transcript. John and Sandra were still arguing. John attempted to be pleasant.

Sandra preferred to be argumentative. The argument lasted all of five pages. It all seemed so petty but so reminiscent of his arguments with Lucy. Sandra complained about her car, the neighbours and the shopping; a shoe repair, the bathroom window latch and the height of the grass out back. Sandra and Lucy must be related, he thought with a fleeting smile. It was very fleeting. What was frustrating Walt was that there was only one tantalising piece of new information regarding Harvey. John had tried to reassure his wife that he would be home soon because they now knew where Harvey lived - but John hadn't mentioned where. Commander Bergman took another Propranolol.

***

As with most days, Sergeant Peter Jean Purchell was dressed in a Milford polo shirt. Not too bright. Not too dull. Just another polo shirt and pair of chinos worn by another young man and, particularly so whilst drinking coffee in The Boat House. The Boat House was not really a boat house at all but a very pleasant restaurant overlooking Town Quay, with the old mill dating from before the Domesday survey of 1086 to the left and the bandstand to the right. On the first floor was a function suite with a wooden balcony on two sides. Downstairs was an excellent bar and lounge-cum-restaurant area with a roaring fire. As with the first floor, on two sides was a substantial wooden veranda with easy furniture and tables and chairs under a candy-stripped awning. It was a relaxing, magical place to sit with uninterrupted views of the river and sail boats and cabin cruisers riding at anchor in single file, as if on a parade ground, with other boats make their lazy progress to and from somewhere to somewhere else, whilst energetic members of the Christchurch Rowing Club were sculling. Some residents shuffled by, others walked their dogs or, maybe, the dogs walked their owners. Tourists wandered unhurriedly, seemingly mimicking the progress of the dozens of swans in a town *'where time is pleasant'*.

They arrived in their black-coloured Mitsubishi Animal Double Cab and parked facing inwards towards the bandstand. The Mitsubishi was big. The other parked cars were small. The occupants of the Mitsubishi were big. Passers-by were much smaller. For a brief moment Jim Hogan and Curt Oslen were uncomfortable, but their arrogance overcame their discomfort as they stepped down from the Double Cab and looked around Town Quay before walking towards the entrance to The Boat House. Sergeant Purchell didn't look around from his stool at the bar. There was no need. He had been alert. He had seen them arrive.

The two Americans walked up to the bar and, after ordering Pacifico Mexican lagers, slouched on the bar looking around at their fellow customers. Peter Purchell checked the menu and ordered a bacon, brie and cranberry panini, chips and another latté. He spoke in English but with a very distinct French accent. He paid and walked out onto the veranda and occupied a two-seat table near the exit. Hogan and Oslen had heard 'the Frenchman' speak and thought that this could be their lucky day. Purchell simply waited. Both Americans ordered Calzone with BBQ sauce. Good choice. Bad mistake. Very soon, the Americans occupied another table further along the veranda. An attentive waitress placed a knife and fork and napkin in front of Sergeant Purchell before walking towards where the Americans' were seated and laid their table too. Excellent, thought the policeman. He would eat a little of his meal, then pretend to answer a phone call and leave. They would follow – he was sure of it.

Purchell's meal arrived first but he didn't hurry eating. Nor did the Americans. They had become complacent. Purchell had not. Twenty minutes passed. Then thirty. Purchell pulled his mobile from his pocket, looked at the screen, smiled and pretended to speak whilst continuing to eat his chips, dipping each one carefully into the tomato sauce. The Americans continued to eat leisurely. When Jim Hogan next looked up, he was in time to see Purchell leave. Both men rose quickly from their table. Jim Hogan attracted the waitress' attention and pointed to a £20 and a £10 note he had left under his plate and went straight to the Mitsubishi whilst Curt Oslen followed Peter Purchell on foot, turning right into the narrow Queen's Avenue with its three large trees in the middle of the pavement. Hogan tried to follow but Queen's Avenue is a one-way street. Not his way. He turned left, then right, only to find himself in another one-way street. Sergeant Purchell strolled into the church yard of The Priory, passed the hundreds of tomb stones and through the great wrought-iron gates, passed quant cottages with quant names: Castle View and Church Hatch and Ye Olde Eight Bells Shoppe, built in 1450.

Along the High Street, Purchell slowed his pace so as to allow Oslen to maintain contact, walked on into Saxon Square and entered The Bay Tree Health Store. Purchell needed to make a purchase and selected a bottle of Potter's Herbal Catarrh Mixture and asked Abby, the assistant, for a large bag. Then he asked for more bags which were stuffed discreetly into the first bag. Abby was bemused but delighted to assist this charming French customer. Purchell stood at the till and, as he paid Abby, he was able to see Oslen across the square, standing under the arches that supported the old Mayor's Parlour.

Sergeant Purchell walked from the store swinging his shopping bag, turned left between Intersport and Costa, down an alley alongside the Christchurch Christian Centre and into the one-way Millham Street. Throughout the follow, Oslen was constantly trying to up-date Hogan as to their location but the narrow, one-way streets where a nightmare for a pursuer. Meanwhile, Purchell had turned left into Ducking Stool Lane and then right onto the elevated pedestrian-only Ducking Stool Walk. This elevated wooden walk-way ran directly alongside the river towards Castle Street, a walk-way that curved to the right about two-thirds along its length. Purchell quickened his pace, walked beyond the curve and, unnoticed, darted right into a little lane giving access to the deliveries' entrance at the rear of the Kings Arms Hotel. But Oslen walked on straight into Castle Street. Purchell walked on straight into the hotel's restaurant. He stood back from the restaurant's windows and was able to see Oslen speaking agitatedly on his mobile. Seven minutes later, Hogan drove the black Mitsubishi into the small car park across the road from the hotel. Oslen stepped up into the Mitsubishi's cab. Purchell took the Mitsubishi's number.

Then he called Faraday: 'Patron, we have two unwelcome customers.'

Chapter 17

Monday, 16th May.

50°36'N 01°56'W and the County of Devon and Christchurch, England.

SKIPPER PAUL DELISILE HAD STUDIES the Admiralty's Nautical 5500 Routeing Guide and braved the chilly, wet night as he crossed the Traffic Separation Scheme operating between Lands End and Ushant in the English Channel. The strong winds had helped his passage. Poor visibility had not. But he was on schedule. He had passed the headland that was Start Point and was now crossing Lyme Bay. The sun had broken through the clouds. He could feel the sun's warmth. He felt good. Tired, but still good. Soon he would see the Bill of Portland, take a bearing on Durlston Head then onwards to the safety of Christchurch Harbour, his final destination.

***

Commander Walt Bergman wasn't so sure of his final destination. He and Lieutenant Lightfoot had raced towards Falmouth. They never reached the town. A signal from NSA directed them back towards the maritime city of Plymouth where Sir Francis Drake had famously continued to play a leisurely game of bowls as the Spanish Armada had approached. Walt wasn't as confident as Sir Francis and his supply of Propranolol was running low – adding to his anxiety. He was now speeding along the A38 towards

Exmouth, NSA's estimated land-fall for the *Angeline*, but Paul Delisile was already approaching the Bill of Portland.

Lieutenant Lightfoot had proved to be an excellent and calm navigator, hardly having to use their GPS. And Walt liked the powerful and comfortable Skoda. But the constant re-routing, with Janet concentrating on her navigation and Walt concentrating on driving on these damn rural roads had meant that there had been little time for small-talk and, frustratingly, he and Janet Lightfoot had only been able to snatch five hours of sleep in a small hotel in Newton Abbot – in separate single bedrooms. The latest signal from Menwith Hill had not lessened his frustration and anxiety. The signal contained the dis-information that Faraday's team had located Harvey's home and bugged it, but the property's exact address had still not been given. Walt just wished that Sandra would argue less and allow John to speak more.

Chapter 19

Wednesday 18th May.

Highcliffe and Christchurch, England.

WALT HAD BEEN RELIEVED. He had received the latest signals at 18:22 GMT the previous evening. NSA had confirmed that the *Angeline* was at anchor in Christchurch Harbour and the signal from Menwith Hill confirmed that Faraday had located Harvey's home. But Walt still had no idea of the exact location of Harvey's home, but he didn't consider that to be vital. He didn't need to know the address. Out of sight and sound of Lieutenant Lightfoot, Walt had contacted Jim Hogan and Curt Oslen, given them the time and place of the hand-over of the package from the *Angeline's* skipper to Harvey, and both Americans has assured Walt that the package would be intercepted way before Harvey ever arrived at his home.

Walt read the transcript again with relief over breakfast at the Lord Bute hotel in near-by Highcliffe.

Reading the transcript was not quite like hearing this husband and wife actually speaking the words. There was no body language to assist Walt to register the frustration and volume, petulance and spite in the words spoken. But, clearly John Butcher had tried to placate his wife, Sandra, whilst she appeared to have little tolerance towards or understanding of his duties, so much like Lucy, he thought.

‘Look, we’re nearly done here,’ John had said, apparently seeking to calm his wife.

‘You keep saying that.’ Walt imagined Sandra’s voice was now a screech.

‘We are nearly done. We are,’ replied John. Walt imagined the frustration etched into his tone. ‘What is it with you?’ he continued. ‘The bloody boat’s arrived and the skipper, some wind-surfer looking guy, is going to leave the bloody parcel in a little café with a stupid name at mid-day.’ Walt imagined more frustration.

‘I don’t know what you’re talking about. What stupid café?’ Sandra seemed to demand.

‘It’s not important.’ Walt imagined a resigned, frustrated John. ‘It’s just a bloody café, the Cheese and Alfies or something like that. It makes no difference what the place is called. Harvey’s going to pick up a parcel there and we will be waiting for him when he gets back to his house. Job done.’

Clearly ‘job done’ was not enough for Sandra. ‘So you’ll be home then - tomorrow?’

‘No, not tomorrow. I won’t be able to get away tomorrow. The next day. It will be the next day, I promise.’

But Sandra didn’t let it end there. The bitter exchange continued for some while, but Walt didn’t mind. Walt was more than relieved. Walt was ecstatic. His clever plan was about to come to fruition. He just had to be patient for a while longer and await the call from Hogan and Oslen. And Walt could be a patient man.

Faraday and his team would need to be patient too. For the moment, Faraday was relieved. All the key dis-information had been included in the heated exchange between Constable and Mrs Butcher and there was little doubt in Faraday's mind that the Americans would take the bait.

***

At eleven-fifteen, John Butcher and Pippa Blanchard walked hand-in-hand along High Street and into Church Lane and stopped to read the menu outside the James and White Bar and Kitchen which was directly opposite The Cheese and Alfies café. They nuzzled their heads together and pulled faces as if the menu was unsuitable. It wasn't. But they pretended it was. They pretended because they had seen Oslen, the man Sergeant Purchell had described to them all, and, what was likely to be another American with a tooth paste smile, in the window seats. For a moment, Hogan fixed her with a stare. Pippa smiled back seductively with a raised eyebrow. Then she pointed Butcher towards the Soho restaurant next to The Cheese and Alfies café, walked across the road to repeat the facade of reading the menu. Window seats were available but to occupy them immediately might seem too obvious, and so they walked a little way to the left and checked-out Pinocchio's menu, only to return to Soho. They occupied a window seat and ordered their lunches. John sat with his back to the window with Pippa looking over his shoulder towards the

James and White. Pippa performed an excellent role as the besotted girlfriend which John felt, well, slightly uncomfortable with. She tweeked his ear, she would laugh, she would feed him some food with her fork. It would have been very easy for Butcher to forget that he was on duty and to become besotted with Pippa. But Pippa never forgot that she was on duty. Her beautiful blue eyes never met John's eyes. Their focus was slightly to the right and on the Americans. Pippa had already sent her message: 'Patron, this is Francesca. Our two customers are seated and are waiting to be served.'

And, elsewhere, preparations had been completed. Kay Yin was in place and the Land Rover Defender had been reversed along the track between the castle and the bowling green.

Now they all waited.

At ten minutes to twelve, Peter Purchell walked from the direction of The Priory and entered The Cheese and Alfies. He had walked up the gentle rise from Castle Bridge towards The Priory. The grass had been recently mowed; gardeners attended meticulously to the roses that grew along the wires of the thirty-five yard long metal pergola that straddled the path; parents played with their children or cared for them as they fed the ducks in the mill stream. It was a peaceful scene. Not a scene for firearms.

The Cheese and Alfies had been well chosen. It was small. Small, narrow and deep. And so the inside appeared dark from the outside. It provided perfect coffee and a tasty menu. With only six tables and seventeen chairs it was a cosy and inviting place, but it was far too small to provide an opportunity inside for covert observations by either the police or the Americans one on the other. And Faraday didn't want those outside to see what was taking place inside. Yes - well chosen.

At one minute to twelve, Faraday wearing a curly blond-coloured wig walked from Wick Lane towards the entrance porch of The Cheese and Alfies. He carried Harvey's green-coloured Mach XT8 angler's rod holdall over his shoulder. He wore jeans. Not shorts. Shorts would show his white legs. He wore deck shoes. He wore a light moss-coloured traditional fisherman's rib knitwear and a blue and navy check shirt underneath. Not short-sleeves. Short sleeves would expose his white arms. He looked about before entering the café and, as he did so, the church bells of The Priory rang out. It was noon. The chimes from these remarkable bells, dating from 1663, seemed to last such a long time. But not as long as Purchell and Faraday remained in the café. At six minutes past twelve, Purchell appeared in the doorway carrying the fisherman's rod holdall, turned left and made his way along the cobbled street towards The Priory.

Sergeant Peter Purchell walked the short distance to The Priory's wrought-iron gates and into the church yard. By the time Peter had reached the gates, Hogan and Oslen had left the James and White bar and were about twenty-five yards behind the officer.

‘This is the Patron. All our customers have now left,’ said Faraday as he discarded his wig and the moss-coloured knitwear in the cafe, and was now about ten yards behind Hogan and Oslen, with Butcher and Blanchard, who would certainly be remembered by the American, behind Faraday but to his left.

Peter Purchell walked on past the tombs of the Rose family: Emily, Frances and Ellen – all so young - and the red marble tombs of Sir William Rose and Field-Marshall Rose, and followed the path as it wound its way gently downwards and to the left towards the pergola. The two gardeners were there with their wheel barrow, now meticulously securing the thick wire along the metal ribs of the thirty-five yard long pergola. Kay Yin was there too, about six yards further on to the right relaxing on the grass, her police baseball cap and expanding baton at her right-hand side concealed from view.

About half-way along the pergola’s enclosed length, Sergeant Purchell slowly came to a halt as if to make a phone call. Hogan and Oslen took the bait. They rushed towards him and Hogan snatched the fisherman’s holdall from his shoulder, then they both ran like American quarter-backs, knees high, arms pumping. Faraday had gauged what was about to happen and was able to begin his sprint seconds before the Americans. He raced forward, shouting: ‘police’. Hogan and Oslen turned and saw Faraday closing with them wearing his police baseball cap. They ran on as Faraday threw himself at Hogan whist John Butcher followed behind. Hogan began to stumble, driving his elbows, left, right, left, right, into Faraday’s shoulders and face, at the same time, throwing the green fisherman's holdall through the air like an American football towards Oslen. But it hit the metal ribs and bounced about inside the pergola. Oslen ran on darting left, then right, followed by Butcher and, with Pippa Blanchard and Peter Purchell, they fell upon Oslen.

Meanwhile, Hogan, the larger and more powerful man, had concussed Faraday and now ran directly towards Kay Yin. He thought he would brush this petite female officer aside. Mistake One. Hogan ran full pelt at the officer who simply stood her ground. Hogan expected her to step aside. Mistake Two. Hogan feinted to the right and then to the left displaying a huge, confident, teeth-laden grin. Kay dropped down onto her right knee and swept her right arm in a clock-wise graceful arc. Her expanding baton expanded, twenty-one inches of aluminium alloy with a heavily weighted tip at the end of the inner-most of the three telescopic sections. The baton shot through the air in a blurred curve parallel to the ground, the knob at the end of the baton striking Hogan's Tibial Nerve on his right calf. The pain was excruciating, immediately disabling his knee function and that of his three larger toes. Hogan lost momentum and pulled his right leg up with both hands towards his chest, turned, bewildered, thinking that he had been shot, and hopped on his left leg as Kay now swept her expanded baton in an anti-clock-wise curve striking Hogan's Common Peroneal Nerve just above his left knee. He went down like a big sack of potatoes.

Kay walked slowly towards Hogan. Hogan wasn't grinning any more. Hogan was in pain. Temporary but disabling pain. For a fleeting moment concern was etched on her face, concerned for her lover. But Peter Purchell understood. He was now with a concussed Faraday. Peter simply nodded enthusiastically and gave her the thumbs up. With Oslen already handcuffed, Kay was joined by Pippa and so she now able to return her full attention back to Hogan.

'You seem to like rolling around on the grass,' she said contemptuously. 'Roll over once more, *just* for me, with your hands behind your back.'

'I'm in pain,' squealed Hogan. And he was. Temporarily. But still in pain. Both legs.

'Man-up,' replied Kay as she cuffed his hands behind his back.

'I want medical attention,' demanded Hogan in an effort to distract her.

But Kay wasn't distracted. 'I just gave you medical attention. Man-up.'

Oslen could walk unaided but Hogan had to be helped to his feet and with some difficulty walked awkwardly along the path towards the awaiting Land Rover Defender. As he did so, he called out. 'Hey. Did you fine people see this police brutality?' But the families on the grass simply continued to applaud loudly.

***

The two prisoners were taken to Christchurch Police Station. There had been one prisoner. Now there were three. The new arrivals were informed that they would be detained incommunicado, that is that they would not be allowed any contact with anyone. Superintendent David Warwick from the local police explained the provisions of Sections 56 and 58 of the Police and Criminal Evidence Act and asked both prisoners to sign their forms accordingly. They refused. Superintendent Warwick endorsed both forms: 'declined', signed the forms himself then went off home for tea.

***

Mark Faraday and Kay Yin had sat in a vacated office and discussed their forthcoming interview strategy. It would be unlikely, they reasoned, that the two Americans had intended to keep the contents of the parcel for any length of time and would pass the parcel on to others. But, if so they wondered, pass it on to whom and why? Would any hand-over be in Christchurch or elsewhere? Would they pass it on quickly or go to ground and wait? True, the parcel had been recovered and three people arrested but, whilst other investigating officers might be content with such a good result, Faraday and Yin were certainly not. They judged that there was little time to lose and they must assume that the handover would be made sooner rather than later. To wait could easily spell disaster.

As a preliminary to the interview, Faraday had asked the escorting officers for their perceptions of both men; he had studied them when they stood before the Custody Sergeant and Superintendent Warwick; he had examined their clothing and the personal property taken from them as well as the contents of their vehicle; and he spoke with Kay and sought her views. Now he felt that he had the measure of them both. As a result of the need for urgency and his assessment of the American prisoners, Faraday made a very controversial decision and took the extremely unusual step of interviewing both prisoners together.

At 1.57pm Mark and Kay entered the interview room. The room was featureless with no natural light. Plain, uncluttered and business-like. Not home-from-home. The prisoners were dressed in blue-coloured forensic one-piece cotton suits. They both sat behind a grey-topped metal table, their hands in view. Handcuffed. Their backs were against the far wall. Two local uniformed officers stood smartly, one to their left, the other to their right. The detectives, both of whom deliberately wore immaculately-tailored blazers and trousers, took their seats, their backs to the only door.

Kay pressed the buttons on the recording machine to her left. Little lights glowed in response.

'Thank you officers,' said Faraday to the two uniformed constables, 'you may step outside, if you would, but remain in the corridor. This interview won't be taking very long.'

The prisoners looked at each other, thinking hard. This was not what they were expecting.

‘For the purpose of the tape, it is now 13:57 and I am Detective Superintendent Mark Faraday,’ adding for effect, ‘of Special Branch.’

‘And I am Detective Chief Inspector Kay Yin.’

‘You have both been cautioned but I shall do so again,’ said Faraday formally to the prisoners. ‘You do not have to say anything, but it may harm your defence if you do not mention when questioned something which you later rely on in Court. Anything you say may be given in evidence.’ Faraday looked at Hogan. ‘For the purpose of the tape, please give us your name?’

‘No comment.’

‘Excellent,’ responded Faraday. He turned towards Oslen. ‘For the purpose of the tape, please tell us *your* name?’

‘No comment.’

‘Again, excellent,’ replied Faraday, their voices now clearly identifiable for the interview.

‘You have already been informed that you have both been arrested in connection with a serious theft and for assaults on police … ‘

Hogan interrupted. ‘We are US citizens and I demand you contacted the United States Embassy right now,’ he said as if he was playing and about to win.

‘Oh. You are Americans demanding contact with the US Embassy?’ remarked Faraday. The policeman leaned back in his chair and looked at each man in turn. There was a very distinct and delayed response as if Faraday was, maybe, anxious and considering his answer. He wasn’t of course. Hogan and Olsen exchanged smiles, anticipating a favourable response. It wasn’t forthcoming.

‘Well,’ continued Faraday, ‘we won’t be contacting anyone. I think Superintendent Warwick has already explained to you, more than adequately, that you are both being detained incommunicado, principally in order to prevent you from alerting others who may be involved in the offences for which you are suspected. That means you don’t speak to anyone other than me. No lawyer, no embassy, no mum or dad.’

Again, this was not what the Americans were expecting. ‘Hey … ‘ protested Hogan, but he didn’t get past the ‘Hey’.

Faraday raised his hand silencing his protest. Faraday was determined to demonstrate to both prisoners from the very beginning that their only way out was through him, that their planning had been flawed, that the cards were now stacked against them and that they would have little choice but to co-operate.

‘So, let me make it very clear to you the position that you both find yourselves,’ said Faraday. ‘Your vehicle is registered to a drilling company. The last drilling you have experienced, I suspect, was whilst attending your dental appointment. Your ridiculously conspicuous vehicle is so clean it may as well have come straight from the showroom. Your heavy duty boots have never experienced heavy duty anywhere and have never visited a drilling site. And so,' he said, as if their protests were of no significance at all, 'do yourselves a big favour and re-enter the real world.'

Both Americans exchanged glances again in silence. They thought of their lack of preparation and care. They were unsettled at this turn of events, as Kay removed a piece of typed paper from her leather file and placed it in front of Faraday.

'Your mobile phones and satnav show some very interesting routes and locations,' she observed, her contribution taking the Americans by surprise. They both became increasingly uncomfortable wondering what the cell site analysis would tell these detectives, or, already had done so.

'You can't keep us here,' said Hogan defiantly and held Faraday's stare but it was unsteady. Faraday studied his man. Hogan was nervous. It was in his voice. It was in his eyes. But there was an underlying confidence in his remark too. Maybe he was nervous that he had somehow fouled-up which would have consequences for him. Maybe he would now not be paid, but, maybe, he also thought that help was at hand. Whatever, Faraday increased the pressure.

'Clearly I can. That's why you are sitting that side of the table in handcuffs and we are sitting this side controlling your *only* exit.' The significance of this remark was not lost on the prisoners. 'The thing is that you have both acted jointly in a criminal enterprise,' he said in an uncompromising tone. 'You have both assaulted police officers.'

'Hey, come on,' scoffed Hogan with a strained laugh, 'it was just a little rough play in the park and this little lady here used a weapon on me and I didn't touch her at all.

'You don't seem to have grasped the subtleties of the Offences Against the Persons Act, do you?' said Faraday addressing his remarks to Hogan. 'In English law you don't have to make physical contact to constitute an assault. An assault is an attempt or offer by force or violence to do bodily harm to another. You must be two-hundred and forty pounds and this officer, whom you yourself described as "little", must be about one-hundred and ten. No. The courts won't like that.' He turned to Kay. 'Nine months do you think?'

'More like twelve I should think, sir,' she replied, her face expressionless.

'Yes, twelve is about right. Then there is the assault on Detective Butcher. And the assault on me.' Faraday pointed with his right hand towards the left side of his face. 'This facial bruising will result in a charge of Actual Bodily Harm.' Mark turned to Kay. 'Two years?'

'Two years would seem about right, sir,' Kay Yin agreed without emotion. The two prisoners moved about in their seats. They looked at each officer in turn, then back again, rather like spectators at a tennis match. They didn't like Faraday's stern formality and they found Kay difficult to read - all they seemed to remember is how this petite detective had brought down Jim Hogan with such ease.

Hogan tried to fold his arms and look relaxed but the handcuffs prevented such a leisurely pose. 'Two years. I don't think so,' he said, shaking his head from side to side – a little too confidently. Yes, thought Mark and Kay, this prisoner is confident that the US 7th Cavalry will be riding to his rescue.

Faraday continued unperturbed. 'Then there is the theft of a medieval manuscript, the property of the Vatican State.'

'We just collected a parcel, that's all,' remarked Hogan with a smug grin.

Faraday ignored the remark but spoke to Kay. 'And the value of the manuscript, Chief Inspector?

'Priceless, sir,' was her crisp response.

'Ten years?' he suggested.

'It is *the* Pope, sir. Fifteen I should think would be more appropriate,' she said as she already began to remove photographs from her black leather file. She placed a photograph carefully on the table in front of the two prisoners. 'Do you know this man?' she asked.

They both glanced down, just for a second. Oslen said nothing. Hogan said: ‘No comment.’

‘Well, I know him. This is Alessio Bianchi. For the tape, I have just shown the prisoners Exhibit JB/31,’ she said, then looked at both men before she continued. ‘Alessio worked in the Archivum Secretum Vaticanum and had a nice little side-line stealing Vatican artefacts and manuscripts. We know that he stole the manuscript that was inside the parcel you were supposed to collect, a priceless manuscript written in 1497 by Giovanni Antonio de Carbonariis, the Deputy Papal Tax Collector in England.’

‘Interesting history lesson, Detective, but we were just told to collect a parcel,’ Hogan said. ‘We have never spoken to this man.’

‘You will certainly have difficulty speaking with him now,’ she said as she produced another photograph of Alessio. ‘For the purpose of the tape I am now showing the prisoners Exhibit JB/32.’

The confident grin instantly vanished from Hogan’s face. The confident grin was replaced by a shocked expression as both men looked at the graphic photograph of the corpse of Alessio Bianchi, his burnt fingers and closed eyes. He looked like a grotesque cyclops, a vision created by a single, up-close, blackened bullet hole in the centre of his forehead.

Oslen broke first. ‘Hey, we don’t know anything about this,’ he protested.

'From this side of the table we think you do,' said Kay in an uncompromising tone. 'Here's the thing. Yesterday we intercepted this vessel, the *Angeline*. I am now showing the prisoners Exhibit JB/11.' She produced the photograph of the beautiful vessel and placed it in front of the two prisoners. She waited for a short moment so as to allow the prisoners to reflect upon the apparent effectiveness of the police before speaking again.

'The *Angeline* had sailed from Rome,' she said. 'We were waiting for her, of course, and we have arrested the skipper, Paul Delisile. Paul, unlike you two, was very eager to give us his details. Paul has told us that he was supposed to hand the manuscript over to a man called Adrian Harvey. Oh yes, it slipped my mind. Adrian Harvey, he's dead too.' The pressure was now bearing down upon the prisoners as if from all sides: left and right, front and back, top and bottom. Kay Yin pulled another two photographs out of her file and placed them before the two Americans, one face up, one face down.

'I am now showing the prisoners Exhibits JB/33. This is Marco Rossi a friend of Alessio Bianchi,' she explained. 'Marco was a pleasant, harmless family man. He had nothing at all to do with thefts, he just happened to know the thief. Marco was married to Carolina. They had two children, Ludovico and Beatriz. But that innocence did not save him. I am now showing the prisoners Exhibit JB/34.'

There was a tense silence as she turned over the second photograph and spoke again. 'As you can both see, Marco was gunned down in a dusty little alleyway near his home late one evening when he was taking his little dog for its regular walk.' She moved the photograph slightly. 'Yes, there you are, the photograph even shows his dog.'

Kay turned the photographs back towards the prisoners. The photograph depicted the murder scene illuminated by police lighting, the lights shining upon the crumpled body of Marco Rossi, his body contorted against a pale plastered wall, a dark stain surrounding the head and upper body of the corpse, a bewildered little dog at its feet. Oslen averted his eyes. Hogan simply stared expressionless. Both men, in their own way, tried to mask something that can never be truly hidden. Fear. Both men didn't like how the interview was progressing: an Italian being tortured and then executed, Mafia-style; an innocent man not spared death.

'We had been waiting for Paul Delisile and the *Angeline,*' said Faraday. 'We had also been waiting for you. The only question that remains is: What were you going to do with the manuscript?'

'No comment,' blustered Hogan.

But Oslen wasn't so confident. He now assumed that the police had been one step, maybe two or three steps, ahead all along. He had been told by Walt that this was a straight-forward job of collecting a parcel. But the police had been waiting for this boat, the *Angeline*. They had been waiting for him too. Curt Oslen was real uncomfortable.

'You have no comment,' said Faraday. 'Okay, then let me make a comment to you both. You *will* appear before the justices tomorrow morning at 9:30 at a special hearing of the Magistrates' Court held in camera. That means, no one outside the courts will know of your appearance. I will then ask the magistrates for you both to be remanded in custody until your trial at The Old Bailey.'

Faraday shuffled his papers together before speaking again. 'I don't know about you two, but I've visited Alcatraz in San Francisco Bay. It's not very impressive, just a little rock with an abandoned, rather shabby prison.' Kay leaned over and collected the photographs and returned them to her black leather file as Faraday continued.

'We have a version of Alcatraz. It's just across the water from here on the Isle of Wight. There's a prison there. Her Majesty's Prison Parkhurst. Unlike Alcatraz, it's open for business and they are expecting you both.'

Faraday stood up and looked towards Kay. 'I think we are done here, Chief Inspector.'

'Hey. Hey,' protested Oslen. 'We are just delivery boys. We were supposed to grab the parcel and hand it over.'

'To whom?' asked Kay leaning on the desk and fixing Oslen with her no-nonsense eyes.

'Commander Walt Bergman,' blurted Oslen, 'out of the US Embassy in London.'

***

Faraday had sent the code '250960' to Assistant Chief Constable Perrin's phone then drove to the phone box with Kay and waited. At exactly four o'clock he phoned his ACC. Perrin was sat at the end of the Clevedon pier and answered the call immediately.

'Hullo Uncle, how's you?' asked Faraday brightly.

'Very good, my boy, and how are you?'

'We're good. The party has been a great success. But we do miss you, of course. As Aunty Joan is away you should really come down. Three guests are already with us and we have to pick up another guest right away, but would love to see you. Could you get down later this evening for a few days?'

'With such an invitation, how could I refuse? You pick up your other guest and I will see you later tonight or tomorrow morning.'

'We have the green light,' said Faraday as he replaced the handset. Kay ran her hands under his jacket and gripped him around his waist. Her presence, her closeness, was intoxicating. They kissed, oblivious to the rain outside their fleeting but precious cramped little world.

***

They both entered the interview room again. Hogan and Oslen were occupying the chairs with their backs against the far. They were still handcuffed. They were still guarded by two uniformed constables.

Kay pressed the buttons again on the recording machine. Faraday spoke first. 'It is now 16:37 and I am Detective Superintendent Mark Faraday.'

'And I am Detective Chief Inspector Kay Yin.'

'I am now asking the two uniformed constables to leave the interview room.' He looked at both officers. 'Thank you, gentlemen. Please wait in the corridor.' The officers shuffled out and the door clattered shut before Faraday continued. 'For the tape, please give us your name, please.'

'I am Jim Hogan,' said Mr Colgate toothpaste smile.

'And your name, please?' asked Faraday.

'I am Curt Oslen,' his voice full of palpable anxiety.'

'Thank you,' said Kay. 'Now, listen in both of you. There are rarely moments like this, but for you two, this will be a game-changer. You have only two choices. What I am offering you is being recorded. Co-operate and I will talk to the Crown Prosecution Service on your behalf and I will speak to the judge in chambers. I will ask for leniency and urge that some of the charges are dropped or lessened. Failure to co-operate, well, everything will be on you. This is decision time. I need an answer now. I don't mind. From you both. Or from just one of you.'

Curt Oslen seemed petrified. He looked towards Jim Hogan.

'Don't look at him, Curt,' cut-in Faraday. 'You have to look after yourself. Will you co-operate?'

'Yes. Yes, I'm co-operating.'

'And what about you, Jim. Are you in or out?' demanded Faraday.

'I'm in. Okay. I'm in.'

'We're glad you are both in,' said Kay. 'Now, how were you going to contact Walt?' she asked, specifically avoiding using his naval title that might imply that the police would be in awe of his position or be prepared to treat Commander Walt Bergman more favourably than themselves.

'We just had to kinda tell him when we had the parcel,' replied a still sullen Jim Hogan.

'Were there any times that were off-limits?' asked Kay.

'No,' replied Curt.

'So you were free to contact him any time you liked?'

'Yes.'

'Call him now.'

‘Now?’

‘Is there a problem with *now*?’ she questioned.

‘No.’

‘Okay, you will call Walt now,’ she said. ‘You will sound chirpy. You know, pleased with yourself. You will boast that the *Angeline’s* skipper had been easy to follow. That the exchange took place in the café. That the English guy had been even easier to follow. And that there had been no problems with relieving the English guy of the parcel. Are we with the script?’ she persisted.

‘We get it,’ replied Hogan.

‘If he asks where you are, you will say that you’re staying in a little bed and breakfast. If he suggest turning up at the bed and breakfast, you say that he can if he wishes but you wouldn’t advise it because the landlady is a nosy bitch. Are we still with the script?’

‘Yes, ma’am,’ Oslen said.

‘Okay, let’s see if you can arrange an RV for tomorrow.’

***

Hogan did all the talking to Commander Walt Bergman in his over-the-top brash way. Bergman suggested an RV at 11.30 the following morning at Long Slade Bottom in the New Forest, near a very cosy hotel in Burley. Clearly, Walt didn't want to get up too early and he seemed preoccupied and distracted. He was. Walt was preoccupied and distracted by the lovely Lieutenant Janet Lightfoot. He just couldn't believe his good fortune. To have Janet finally in his grasp – literally - and the manuscript so nearly in his grasp.

Chapter 20

Thursday 19th May

Christchurch, Dorset and the New Forest, Hampshire, England.

RAIN WAS GOOD. MUD WAS GOOD. For the police, that is. Rain ensured that Walt's driving vision was restricted particularly to the sides of his Skoda Superb rental. Right, left and to the rear. Walt would have to concentrate essentially to the front when driving, particularly in the New Forest where the roads were narrow and twisting with drainage ditches and bogs, unexpected New Forest ponies and roaming cattle.

Rain would also mask from the curious the officers waiting in their Land Rovers and mud had been good for the officers too. The police drivers delighted in going off-road and, as Kay suggested: 'grub-up your vehicles'. The officers were pleased to obey without question such an order. As a consequence, the Land Rovers looked as if they had spent most of their lives on working farms or with the Forestry Commission. Now the police waited, hull-down, at Wilverley Enclosure between Burley and Sway and atop Oaken Brow.

At 9.30am Detective Sergeant Pippa Blanchard was already in place at Wilverley Enclosure, some three miles from Burley and less than two miles from Long Slade Bottom, whilst Detective Chief Inspector Kay Yin and Sergeant Peter

Burchell were less than a third of a mile away at Oaken Brow. At 11am Faraday, with Detective Constable Butcher, drove the black Mitsubishi Animal into the small visitors' car park at Long Slade Bottom and parked, facing away from the road and facing towards Hinchelsea Wood. Side-lights on.

Police work often requires long periods of waiting. They waited a long period.

Walt Bergman and Janet Lightfoot were running late. Walt wasn't concentrating. Well, he was concentrating but on the wrong subject. He should have been alert. He should have been cautious. He should have been early. But he wasn't. His late evening and night-time sexual endeavours and exertions had resulted in him becoming smug and complacent. Arrogance and renewed confidence had already begun to contort his judgement. Now he had convinced himself that everything was coming together. He had another fisherman's rod holdall in the car's trunk which he had ensured was damp with salt water from further down the coast and contained some old, rolled-up maps from the Portabella Road. Perfect. The master plan conceived by the 'Master' himself was soon to come to fruition.

The police continued to wait. It was a tense wait. The volume of traffic was never going to be heavy in the New Forest but they didn't know what vehicle Walt would be using and they assumed that he would be alone. But Pippa was concentrating. And she was alert. Pippa was concentrating not only on vehicles but also on the manner in which vehicles were driven. If Walt, an American, had driven from London, Pippa assumed that the vehicle would not be small, it would not be 'grubbed-up', the driver would be uncertain of the roads and his driving would be equally uncertain. And it was. Bergman was driving right to left from Burley towards Long Slade Bottom. Pippa adjusted her binoculars. She couldn't see the driver but she was sure that the passenger was female. Now Pippa was on the move.

'Patron, this is Francesca. I'm sure our VIP customer is about to call in with a lady companion.'

Both police Land Rovers rentals were brand-new and had day-time driving lights, but these fuses had been pulled. Kay waited, the silence only broken by the throbbing, impatient engine.

Walt wrestled with the right-hand drive and the poor visibility. At the T-junction he peered to his right. The road was clear and he drove out, spinning his tyres a little and then slowed quickly as he saw the red tail-lights of the Mitsubishi at Long Slade Bottom. He jerked the steering wheel to the left and lumbered into the carpark triumphantly and slid to a halt. He swung open his driver's door and swaggered confidently towards the Mitsubishi. Faraday opened his driver's door and stepped out, his Glock pointing directly at the American as DC Butcher moved quietly towards the passenger door of the Skoda and Janet Lightfoot. Walt looked frantically around stunned, uncomprehending confusion etched on his face, the confusion being replaced by utter shock as Kay's Land Rover seemed to launch itself towards him, bouncing across the pot holes and uneven gravel of the carpark, lights blazing, followed by Pippa and her four-track.

'I am Superintendent Mark Faraday and you, Commander Walt Bergman, are under arrest,' said Faraday through gritted teeth, 'Now assume the position against your vehicle.'

***

At the police station both Bergman and Lightfoot were stripped searched. Every piece of clothing and every item of jewellery were removed before they were dressed in the pale-blue, baggy, unflattering forensic suits. All of their clothing and personal possessions and the Skoda were meticulously examined, with everything bagged, tagged and logged. The officers didn't interview their new arrivals immediately. Meticulous searching takes time as do internet searches and phone calls.

Meanwhile, Mark Faraday and Kay Yin had returned to the Coastguard Centre and briefed ACC Perrin who was intrigued, questioning and contemplative. Perrin drank a mug of tea as he speed-read the interview transcripts produced by an over-worked Jane Flood. Then he asked more questions about the sequences of events, the arrests and the manner and demeanour of the prisoners. Satisfied, he examined some of the personal possessions of the prisoners.

'Oops,' said Faraday as he used a pair of scissors to snip through some ties binding the course cloth wrapping around the medieval document. 'I probably should have asked you, sir, but you will probably have to inform the local ACC that we, potentially, have one or two prisoners in custody who may have diplomatic status. If we don't have some idea of the contents we will run out of time.'

'But the naval commander is denying that he is US Navy and his partner is saying nothing,' reassured Perrin.

'I'm not sure the local ACC will see it in such a helpful way and I suspect that the Custody Sergeant will have told her of the two new arrivals.'

'I'm sure you are right,' acknowledged Perrin with a knowing grin, 'so, as we seem to have already *accidentally* cut the ties, we may as well see what we've got.'

Mark was eager to open the older parcel first, but Perrin was more cautious. 'The newer parcel first, Mark,' suggested Perrin. 'You don't think it will contain much, do you? Then if the contents are of no real value it would be quite reasonable to move onto the second, only to be surprised when we look inside. Well, that's what I am going to say anyway.'

In the Mess Room there were now two rows of three trestle tables, laid out alongside each other like a dual-carriageway, illuminated by eight 100w light bulbs in eight old-fashioned light fittings with metal shades, hanging from long wires from the ceiling. On the row of trestle tables to the left was the older manuscript. On the right, the newer. They concentrated on the right. They removed six old maps and charts and eleven old prints depicting black and white seascapes from the angler's holdall. The contents were in various sizes and the officers laid them out like a patchwork-quilt.

'What do you think?' Faraday queried.

'I wouldn't know, Mark ... sir,' responded Kay, Robert Perrin smiling at the slip.

'Go on, Mark,' encouraged Perrin.

'They are prints,' said Faraday. 'Quite nice, the sort of thing you see in a rear corridors or backstairs of an old National Trust house, just something to fill up a plain wall. You could probably pick this sort of thing up at any bric-a-brac store in Highcliffe or Bournemouth, Bath or Bristol.'

'Well, now we can look at the other,' suggested Perrin.

ACC Perrin assisted Mark and Kay as they carefully removed the course cloth wrapping and rolled the contents out over the left-hand row of trestle tables. 'What a surprise,' said Perrin with a wilful smile. 'And I had assumed that this would be much of the same as the one we have already opened. Maybe, we shouldn't have opened it, but we have, and so we better get on with it. You do it, Kay. We want a woman's touch, although I don't suppose I should say that sort of thing nowadays. Whatever, Kay, you will be much more careful than two clumsy men.'

They crowded around the table, their bodies casting gentle shadows over the ochre-cum-grey parchment. Kay rolled what appeared to be parchment the full length of the three trestle tables. As she did so, fine particles gently rose like grey coffin dust. The parchment was one continuous document, a little less than three feet wide. Clearly, during its long life it had been folded and there was some damage running along the right-hand side and amongst the folds. The folding had resulted in some cracking and, in four or five places, the cracking had been complete as if torn. The two male officers stood back, intuitively allowing Kay to almost reverently adjust the document so as to allow it to rest upon the three tables. As she did so, little sparkles of dust seemed to dance in the shafts of light, then twirl in the disturbed air as her tiny hands carefully caressed the document and adjusted its line. Then she stood back.

'Well?' asked the ACC. They didn't answer immediately. They were thinking. 'Mark?'

'It appears to be written in Latin. I assume it's Latin, but not illuminated like a Bible of this age would have been. The way it's set out is more like a record, an account, a ledger,' suggested Faraday, 'but, the truth is, sir, I don't have a clue. We need an expert in the mix.'

'Okay. I agree. I am going to have to inform Miss Downs , the local ACC, and I will suggest to her that we inform MI5.' He paused, then added, 'I don't think we can do much more now.' He looked at both officers whose body language could sometimes be awful. 'You clearly don't think so?'
'Go on, Kay,' suggested Faraday.

‘We have talked about this on the way over, sir. Seeing this now, I think there is something else we can do.’

‘Well, that cup of tea was excellent and the journey was a little tiring for me,’ said Perrin with his mischievous grin. ‘I think I need to sit for a while.’ He moved away from the tables and occupied an easy chair. Then added more seriously. ‘I can give you another thirty minutes. Forty-five tops. Off you both go.’

***

At the police station interview room, Kay and Pippa had covered the legal formalities for the interview. Now they sat across the grey interview table from Janet Lightfoot. A table covered with exhibit bags. Small. Medium. Large. Bags containing every single item taken from the prisoner.

‘You claim that you are employed by Native Antiquities of Missouri, as does the man you were arrested with. Is that correct?’ asked Kay.

‘Yes.’

‘And what does Native Antiquities specialise in?’

‘As it says on my card.’

Kay read the card. ‘Native Indian wallpapers, prints, ceramics, arrow and spear heads, that sort of thing?’

‘That’s correct.’

‘And your colleague, Walt?’

‘It’s not Walt. He is Mr Dexter White and the European sales director.’

‘Well, that’s not the case is it? The guy you were arrested with is Commander Walt Bergman.’

‘I’ve told you his name is Dexter White. You will find that on his business card too.’

But Pippa and Peter had researched the one photograph is Walt’s wallet, a photograph showing his daughter, Debbie-Jane, just head and shoulders, but it was enough. Debbie-Jane was wearing a distinctive university graduation cap and gown. It hadn’t been difficult to identify the university and search the year books.

‘No,’ said Kay. ‘Walt isn’t Dexter, he’s Walt. Wife: Lucy and daughter: Debbie-Jane. Are you still saying that you are Eleanor Perot and that you are Dexter’s colleague?’

She thought for a quiet moment, then kept to her ‘cover’. ‘It’s Elli and I am Mr White’s colleague.’

‘But how can that be?’ Kay questioned.

‘I don’t follow.’

‘Well, Dexter White is Walt Bergman. We know that. Your hire car is registered in the name of Dexter White and he booked into your little hotel in Newton Abbot as Dexter White.'

'There you are. Dexter White is Dexter White,' she replied with a practiced smile, the practiced smile of a lawyer. But she was nervous. Her voice was thick with anxiety. She knew what was coming.

'But he booked into the Lord Bute hotel and the Burley hotel as Frank Seitz and you booked in as Miss Donna Valdinoci. Why should that be?' probed Kay.

'I have no comment.'

'You were sleeping together.'

'We had separate rooms.'

'Yes, but you didn't sleep in separate beds. Not according to the maids. I doubt whether your superiors will look kindly upon that indiscretion.'

The officers waited a few heart beats as the prisoner swallowed and averted her eyes. The ramifications of her conduct and Walt's conduct had already been filling her mind. Now it was pretty full.

'You are not Elenor Perot nor are you Donna Valdinoci,' Kay said.

Lightfoot didn't answer.

'You see,' persisted Kay, 'your satnav, your GPS that is, tells us where you have been and most of the answers about *you* are here on this table.'

Kay picked up the exhibit bags containing Lightfoot's blouse, her bra and her underwear. Kay appeared to examine each item dismissively in turn. Having her intimate clothes touched made Lightfoot feel vulnerable – as was intended. Kay picked up Lightfoot's wrist watch and her belt; her purse and its content.

'All of your possessions are of average quality. Nothing too expensive. Nothing too cheap. Your wristwatch is a Casino. It can be purchased in any store as can all of your clothing. But you made a mistake, didn't you?'

'Did I?' she responded defiantly but with a little less confidence.

'Let me tell you what has happened here,' continued Kay. 'You probably hold lieutenant rank. The last few days have been a ride-along with the commander. An exercise. A field-training exercise, maybe. An exercise for you. But not the same exercise for Walt. I think that he was on a very different exercise regime.'

'You were given a "cover" for the short-term. Not a "legend" for the long-term,' said Pippa.

Lightfoot was, for a moment, taken off-guard with the change of interviewer.

'Your short-term "cover" would have been more than adequate if you had been involved in a simple road traffic accident or even arrested for possession of your firearm,' suggested Pippa. 'The local police would have made some calls, to the number on your business card, to the car rental company. The recipients of your calls would have immediately notified your embassy, the embassy would have liaised with the Home Office and the Home Office would have contacted the local Chief Constable. The field-training exercise would have served to explain everything away. The local police would have been pissed-off, of course, but the tolerant and accommodating Home Office and the Foreign and Commonwealth Office would have had conversations, hands would have been shaken, backs would have been patted and you would have been on your way. The "special relationship" maintained. But ... the short-term has grown into a long-term. Why?'

'You tell me?' Still defiant, trawling for the information the police held.

'Because,' said Kay, 'Commander Walt Bergman is a traitor to his country. The question is: are you a traitor too?'

Lightfoot leaned back into her seat. She had been trained, but was not practiced. A little training to cope with hostile questioning was one thing. A little training in tradecraft was another. But coping with the prospect of being a traitor was something way out there. The significance of the words seemed to paralyses her thoughts, confirming those little nagging doubts she had harboured about her commander. She recovered sufficiently to say: 'I've told you that we are US citizens.' Trawling again. Saying little, listening more.

Of course, the detectives weren't sure that Bergman was a traitor but they were sure that he was engaged in some sort of dishonest, if not criminal, enterprise. They were determined to find out what it was. They persisted.

'These aren't your daily clothes are they?' asked Kay.

'They are,' she replied, still defiant.

'No, these were issued for field operations?'

'No, I've had the clothes for months.'

Kay picked up Lightfoot's loafers and examined them carefully. 'No scuff marks on the uppers, virtually no wear on the soles or the heels.' She replaced the shoes neatly on the table, side by side, and pushed them, toes first, towards Lightfoot. 'You have hardly worn these shoes.'

'I bought them a few weeks back,' she replied uncomfortably, her lies unsettled by the truth.

'No. No,' said Kay shaking her head as if in disbelief. 'We have spoken with Marks and Spencer.' She paused for a long moment. 'You see, this particular range of shoes, the style and colour, were removed from the shelves thirteen months ago.'

Lightfoot remained silent. They were getting closer and Lightfoot didn't like how this was going but wanted to hang in there and gauge where it would go.

'I guess you were told to go out and buy some suitable clothing when you were posted here that couldn't be traced back to the embassy,' suggested Kay.

'You are right,' volunteered Lightfoot. 'I did buy these months ago. You've gotten me confused. I buy a lot of shoes.'

'Is Walt confused?' asked Pippa.

For the first time Lightfoot didn't object to Walt being referred to as Walt. Maybe the first indication that Lightfoot was breaking.

'I don't understand what you mean?' Trawling again. Hopeful.

'Why do you think Walt had a fisherman's rod holdall in the boot, the trunk that is, of your rental?' Pippa asked.

'He had a case, that's all.'

'It wasn't just any case,' explained Pippa. 'You see, Walt had a fisherman's holdall, a JRC Contact 3, which was filled with rubbish and *you* both had travelled to Long Slade Bottom to RV with Jim Hogan and Curt Oslen and collect a medieval document in a Mach XT8 fisherman's holdall,' adding so as to impress upon Lightfoot the police knowledge of events, 'which came down from the city of Bristol. Why should that be?'

Lightfoot realised that she had been wrapped into some plan by Bergman. Maybe treason. Her mouth became dry as she thought of the provisions of the Patriot Act. She knew she was in trouble. Real deep trouble. Hope fading.

Kay spoke. 'It is now 13:21. I am terminating this interview in order that I can take the prisoner to HM Coastguard station where she will be shown Exhibit PP/4, JB/2, MF/2 and MF/3.'

***

They travelled in the Land Rover Defender. In the back compartment with the rear door and double-facing seats sat a Dorset detective with a Heckler and Kotch resting in his lap, but alert and watchful, right index finger across the trigger guard. In the rear seats were Pippa handcuffed to Lightfoot. The Land Rover was driven by Kay. As they approached the Coastguard gates, these were opened by another Dorset detective, his automatic concealed from view.

'Good afternoon, ma'am,' said the detective. 'And you, sergeant,' he said acknowledging Pippa Blanchard. He waved them through and Kay drove out of sight and hurried Lightfoot into the Mess Room. Perrin was there, in a shadow, in an easy chair, sipping more tea. Just listening.

Lightfoot was walked to the head of the parallel tables.

‘Let me clarify for you, so that you are in no doubt,’ said Detective Chief Inspector Yin, ‘The police, that’s us, aren’t running out of time because the prisoner, that’s you, will be appearing before the court tomorrow. Why? Because you have given different names. Because we don’t know who you are. You were carrying a firearm which is illegal here. You are involved in a theft and possibly two murders. And treason. And so, *you* are running out of time. As we speak, a police motor cyclist from Scotland Yard is about thirty minutes away with his paniers filled with the details of all staff accredited to the US embassy. I am sure that your mug shot, and Walt’s, will be there amongst the photo gallery. When the motor cyclist arrives, the deal is off the table.’

‘What deal?’ asked Janet Lightfoot, composed but not relaxed. Maybe it was the shock of her arrest or the rapidity of the events unfolding, the enormity of the difficulties in which she had been plunged or her betrayal by Bergman. Whatever, her defiance was ebbing away. A deal? Hope, maybe, returning.

‘What do you see on the tables to the right?’ asked Kay.

‘There’s old pictures and charts.’

‘And here?’ asked Kay pointing to the left-hand set of tables.

‘Some sort of manuscript.’

'Let me tell you some of what we know,' continued Kay standing with her arms folded facing Lightfoot. 'We know that a man named Alessio Bianchi stole this priceless manuscript from the Vatican. He was tortured and then shot in the head. His friend, Marco Rossi was also murdered. He had nothing to do with the theft. But, it made no difference. They just killed him anyway. The manuscript, this manuscript here,' she said casting her arms across the left-hand row of tables, 'was then given to a man by the name of Paul Delisile. He was the skipper of a boat, the *Angeline*. His boat has been seized by us and now rides at anchor in Christchurch harbour. Skipper Delisile was arrested and is occupying a cell a little way along the corridor from *your* cell. Delisile was to have handed this manuscript to two Americans. We have arrested them and they are making themselves at home along the cell corridor from you and Walt. Walt was supposed to collect this valuable manuscript from the two Americans but met up with us instead. In Walt's boot, the trunk that is, were these old prints in the JRC fisherman's holdall. Why you might ask?'

Kay looked down towards the manuscript, paused, then looked up with her dark, penetrating feline eyes. 'There can only be one explanation. Walt was going to hand over the old prints and keep the valuable manuscript for himself. And that's where the treason bit comes in, doesn't it?'

'Does it?'

'I think so. And you know so,' said Kay confidently.

'You can't be sure, can you?' Defiance had returned. 'All of this is conjecture.'

'What I *can* be sure about,' replied Kay, 'is that all of this must have been sanctioned at some senior level by your embassy. Your people wanted the manuscript. Now your people don't have it. We have it. And, we have you, oh, and Walt.'

Kay moved and sat on a chair alongside the manuscript. Lightfoot remained standing. 'Your mission failure and your conduct with Walt, will embarrass your service, the United States of America and your President.'

Lightfoot said nothing as the harsh words hit home to this otherwise loyal American. Her shoulders sank a little, the advantage passing back to Kay Yin.

'You have,' said Pippa at Lightfoot's side, 'about ten minutes to decide whether you want to be eventually charged with treason … .'

Lightfoot interrupted. 'They won't charge me with treason.' Her remark was part hope, part bitterness. Lightfoot was realising that her promising career had been harmed. Harmed by Commander Bergman.

'Won't they?' countered Kay. 'I'm sure that you are much more familiar with The Patriot Act than I am. If I am correct, the Act is designed to quotes: "deter and punish terrorist acts in the United States and around the world" and, oh, these are the words you need to remember: "and any other purpose". I understand that The Patriot Act is a very flexible piece of legislation that your government has controversially applied to all sorts of people who have displeased them.'

Kay paused so as to allow Lightfoot to reflect upon the significance of The Patriot Act before she spoke again.

'You only have about five minutes so let me re-wind. *You* need to decide whether *you* want to risk being charged, along with Walt, with treason during which your sordid little romp in the Burley hotel is revealed to all, or, that *you* have demonstrated that this, as far as you were concerned, was a drive-along exercise and you have been shocked by these revelations.'

Lightfoot quickly thought through her options. Limited options. Her response was more conciliatory. 'But I can't prove that I knew nothing about this.'

'You can,' suggested Kay. 'You can by telling me where Walt was heading next.'

***

Janet Lightfoot told the officers that she was Lieutenant Janet Lightfoot. Janet Lightfoot told the officers that Walt's intention was to head on back to London but take a detour through Milton Keynes. Walt had already given her the road's postal code although the specific premises were not known to her. Jane and Peter identified eighty-six companies that had offices or units at this postal code.

‘Find one that will interest me,’ Faraday had asked his officers.

Meanwhile, ACC Downs had been informed of the revelations made by Lieutenant Lightfoot. She in turn had contacted the Home Office. The Home Office officials were alarmed. There then followed a pantomime that was reminiscent of a bureaucratic combination of ‘pass-the-parcel’ and ‘musical chairs’. The officials played for time and requested the immediate attendance of both Assistant Chief Constables at the Home Office, London. This response gave the impression to the uninitiated that the Home Office had timely determination and steely resolve. Perrin had suggested that experts should be called to examine the manuscript. The Home Office promptly agreed, pleased that they would be shown as decisive and able to take credit for calling in Dr Heather Carringdon of the University of York’s Centre for Medieval Studies and Dr John Ellis of the University of Leeds’ Institute for Medieval Studies.

Chapter 21

Friday, 20th May.

Christchurch, England.

THE TWO ASSISTANT CHIEF CONSTABLES had spent much of the previous evening waiting for an interview with the Home Secretary. No interview was forthcoming. Clearly, the Home Secretary intended to distance himself from this matter, at least for the present, and allowed a junior minister a decision-making role whilst the Home Secretary dined with the Foreign and Commonwealth Secretary at the latter's club.

The United States Embassy had been informed. They were informed that two of their staff, Commander Walt Bergman and Lieutenant Janet Lightfoot, had been involved in some sort of, as yet unclear, dispute with local police. Bergman and Lightfoot had been found in possession of automatic weapons and had been arrested. Neither the Americans nor the local police had been badly injured and the media were unaware. The embassy was relieved, although concerned and guardedly apologetic. The embassy thanked the junior minister for his skilful handling of this unfortunate incident but requested an up-date by noon on Friday. The Home Office junior minister agreed. The Home Office junior minister did not, however, reveal anything regarding the medieval manuscript nor that two eminent experts were on their way to Christchurch. Nor did he mention that Agent Helen Cave of MI5 was also heading for Christchurch.

***

Faraday's team were now completely snowed-under with preparing the report for the Chief Constables and papers for the Magistrates' Court. Dorset Police had provided Faraday with two typists from their Special Branch office to assist. Enquiries continued at hotels in Newton Abbot, Highcliffe and Burley. The Skoda Superb and the *Angeline* were examined thoroughly and enquiries continued at Milton Keynes.

Agent Helen Cave from MI5 arrived in Christchurch at five past ten in time for morning coffee. She had had a relaxed trip. Not so two experts. Dr Corrington from York and Dr Ellis from Leeds were later, arriving at a little after 11.15am. Both doctors had had a unique experience. One had travelled from York in an unmarked police Range Rover at speeds she had never experienced in her life. Not an entirely relaxing journey but one she found exciting. The other had travelled from Leeds in an unmarked police BMW at speeds that he could have, hitherto, only imagined. After the initial shock, he had enjoyed the ride.

Both doctors, after hasty visits to the toilets and then having coffee, were allowed to quietly examine the manuscript. The examination took just over two hours. There was close examination with magnifying glasses. There was much kneeling on the floor alongside the trestle tables. They used forensic-type brushes on the manuscript's surface. They huddled and mumbled together. They shook heads or nodded in unison. They scribbled notes.

Dr John Ellis was deputed to speak to the police officers. He was quietly spoken with a soft, Welsh accent. He spoke without pomposity as if talking to fellow academics.

'You referred originally to the manuscript being of parchment,' said Dr Ellis. 'It's not vital, but we believe it to be vellum, calf skin that is. The facilities here are limited and further tests would need to be carried out. The important conclusion is that Dr Carrington and I believe that the manuscript is from about 1497. Probably 1497 and 1498. We say that because the script does contain dates, but there are also alterations or later additions. This is no surprise, indeed, it often happened. It is difficult to be any more precise at the moment because the script is, in fact, heavily abbreviated Medieval Latin. Again, this would not have been unusual given what we think the manuscript actually is.'

'And that would be what, Dr Ellis?' asked Perrin full of curiosity.

'This appears to be part of an account of a voyage to North America and the subsequent establishment of a small colony there. Much of the content concerns an audit of the voyage, the crew's obedient reliance upon God, the hardships they faced, their human weakness but their resolution inspired by the Almighty. Additionally there is an emphasis upon their achievements in their contact with, and conversion of, the indigenous population.'

'Do you know by whom it was written?' asked Faraday of both experts.

'Oh, yes,' volunteered Heather Corrington, 'this was undoubtedly written by Father Giovanni Antonio de Carbonariis.'

'And who was he exactly, Doctor?' Perrin asked, although the police already knew something of this cleric.

Dr Corrington smiled, pleased to speak of a man whom she had studied for many years.

'He was a banker from Milan, but also an Augustinian friar who was England's Deputy Papal Tax Collector. More importantly, we know that he accompanied John Cabot on his explorations. His task was two-fold. Firstly, he was the Pope's eyes and ears, particularly when it came to wealth – either spending it or finding it,' she said with an attractive but cynical smile. 'Secondly, it was his role, his duty no less, to spread God's word and convert all those whom they encountered. It appears that he was very eager to assure the Pope of his diligence and success in this regard.'

'If you don't mind me asking. Are you sure that this manuscript is genuine?' asked Perrin.

'Ninety per cent sure,' replied Dr Ellis. 'You would probably wish to have a papyrologist or a palaeographist brought in, but I am almost certain.' John Ellis moved around the table as he explained. 'You see the scudding wasn't perfect here.'

'The "scudding"?' queried Perrin.

'Yes, scudding was the process used to remove hairs from the skin. And here is very clear evidence of pricking. Prickings are these little needle holes here and here on each side of the velum,' he said, leaning down, pointing to little pin-prick holes that no one else could really discern. 'These little holes were made in preparation for ruling lines. The scribe would then use these lines as he wrote. I could carrying on, but let me say that we are both pretty certain that this is genuine.'

'Would it be too much to ask you to make a quick verbal translation now?' asked Helen Cave exhibiting her most encouraging smile.

'I think we could. It will probably be punctuated by lots of pauses. But we could give it a try.'

And they did.

After just over forty minutes the two doctors had finished. The assembled group asked a few questions that the doctors answered with casual clarity. Helen Cave thanked them for their expertise, explaining that they would both be taken to The Christchurch Harbour Hotel for the night, collected the following day and taken to Bournemouth rail station for their journeys home. Both doctors were charming and pleased with the arrangements that had been made and expenses paid them, although, neither were as pleased when Helen Cave requested Dr Ellis' scribbled notes and reminded them both of the provisions of The Official Secrets Act.

Helen Cave turned to Mark Faraday with her most engaging of smiles and handed the note pad to him. 'Burn bag I should think, Mark.'

***

The dock contained five prisoners. The court itself a further thirteen participants. Perrin, Faraday and Yin were present, together with ACC Downs and Superintendent Warwick, both in full uniform, to provide a prominent local flavour, with a uniformed constable escorting each prisoner, the clerk and two prosecuting solicitors. The Severnside officers stood back from the Dorset officers, knowing that the local magistrates may resent any perception that 'outsiders' were seeking to influence the local force and the impartiality of their court.

Mr John Picton of the Crown Prosecution Service informed the three magistrates that the case was complex. The case involved the Vatican and the Vatican's police, the Corpo della Gendarmeria; the Severnside Police; the Dorset Police; the Metropolitan Police Service; The Security Service; the Director of Public Prosecutions and the United States Embassy. The charges against the defendants were holding charges.

The three magistrates were a mixed bag. The chair had been conveniently selected – a retired major-general. The female member was a director of a yacht brokerage and the male, a greengrocer from Fordingbridge.

After only eleven minutes, all the prisoners were remanded in police custody until Monday morning at nine-thirty.

Whilst the police officers had been attending the magistrates' court, Helen Cave had been attending the elite of MI5 and MI6.

When the police returned to the Coastguard Centre, the atmosphere was amicable enough, but MI5 and MI6 were guarded. An Assistant Director of MI5, David Weaver, held a long conversation with Perrin, Faraday and Yin, expressing surprise that the United States would not be playing the diplomatic immunity card and seeking the release of their nationals, at least Bergman and Lightfoot, if not the other two.

Faraday queried the process to be followed. Weaver was laid back. 'You haven't been involved with the arrest of Americans before?'

'No, sir.'

'It's straight forward really, Superintendent,' replied Weaver in a charming, nonchalance manner. 'Just deal with the unusual in the usual way.'

‘Okay, but there is one other thing, Mr Weaver?’ asked Faraday.

‘Of course. How can I help?’ he asked as if any request would be a delight to fulfil.

‘The manuscript isn’t here. Is it with the other exhibits?’

‘Oh, good God no. Far too valuable,’ he replied reasonably. ‘On route to the FCO.’

‘But the manuscript will be needed so as to present the court with “best” evidence.’

‘Yes, of course. Ordinarily it would. But presenting it unnecessarily to the court is one thing. To present it necessarily to the Pope is quite another.’

‘I’m not sure I understand, Mr Weaver?’ asked Faraday.

‘We should have said,’ replied Weaver as if the matter had accidentally slipped his mind. It hadn’t of course. The explanation was held in reserve, just in case. ‘The manuscript is going to be presented to His Holiness when Prince Charles visits the Vatican next month. But don’t concern yourself, Superintendent, we have had comprehensive photographs taken. Helen had them. I think Helen gave an album to Detective Chief Inspector Yin. They would be quite acceptable to the courts as “secondary” evidence. Have a chat to Helen. Anyway, must go.’ Weaver turned towards Perrin and extended his hand. ‘It’s been such a pleasure to have met with you Mr Perrin, and with your excellent team here. A splendid job all round.'

No further discussion was encouraged. The visitors made their way out to their vehicles, although Helen Cave asked to be driven to her hotel, The Captain's Club - no expense spared.

Kay Yin declined to be party to the farewells. Kay was troubled. Kay examined the photographs again. Kay was still troubled.

Faraday walked across to Kay. 'What's the matter, darling?' he enquired.

'Tell me if I am wrong?' she asked. 'When the manuscript was laid out on these tables, did it not virtually cover the whole length?'

'Yes,' replied Faraday. 'All but about two or three feet at this end.'

Perrin noticed the body language and approached the two detectives. 'Everything okay?' he enquired.

'I don't think so, sir,' replied Kay as she positioned herself between the two men whose size seemed to engulf her. She turned over each photograph in the exhibit album, close-ups of various sections. Then she returned to the photograph that showed the manuscript laid out the full length of the tables.

'Some of its missing,' exclaimed Perrin.

'Yes there is,' replied Kay, 'about three feet I should think.'

'We need to check the burn-bag,' said Faraday to no one in particular, as he crossed the room. Faraday didn't have to poke about in the black bag too much. It was there. Awaiting incineration. Faraday retrieved the pad.

'I have a bad taste in my mouth,' said Perrin. 'Let's have some coffee.'

Over coffee, the three police officers presented various hypothesises and scenarios. Their conclusion was unanimous.

'Helen Cave didn't realise the significance of the document or she wouldn't have been so cavalier with the doctor's note pad,' said Perrin as he got up from his chair. He walked around in a small circle, thinking. 'Normally, the United States would want to get their nationals back State-side to demonstrate that they had reach and, in any event, would want to interrogate them.' He was silent for a little while longer as he pondered again. 'And they would go to the ends of the earth to avoid bad PR. Yet, they make no great efforts to hinder or delay our legal process.' Perrin flopped into his chair again.

'The Americans want to know what the manuscript contains,' suggested Faraday.

Perrin didn't answer, but Kay spoke. 'The way they can do that is throw their people to the dogs, allow the court case to progress … .'

'And ask for the manuscript to be produced as evidence,' said Perrin. 'Then they will have an opportunity to read it.'

'And that is the reason for the photographs,' suggested Kay.

'Yes,' speculated Mark, 'the FCO, MI5 and M16 have had the photographs taken because they don't want the manuscript to be produced at court. They will have the CPS in the mix and will argue that the document is far too fragile and valuable to bring backwards and forwards to a court when the content is not key to the case, although the manuscript as an item of theft is.'

'And any judge will rule in favour of the prosecution,' said Perrin, 'and the defence will have to accept "secondary" evidence, that is, the photographs.'

'Photographs that don't show the complete manuscript,' said Kay.

'As always,' said Perrin, 'the question is why?'

'The note pad should tell us,' replied Faraday. And it did.

They slowly read Dr Ellis' notes. They remarked that he must be a doctor because they could hardly read his writing! But the gist of his notes was clear.

Back in the fifteenth century, a king's ultimate power flowed from the Holy See. Father Giovanni Antonio de Carbonariis' presence on the expedition served to remind John Cabot and his crew of the Holy Father's supreme authority, but Father Giovanni was also required to provide a detailed account of the voyage and the establishment and success of their mission stations. All of this was recorded in graphic detail, particularly how their faith had sustained them as they crossed The Sea of Darkness and their success in pursuit of the 'Conquest of Souls' – that was their sacred duty to spread the word of God - whilst, at the same time, seeking and securing wealth. These activities brought them into contact with the indigenous Cree, Montagnais, Naskapi, Inuits and Huron. Verbal communication with the local people was difficult, written language limited or non-existent, although oral history was the cement that secured their history and heritage.

What appeared to be clear from the doctor's notes was that solemn agreements had been entered into with King Henry VII guaranteeing the land rights of the indigenous people, in perpetuity, in exchange for mining, trapping and fishing concessions, together with permission to build mission stations.

But what attracted the police officers' attention was a side note scribbled by Dr Ellis:

'What does this mean for present-day oil and gas exploration?'

Perrin spoke to Faraday. 'Don't lose the note pad, Mark, but for now I think you two had better go and see Commander Walt Bergman.'

***

It was twenty past six when Mark Faraday and Kay Yin entered the interview room. Bergman had eaten. He had asked for a McDonald's Big Tasty, fries and a coffee. He got a McDonald's Big Tasty, fries and a coffee.

Bergman was reflective. Two days ago his master plan was working – or so he believed. Since then he had been arrested, strip searched, interviewed, appeared before a closed court and been remanded in custody. His head was in his hands. He was thinking of HM Prison Parkhurst followed by an inevitable court martial and his equally inevitable incarceration in the Naval Brig at Norfolk, Virginia; his loss of his naval pension; a gloating Lucy and tearful Debbie-Anne. Walt didn't think it was looking good for Walt.

The two detectives commenced with the legal preamble. Then they began their questioning.

'Walt,' said Faraday. 'I want you to listen to me very carefully.' Walt's head remained firmly clasped between his hands, elbows on the grey table.

'Walt. Look at me.' Walt looked up. Walt looked terrible.

‘I don’t have any idea what you are going through,’ Faraday said patiently. ‘I could guess, but I suspect it wouldn’t come close.’ Walt nodded his head as if he was about to burst into tears.

‘Let me make it clear to you. We are not here to destroy you. We would prefer to be pursuing the bad guys. I don’t think you are a bad guy.’ Walt looked up sorrowfully at that.

‘A bit of a mug, maybe. But not bad.’ Walt nodded slowly in agreement.

‘I can help you a little. Not a lot. But a little. We can emphasise to the court that you didn’t assault this young officer here like the others.’ Walt’s blood-shot eyes drifted sorrowfully over towards Kay Yin and he nodded a little more.

‘You didn’t assault me like Jim Hogan did.’ There was more nodding from Walt, a little like one of those toy dogs you see in the back window of a car.

‘You didn’t draw your weapon or resist arrest.’ More nodding and a trace of a thankful grin began to show on Walt’s face.

‘I think you are now remorseful.’ Walt’s nodding became more energetic, mainly because he had not shown the slightest remorse since his arrest. In fact, Walt had shown no guilt regarding his treachery, only acute anxiety as to his fate.

‘There is no evidential value in us revealing to the court that you abused your rank and slept with Lieutenant Lightfoot,’ reassured Faraday.

Walt’s nodding was interrupted by a look of relief. He mumbled a ‘thank you’.

‘I’m sure you wouldn’t want Janet’s career to be ruined.’ Walt shook his head limply from side to side.

‘You are too much of a gentleman for that.’ Walt reverted to sorrowful nodding.

‘I only want to ask you one question.’ Faraday paused to attract Walt’s attention. Walt paid attention. ‘How did you get into this?’ he asked.

Walt Bergman slouched back in his chair. A sad man. A man with his treacherous and unrealistic dreams shattered. Walt began to snigger. A silly expression held his face as he shook his head from side to side as if in disbelief.

‘It was the number 35 bus,’ he said. He was still sniggering.

‘The number 35 bus?’ asked Faraday.

‘Yep,’ he said with a resigned sigh. ‘That was it.’ He thought a little longer as if detached from reality. ‘The number 35 bus,’ he said as if recalling a dream. ‘I saw this bus come by and it reminded me of a research task I had undertaken at the Pentagon. I was told to research Section 35 of the Constitution Act. It was just a piece of God-damn research regarding Canada's indigenous peoples. I researched and then forgot about it until I came over and a note was brought to my desk from one of our guys in Rome.' His voice began to trail off. 'Just time and chance,' he said, almost in a whisper. Walt resumed his dejected pose, elbows on the desk, head in hands.

'Okay, Walt. Thank you for that,' Faraday said. 'This conversation has been taped but it is of no evidential value to the hearing on Monday. You must know that you are in enough trouble with your own people, but, I will see what I can do about the charges. Is there anything you want?'

'No, just to go home … but I don't know where home is now,' he said mournfully.

Commander Walt Bergman USN looked up as tears of self-pity cascaded down his cheeks as he thought of his career as a lawyer, as a naval officer; his life as a husband, as a father; and the loss of home, his pension, his reputation.

'Okay. Let me walk you back to your cell, Walt.'

And they walked him down the corridor. But before Faraday left the station he spoke with the Custody Sergeant.

'Sergeant, put Commander Bergman on suicide watch – now, if you please.'

Chapter 22

Saturday, 21st May.

Christchurch, Dorset and Edlington, Lincolnshire, England.

THAT MORNING, ASSISTANT CHIEF CONSTABLE PERRIN thanked Faraday's team. He had been well briefed. He spoke of the plucky behaviour of the arresting officers; the long hours worked by all; the tolerance of their rudimentary living quarters; the excellence of the diligent and perceptive research undertaken by Sergeants Blanchard and Purchell and Constable Butcher and the research, administration and mammoth typing burden borne by Jane Flood.

But the work in preparing the papers for court went on. And DC Butcher went home.

That evening, Paul Delisile was charged with Handling Stolen Property. Jim Hogan and Curt Oslen were charged with Assualt on Police and Conspiracy in respect of the theft of a manuscript, the property of the Vatican State. Commander Walt Bergman and Lieutenant Janet Lightfoot were charged with Unlawful Possession of Part One Firearms and Conspiracy.

***

It was a big house. William J L Kemper called it his English 'home'. It wasn't a home. It was a big house. A status thing. Modern with a Victorian walled garden. There were six bedrooms, all en-suite; a study-cum-library; a snooker room and bar; a mini-cinema and another bar; a lounge with beamed ceiling and stone fireplace giving a panoramic view over the lawns to the south; a dining room with French windows giving a panoramic view over the lawns to the west; a sitting room leading into a huge conservatory giving a pleasant view over the rose garden. William liked the rose garden – just like the White House he thought. William liked to show guests his rose garden. There was also an indoor swimming pool and gym; garaging for seven cars and a paddock.

He liked the house and felt comfortable there. But he didn't like his staffer's latest message which made him feel less comfortable. That bumbling faggot Bergman, he determined, had failed to deliver. Now the Nigerians had attributed this failure to William J L Kemper. They wanted reassurance. They needed to know that William J L Kemper was still in control of events. They wanted William J L Kemper to demonstrate that control.

Chapter 23

Thursday, 9th June.

Little Chalfont, Buckinghamshire, England.

IT WAS A PLEASANT DRIVE. A little more that eighty miles in glorious sunshine. The Jaguar staff car turned off the main road, through opened wrought-iron gates, down and along a sweeping two-mile long drive past grazing deer and English oaks. As is so often the case with such magnificent estates, trees concealed the Grade II* listed Georgian house, but, as a visitor approached this house along the tree-lined drive, staged gaps appeared in the trees to reveal tantalising glimpses of the beautiful house. At first, the glimpse were merely for just seconds, then the gaps in the trees became incrementally longer until, finally, the visitor would arrive and gasp as the driveway broke out into an open space of finely manicured lawns and urns, neat trees and wild flowers.

It was a big house and also a home but, nevertheless, clearly intended to impress. Assistant Chief Constable Perrin, Detective Superintendent Faraday and Detective Chief Inspector Yin were impressed.

The staff car drew to a gentle halt at the pillared front door and, with perfect timing, a butler appeared.

'Good morning, gentlemen. Madam. We will look after your driver. Meanwhile, if you would care to follow me please.' The police officers entered and walked across the stone hall with its neo-classical chimneypiece and the aroma of burnt logs, into the hall with its sweeping staircase and a painting, 'After the Fair', by Sir Alfred Munnings. They walked on with no time to study each room, until they entered The Great Room, now the library, the bookcases being installed in 1891, and dominated by a very fine painting of the RYS Schooner *Gelert* by Captain James Haughton Forrest. Not a large work but still dominant. The room was beautifully furnished with well-worn, brown leather button-backed chairs surrounding a low table with cups and saucers neatly arranged and coffee, un-poured. The chairs were occupied by Sir Justinian Howe, Miss Abigail Jarret and Mr David Weaver. They all stood as the police officers entered.

'If I may, Sir Justinian,' said Weaver, 'as I know these police officers, maybe, it would be easier if I made the introductions.' But he didn't immediately. Firstly, he welcomed the officers as if they were his closest of friends. Then he did the introductions.

'This is Sir Justinian Howe of the Home Office and Miss Abigail Jarret, US Embassy Minister.' He then turned expansively towards the officers. 'This is Assistant Chief Constable Robert Perrin, Detective Superintendent Mark Faraday and Detective Chief Inspector Kay Yin.' They rather awkwardly manoeuvred so as to shake hands.

'Shall we sit,' suggested Sir Justinian with a smile set in a jovial face. He was a small, rather rotund, man with grey hair and a heavy voice. As he resumed his seat he appeared hemmed in by the chair's large arms, but it in no way diminished his aura of authority. In fact his authority was probably enhanced by it. He appeared at home and very much at ease in the surroundings.

Miss Jarret was very tall, sophisticated and elegant. She was comfortable in her chair and comfortable in her role as the 'number two' at the United States embassy in London. Weaver, who was shorter than Perrin and could have been his cousin, was also comfortable, comfortable at what this meeting had in prospect.

ACC Perrin had anticipated what the meeting would hold and was prepared. He had also prepared Mark and Kay. Throughout the meeting, he had advised, they would display either poker faces or smiles or, ideally, a skilful combination of both. Perrin knew that the meeting was a courtesy; there would be compliments and an olive branch extended, but there would be no negotiations.

David Weaver poured coffee. He was gracious and charming. Then he began, addressing his words to the police officers.

'Over the last few months, we, all of us here, have had a problem. It has been a problem that has impacted upon the Vatican, the United States, Canada and the United Kingdom. Mainly because of the splendid work of the police –that is *your* splendid work - the problem has been contained. MI5 didn't contain it. The United States didn't contain it. You, all of you, have contained it.'

That was the compliment. The officers smiled appreciatively on cue.

Weaver replaced his cup and saucer on the table. Sir Justinian gestured as if to offer more coffee, but Weaver shook his head before he continued.

'I don't really expect any of you to believe me. If I was sat in your seats, I'm not sure I would believe me either.'

That was the olive branch. The officers appropriately displayed a combination of a poker face together with a hint of a smile.

'But,' continued Weaver, 'this is such an important matter that we would all much prefer you to be inside the tent, than outside.'

That was a second olive branch. The officers nodded in grateful unison.

'Let me start by going back,' said Weaver as he unbuttoned his jacket. 'It really all began with a simple plasterer in Rome, a very skilled man but a plasterer none the less, not a master spy or master crook. His name was Alessio Bianchi. He had worked in the UK, France and Austria and, of course, Italy. He had been employed for many years in the Vatican. There has been a great deal of renovation for Bianchi to undertake, particularly in the Sistine Hall Library and the Archivum Secretum Vaticanum. It is quite astonishing, but there are seventy thousand books and one hundred and fifty thousand volumes of manuscripts on fifty-two miles of shelving in the Vatican. In fact, before the 1930s there was little attempt at cataloguing. As no one really had a clue what was on the shelves, Bianchi was able to supplement his income by stealing manuscripts. Little ones at first which he would sell on to back street antique shops. However, his activities came to the notice of a variety of high-end antique dealers and the security agencies. Bianchi was asked to steal manuscripts written by a Father Giovanni Antonio de Carbonaris who had accompanied John Cabot on his travels, in fact, ironically, he sailed from Bristol in 1497. He actually stole five manuscripts by Carbonaris. And, as you know, Bianchi and a fellow plaster by the name of Rossi were murdered after the theft of the fifth and vital manuscript. MI5 and MI6 discovered that the manuscript was to be taken to the UK and to be handed to Adrian Harvey, the MoD researcher.' David Weaver moved and made himself more comfortable in his chair before speaking again.

'I need to be open with everyone around this table,' he said, although continuing to address his words primarily to the police officers. 'MI5 wasn't exactly sure what involvement the United States had in this affair and whether they could be trusted. It transpires that this lack of trust was, to some extent, justified. There's a saying, Mr Perrin, in the security world: "there is always someone on the inside". Perrin nodded in acknowledgment.

'Our lack of trust in the United States on this occasion has been mirrored over the years by a justifiable lack of trust in us by the United States. Whatever, knowing of the reputation of Mark and Kay for dogged determination and their abilities as detectives, and your reputation, Mr Perrin, for supporting your staff … .'

'Goodness,' said Perrin, 'am I that transparent?'

'It's not a bad quality to have, Mr Perrin,' remarked Sir Justinian in a quiet by gravelly tone, 'and, I suspect that these very capable officers would not have been able to have operated so effectively without your actual or tacit support.'

'It has never been difficult to support such excellent officers,' responded Perrin.

Sir Justinian nodded in agreement but also as a signal for Weaver to continue.

'We were sure that would be the case, Mr Perrin, and were prepared,' said Weaver, 'to allow you to pursue your enquiries and, hopefully, recover the manuscript. What is the significance of this document?' he asked rhetorically.

'Shall I answer, David?' suggested Abigail Jarret.

'Of course,' he replied, with the perfect timing of conspirators suspected the police officers, all three of whom were all smiles and appropriate curiosity.

'There is a desire in many parts of the world for local autonomy or total independence. We see this in Palestine and Kurdistan and the results are bloody. On a less vicious level, the Venetians want to break-away from Italy, as does

Catalan from greater Spain. Scotland seeks an independence from the United Kingdom and some in Quebec wish for independence from the rest of Canada. The United States feels safe on its northern border because of the close ties we have with Canada. Canadians are happy with us to the south, particularly as two-thirds of Canada's trade is with the US. The aims of the French Separatist impact upon our national interests and security. The United States would not welcome instability north of the border.' Abigail Jarret paused to give weight to her words before continuing.

'Father Carbonaris' fifth manuscript was believed to have contained details of a treaty between the First Nation people of eastern Canada and your King Henry VII that could, potentially, facilitate or fuel such desires and instability. The United States was keen to study the document,' she explained, 'but the manuscript contains no reference to any sort of treaty, merely a detailed record of the voyage, the establishment of a settlement and the attempts to convert the ingenious peoples.' The officers deployed appropriate poker faces.

'Thank you, Abigail,' said David Weaver. 'It would appear that Harvey was aware of the potential that this manuscript could have contained and intended to pass it on to the French Consul, a *Québécois*, in Bristol. Meanwhile, Commander Bergman was following his own agenda and hoping to sell the manuscript to Atlas International Associates. Why? Because Atlas, a subsidiary of a US company, was hoping to make a lucrative deal regarding the oil and mineral wealth directly with the First Nation peoples in accord with Section 35 of the 1982 Constitution Act or, simply, to facilitate independence for their own ends. Whatever, for Atlas, this would have been a huge prize. There are estimated to be 800 billion barrels of oil off-shore Newfoundland. And recently, the Nova Scotia government granted an exploration licence to an oil company for one billion dollars.'

'There are two further matters, Mr Perrin,' said Sir Justinian. 'The Attorney General has been consulted and it has been determined that Mr Paul Delisile will only be charged with Handling Stolen Goods. I understand that he wisely intends to plead guilty and would accept a prison term of two years, which means he will actually only serve another seven months. Meanwhile, his beloved vessel, the *Angeline*, has been seized because it was used in the commission of a crime. However, Mr Delisile will be re-united with his vessel upon his release. The *Angeline* will, of course, remain the property of Her Majesty, but he can continue to be her skipper as long as he wishes - *provided* he keeps his mouth firmly shut. The Attorney General's view is that any further prosecutions would not be in the public interest.' Sir Justinian changed tack slightly.

'In respect of those two thugs, Hogan and Oslen,' said Sir Justinian, 'they have agreed to accompany US Marshalls back to the United States and are to be released from HM Prison Wandsworth. The fate of Commander Bergman is less inviting. He will soon be transferred to the custody of the US Diplomatic Security Service and has already entered into some sort of plea bargain and will serve sixteen years.'

Clearly, there would be no negotiations regarding these arrangements, but Kay carefully asked: 'And Lieutenant Lightfoot, sir?'

'Ah yes, as you say, Lieutenant Lightfoot,' said Sir Justinian in his gravelly voice. 'The United States is very grateful for your report, Chief Inspector, which they accept in its entirety. The lieutenant was unaware of Berman's treacherous antics and, otherwise, clearly conducted herself with propriety and dignity. She will be reassigned to … .'

'Paris,' said Abigail helpfully.

'Yes, quite so. Paris. Very nice too,' mumbled Sir Justinian.

'You said, sir, if I may,' asked Faraday, 'that there were two matters.'

'Yes. Two matters. I think you best take this one, Abigail,' suggested Sir Justinian.

'Superintendent, you are quite correct. There was one other matter which directly affects you,' she said. 'Atlas International Associates have been on our radar for some time. If there is a trouble spot or instability on the planet, you are very likely to find Atlas amongst it. Atlas will use any local unrest or regional instability as a smoke screen for money laundering; drugs, diamond and people smuggling; asset-stripping and hostile take-overs. The company has a reputation for bribery and bullying and, we suspect, murder. In fact, we believe that an Atlas operative murdered Alessio Bianchi and Marco Rossi. Their reputation is reinforced by ruthless violence. Our security services have been paying attention to Atlas and NSA and GCHQ are actively monitoring the company. Our information is that a Mr Kempler, their Vice-President, has assured the Nigerians that Atlas will shortly demonstrate their ruthless commitment to their client's needs and are keen to reassure them that no one gets in the way of Atlas International. Consequently, I have to inform you, Superintendent, that there is a contract out on your life.

Chapter 24

Tuesday, 21st June.

Bristol, England.

THEY HAD AGREED. ACC Perrin had authorised that both Mark and Kay should be armed at all times. GCHQ had been monitoring all communication channels used by William J L Kemper of Atlas International Associates and it could be reasonably predicted that the contract would be carried out prior to the 23rd June, the date of a key meeting between Atlas and the Nigerians. The police Operational Order did not include the options of relocating Faraday or providing Faraday with high visibility and heavy personal protection. Faraday had dismissed the option of relocation. The option of some sort of close protection was considered to be unrealistic in the long-term and would, therefore, potentially provide a much wider window of opportunity to a would-be assassin. Instead, the Order recognised the need to restrict the opportunities for an assassination.

It was assumed that any assassin would have had very limited knowledge of Faraday's work or social routines prior to the week commencing the 6th June, and so Faraday would adjust his routines. With the understanding of ACC Robert Perrin, and the ACC alone, Kay and Mark would not stay in each other's apartments and Mark would act as normally as possible, just like any other guy in the street. However, from here on in, Mark would only frequent petrol stations, super-markets and public places which were well served by CCTV and in the open as far as possible. When travelling to and from his apartment at Avon View Court and police headquarters, Mark's car would be followed conspicuously by an un-marked police car containing uniformed firearms officers. Mark would confine his off-duty time predominantly to Avon View Court where MI5 had parked, in the visitors' bay, a standard Volvo V70. But it wasn't standard. The front and rear parking sensors had been replaced by mini-cameras which were able to provide 180° coverage at the front and rear of the vehicle, although not at the immediate sides, left and right. As a result of the vehicle's positioning, the front cameras did cover the entrance drive from the road, with the rear cameras covering the entrance doorway to Avon View Court. These cameras would be monitored 24/7.

Kay had visited Avon View Court. Not Faraday's apartment. Just the reception desk. She was reassured by the estate's lighting which activated along the driveway as vehicles or pedestrians walked along. But there were shrubs, trees and bushes which provided opportunities for ominous seclusion. And the blind spots at the sides of the Volvo concerned her too. But there was little alternative, other than some sort of unacceptable domestic, solitary confinement for Mark. Kay would think some more, drove home uneasily and considered what would be an assassin's best place and time to mount an attack.

***

At twenty to nine, Faraday drove into Avon View Court. The police escort car that had followed him parked across the entrance way until Faraday stopped in front of his garage and activated the remote control. The heavy wooden door shuddered as the motor engaged, then rose gently up. Faraday drove his Audi inside. He shut down the engine and walked to the boot. As he did so, he gave the thumbs up to the escort car. He closed the boot and the police car drove away as the garage door slowly lowered to a close.

She had considered what would be the best place to mount an attack. The driveway lights provided excellent illumination for pedestrians, but they did not provide security. Far from it. The lights provided the darkest of shadows amongst the shrubs and bushes, perfect for an assassin. She stepped from the shadows, but wasn't sure if she should speak in case she spooked him. It would be so ridiculously easy. Such an easy target, she thought. She stepped two paces closer.

'Police', called Kay.

Her beautiful legs and care-free blond hair were illuminated by the driveway lights. She turned swiftly. Maybe Faraday had not been such an easy target after all. Her smile was no longer captivating; her mouth was unsmiling, firm and uncompromising; her small, black Smith and Wesson 2213 automatic was held easily in her hand. As the assassin raised her weapon, Kay fired her Glock 26. The noise was deafening, the surrounding trees seemed to shudder as they contained the explosion as if in an amphitheatre.

There was only one shot. One was enough. No 'double-tap'. The beautiful young woman who had so callously murdered Alessio Bianchi and Marco Rossi was hit and now lay on the earth amongst the shrubs in agony. The firing of the 9mm Parabellum round created a modest recoil although it travelled at over 1300 feet per second. The round had torn into her right Subscapularis muscle, shattering the Great and Lesser Tubercle of the Humerus bone and dislocating the Clavicle. Mark and Kay looked down at her. There was no sympathy for her. She deserved none, but she was in agony and they rendered first aid as their office obliged them to do, as Kay called headquarters.

'This is Alpha Charlie Four. I need an ambulance at Avon View Court. One suspect with a severe gun-shot wound. Scene secured. Superintendent Faraday on scene. No police injuries. Please inform ACC Perrin.'

Chapter 25

Friday, 24th June.

Bristol Royal Infirmary and Police Headquarters, Bristol, England.

DETECTIVE CHIEF INSPECTOR KAY YIN walked along the hospital corridor. She wore a Comptoir des Cotonnies dark-grey jacket and trousers. She was relaxed. True, there would be an investigation by the Independent Police Complaints Commission, as there always was in such cases were the police had discharged a firearm. But the case regarding the medieval manuscript had been completed successfully and Mark was safe. That was all that really mattered to her.

Kay didn't have to look for the private room. The presence of uniformed, armed officer told her where Brandy Myers lay recovering from her operation.

The uniformed officer nodded admiringly at this delicate but determined detective. 'Good morning, ma'am.'

'Good morning, Barry,' she said softly.

He opened the door for her. She stepped through. There were two other armed, uniformed officers in the room. One sitting at the door, facing the window. The other sitting at the window, facing the door. Both were armed with a Heckler and Koch.

‘Good morning, ma’am,’ they said, virtually in unison as they stood.

‘Anything to report, gentlemen?’

‘No, ma’am. Everything is good,’ replied Constable Giles at the window.

Brandy Myers was lying in bed. She looked pale. Her right shoulder was heavily bandaged and supported in some way. An intravenous line led through a Cardinal GP monitor to a cannula in her left forearm; and wires seemed to lead from everywhere under the bed sheets as a Philips MX700 monitor monitored, displaying tell-tale lines and figures. But she would recover. Her right wrist was handcuffed to the bed. Objections from the doctors for the need to handcuff the prisoner were firmly over-ruled. Myers would remain handcuffed. She opened her eyes. There was silence as she studied the officer. Then she spoke.

‘You should have killed me.’

‘And why should I want to do that?’ asked Kay softly from the side of her bed.

Myers didn’t answer that question. She posed another. ‘They will come after that cop, you know that?’ She attempted a contemptuous grin. The contempt was there, but not the grin.

‘I thought I would come along,’ said Kay, ‘and tell you what’s been happening whilst you have been here. You will get, I should think, fifteen to twenty for the attempted murder of Superintendent Faraday. Then, once your sentence here is completed, you will be extradited to Italy and stand trial for the murders of Alessio Bianchi and Marco Rossi. This morning at four-thirty, when you were nicely tucked-up in bed, the offices of Atlas International Associates were raided by Scotland Yard as was the home of your paymaster, William Kemper. Simultaneously, the offices of Atlas International in Houston, Anchorage and Boston were raided by the FBI.' Kay walked to the foot of the bed. 'No one will be coming after the Superintendent. But they will be coming after *you*. Why? Because you failed and you know too much. And, whatever security we put in place, they *will* find you.'

Kay turned and walked to the door. Constable Brian Day opened the door for her. But she stopped and looked at both officers. 'Watch this prisoner. Don't be distracted by the fact that you may think her a beautiful woman who looks so vulnerable. Away from here, she tortures and kills people for a living. So, watch her and watch your backs.'

Kay walked along the hospital corridor, down two flights of stairs, away from the good guys who were guarding the bad and wicked, and outside towards a little garden.

She stood in the garden for a while. In the warm sunshine. Amongst patients and friends - some relieved, some hopeful, others anxious or distressed. Yet, it was strangely calm and peaceful there. And the air was clean.

***

Later that afternoon, the buzzer sounded discretely. The PA looked up. 'Mr Perrin can see you both, now.'

Detective Superintendent Mark Faraday and Detective Chief Inspector Kay Yin, tapped on the doors and entered the Assistant Chief Constable's suite.

'Well, what do I owe this pleasure,' he said expansively, just like that Italian prime minister. 'I thought I had seen the back of you two. Shall we sit?'

'We would prefer to stand if you don't mind, sir,' replied Faraday.

Perrin wondered for a short moment what the purpose of the officers' visit could be. 'So, how can I help?'

'We thought that we should thank you,' said Faraday. 'What Sir Justinian said was absolutely true. Without the reassurance of your backing, the operation could not have succeeded. And, I don't think any other ACC would have stepped up to the plate as you did. And so, thank you, sir.'

'Mark, you said to me once that your father had said that he was proud of you but wouldn't be quite so proud if you let your people down. I think your father and I would have got on very well together.' He returned to his desk and pulled open the right hand draw and retrieved a blue coloured case. He opened it and looked at the silver medal it contained. 'This is the Queen's Police Medal that Her Majesty presented to me at Windsor Castle. On the obverse is the profile of the Queen, of course. On the reverse is depicted a crusader knight leaning on a great battle shield. He looks tired but also alert, maybe because there is still so much more to do. Around the rim are the words "For Distinguished Police Service". But, to me, the really important words are those on the knight's shield: "To Guard My People". Most believe this simply recognises the key role the police have for protecting the Queen's subjects. But I think it goes, or should go, much further than that. To me those words are also about protecting your subordinate officers, those who are actually doing the job, those good people, like you both, who actually make a difference on a daily basis. That's what I try and do from here. It is nothing about covering-up misconduct or ineptitude. Unhappily, there are some who are not worth guarding at all. Only a few. Still too many. But you, both of you, are worth guarding.' He replaced the medal in its presentation case back into the drawer. 'Anyway, thank you for coming in.'

'There is one other thing, sir,' said Kay.

'Oh. Go on,' he replied, although he had anticipated what she was about to say. Not what she was about to ask.

'It's a good thing, sir,' she said reassuringly. 'Mark has asked to marry me and, of course, I have said yes.' She stretched her right hand out and grasped his left hand. As she did so Perrin smile. A huge smile. A delighted smile as Kay continued.

'The wedding will be a small affair, sir, and my mother will be coming from Hong Kong. As you know, I lost my father last year. I have no uncles or brothers. But I have always understood that I should ask someone to stand with me who will bring honour to our wedding and so I was wondering if you would be kind enough to walk me up the aisle?'

***

Epilogue

One year on.

DETECTIVE SUPERINTENDENT MARK FARADAY MBE remains as the Head of Special Branch and attended the Senior Command Course at the Police Staff College. He and Kay follow the FBI's simple dictum: '*Stay Alert. Stay Alive*.'

DETECTIVE CHIEF INSPECTOR KAY YIN was nominated to attend the Intermediate Command Course by her Force and is awaiting the national selection interview. Kay married Mark, moved into Avon View Court and reconfigured the garden and driveway lighting.

ASSISTANT CHIEF CONSTABLE ROBERT PERRIN QPM gave Kay away and at the reception held at The Royal Hotel punctuated his speech with Italian jokes.

DETECTIVE SERGEANT PIPPA BLANCHARD is expecting her first child.

SERGEANT PETER JEAN PURCHELL successfully appeared before an internal promotion board and is awaiting promotion to the rank of Inspector.

DETECTIVE CONSTABLE JOHN BUTCHER has separated from his wife.

JANE FLOOD returned to administrative duties within Special Branch.

SNOWY, Jane's West Highland Terrier, after whom the Operation was code named, was a loyal companion and grand old lady. Snowy passed away peacefully in her 17th year.

CHIEF CONSTABLE'S COMMENDATIONS were presented to all members of Operation Snowy.

COMMANDER WALT BERGMAN is still serving his sentence at the Naval Brig, Norfolk, Virginia.

MISS DEBBIE-ANNE BERGMAN obtained her Master's degree and visits her father every month.

MRS LUCY BERGMAN became bored with Colonel Clarke Jackson and is now partying with Brigadier-General Bob Langston – and buying more shoes.

LIEUTENANT JANET LIGHFOOT continues to serve her country.

JIM HOGAN and CURT OSLEN voluntarily returned to the United States with US Marshalls. They continue to undertake contract work – for who-ever.

ANGELINE is now in service with MI6.

PAUL DELISILE served only four months as a result of 'additional good behaviour' which allowed him to become an MI6 asset. He now skippers the *Angeline* on their behalf.

HELEN CAVE remains with MI5.

MISS UNDERSTANDING continues to enjoy the business benefits associated with Suite 511. The hotel's general manager continues to enjoy the personal services that Miss Understanding provides, as does the Assistant Chief Officer (Colonel Michael Thorne) and the French Consul. All are now closely monitored by MI5 and Special Branch.

MISS VERA WINIFRED KANE sold her painting of the *Angeline* to Kay Yin for £575. The painting, Kay's wedding present to Mark, now hangs in their lounge at Avon View Court.

BRANDY MYERS was found hanged in her cell at HM Prison Holloway. A female prison officer, who was being investigated in connection with the death, was later found dead in her burnt-out Renault Cleo. A fellow prisoner, on home leave, was later found stabbed to death, near the entrance to Caledonian Park, London, amongst the trees, in the darkest of shadows.

***

Author's Note

John Cabot: *fact: aka Giovanni Caboto aka Zuan Chabottot, 1450-1500; citizen of Venice. Second voyage from Bristol discovered Cape Bonavista, Newfoundland on St John the Baptist Day. Fiction: he did plant two flags, one of England, one of St Mark (the patron Saint of Venice), not the Papal flag as stated in the text.*

St John the Baptist Day: *fact: 24th June 1497.*

Father Giovanni Antonio de Carbonaris: *fact: England's Deputy Papal Tax Collector, priest and banker.*

Archivun Secretum Vaticanum: *fact.*

Sistine Hall of the Vatican Library: *fact.*

Corpo della Gendarmeria: *fact: the 130-strong police and security force of the Vatican City.*

MI5: *The UK's domestic counter-intelligence Security Service.*

MI6: *The UK's foreign Secret Intelligence Service.*

MOD Abbeywood: *fact.*

GCHQ: *The UK's Government Communications HQ, responsible for communications intelligence gathering.*

RAF Menwith Hill: *fact.*

NSA: *The USA's National Security Agency responsible for global communications intelligence gathering.*

CIA: *The USA's Central Intelligence Agency responsible for gathering intelligence world-wide, primarily through human assets.*

ONI: *The USA's Office of Naval Intelligence.*

Radio Londres: *fact.*

'Stoneghost': *fact.*

'Stateroom': *fact.*

Severnside Police: *fiction.*

Bristol Central Police HQ, The Grove: *fiction, but on the site of the old Bristol Constabulary's River Station.*
Dorset Police: *fact.*
Special Branch: *The unit responsible, within local UK police forces, for gathering intelligence and mounting operations in respect of the protection of the State.*
The Queen's Police Medal: *fact.*
HM Coastguard, Steamer Point: *fact.*
HM Coastguard, Hengistbury Head: *fact.*
Christchurch Harbour Double Tides: *fact.*
International Maritime Signal Flags: *fact.*
HMS Serpent: *fact.*
MV Angeline: *the name is fiction but everything else about the Ormidale-class vessel is fact.*
Highcliffe Castle: *fact.*
The Priory Church: *fact.*
Stanpit Marsh: *fact.*
Section 35 Constitution Act: *fact.*
Angel in the Field public house: *fact.*
Lord Bute Hotel: *fact.*
The Captains Club: *fact.*
The Boat House: *fact.*
The Trans-European Hotel: *fiction.*
The Cheese and Alfies café: *fact.*
James and White Bar: *fact.*
The Golden Oasis: *fiction.*
The Green House: *fact.*
The Salon Kitty: *fact.*
Belfast City Council v Miss Behavin' Ltd 2007: *fact.*
Glock 17: *fact.*
Glock 26: *fact.*
Smith and Wesson 2213: *fact.*

Parabellum: *fact; widely used by law enforcement agencies, designed by Georg Luger.*
Papyrologist: *fact; study of ancient and historical documents.*
Palaeographist*: fact; the study of ancient and historical hand writing.*
Atlas International Associates*: fiction.*

The first ***Mark Faraday Collection*** crime novel

International intrigue and brutal murder

DIRTY Business

by Richard Allen

IN THE ABSENCE of his superintendent, Chief Inspector Mark Faraday takes command of the Bristol Central District just as MI6 move in to conduct a covert and unauthorised surveillance operation on his district. To make matters worse, Faraday is required to share his office with the beautiful Helen Cave of MI5.

But when one of Faraday's best young officers is murdered an intricately woven plot is uncovered involving secret bank accounts and a dissident Irish terrorist group. From County Wicklow and the rarefied atmosphere of an exclusive London club to Salisbury Plain and the streets of Bristol, and against a background of brutal murder and international intrigue, a deadly clock is ticking as Mark Faraday and Helen Cave race against time to prevent the nuclear devastation that threatens the West Country

The second ***Mark Faraday Collection*** crime novel

Heartless murder and ruthless self interest

DIE Back

by Richard Allen

WHEN SUPERINTENDENT Mark Faraday defies orders and begins to investigate the disappearance of a local lorry driver, a top secret US and UK intelligence operation, designed to destroy the poppy fields of Afghanistan, is unwittingly undermined.

As Faraday is drawn deeper into the secret world of intelligence, he confronts his own senior officers and foreign law enforcement agencies, cynical self-interest and murder.

From the splendour of the House of Lords and the beauty of the Venetian palazzos to the vastness of the deserts of Western Australia, Mark Faraday relentlessly pursues his investigation, haunted by the murder of one colleague and mesmerised by the beauty of another.

Available as eBook or paperback direct from
www.amazon.com or www.amazon.co.uk

COMING SOON:

The fifth ***Mark Faraday Collection*** crime novel

Arrogance and jealousy, treachery and murder

DEADLY Inheritance

by Richard Allen

AT THE SCENE OF A BRUTAL STABBING, Detective Superintendent Kay Yin questions whether the deceased was the intended victim. Together with Chief Superintendent Mark Faraday, Kay's investigations centre upon a quartet of suspects: a successful English property entrepreneur and his Italian wife, a European Union lawyer; a highly respected wine merchant from Madeira and an unsavoury Gibraltarian estate agent.

Mark and Kay's enquiries take them from the shadows of a circus car park in Bristol to the splendour of the Foreign and Commonwealth Office in London; from the dramatic Rock of Gibraltar to the waters of Cabo Girao in Madeira and from the extraordinary Russel-Cotes Museum to the Brecon Beacons in Wales where, at every turn, they encounter arrogance and egotism, envy and jealousy, treachery and hatred – where nothing is as it seems.

Available as eBook or paperback direct from
www.amazon.com, or www.amazon.co.uk

40822581R00183

Printed in Poland
by Amazon Fulfillment
Poland Sp. z o.o., Wrocław